In the Time of Spirits
Beth Ford

Copyright © 2024 by Beth Ford

All rights reserved.

No part of this publication may be reproduced, distributed, or transmitted in any form or by any means, including photocopying, recording, or other electronic or mechanical methods, without the prior written permission of the publisher, except as permitted by U.S. copyright law. For permission requests, contact beth@bethfordauthor.com.

The story, all names, characters, and incidents portrayed in this production are fictitious. No identification with actual persons (living or deceased), places, buildings, and products is intended or should be inferred.

Part I

Chapter 1

The still curtains against the open windows in the stifling room evinced the flatness and stasis of the day. Addy let the novel she had been reading collapse into her lap. She could barely think, let alone concentrate, in the sticky Washington, DC, mid-July heat.

She sighed and flapped the pages of the book close to her face to cool herself. Across the room, her mother stayed silent and still, never liking to complain, but the redness of her face as she bent over her needlework showed that she, too, felt the heat.

A faint knock sounded at the front door. Addy heard Sally, the maid, answer it, and she recognized the voice that responded. Her mother peeked up from her cross-stitching, having heard it as well, but her gaze quickly returned to the needle. Addy rolled her eyes and sank back in her chair. As much as her mother would pretend not to interfere, Addy knew she would be cataloging and judging the entire encounter for discussion later, jumping in when she thought it necessary, hoping to force some change in Addy's feelings toward her childhood companion turned suitor.

"Mr. Arthur Simmons," Sally announced, stepping into the threshold of the parlor and then just as quickly disappearing.

Arthur, short and blond, with a wisp of a mustache curling across his lip, walked in and bowed. "Miss Cohart, Mrs. Cohart," he said, formal as always.

"Hello, Arthur," Addy's mother replied, though she still only looked at him from the corner of her eye, as if not wishing to impose even her gaze on the young people's conversation.

Addy just nodded and smiled up at him, motioning toward a blue-patterned chair across from her. Arthur settled in. Beads of sweat weighed down the thin hairs of his mustache.

"You're brave going out in this heat," she said companionably. "I think I'd melt."

"Adalinda," her mother said, using her daughter's full name as a warning, "perhaps you'd like to ask our guest if he wants some iced tea."

Addy pursed her lips to keep from answering back, but she couldn't help herself. "Perhaps you can ask him yourself since you're in the same room as him, too." Her mother's expression turned tight and sour with the rapidity of a turtle snapping its head inside its shell. *"Arthur,"* Addy continued with unnecessary emphasis on each syllable, "would you like some iced tea?"

"That would be lovely, thank you." He gave an uneasy laugh, unsure if he was in on the joke.

Addy rang the bell to call for drinks as a clattering in the street outside announced her father's return in the carriage.

He stomped inside, dust flying off his jacket. "What we need is some blasted rain," he said as all six foot three inches of him entered the parlor. "I think I could fry an egg on my forehead right now." Noticing the guest, he said, "Ah! Arthur!" He clapped the young man on the shoulder by way of greeting, then bent down to kiss the top of Addy's head. He crossed to the chair beside his wife and threw himself down. He pulled off his jacket, tossed it over the end table, and began to roll up his shirtsleeves.

"Nathan, don't—"

He cut his wife off, guessing the reprimand would be for dressing down in front of their guest. "Oh, for heaven's sake, Marty, it's only Arthur. And I have to get it off before I melt."

"Addy was just saying the same thing about melting," Arthur said, to redirect the conversation.

"Was she? Well, like father, like daughter. Neither of us can take this heat—can we, dear? I saw Sally going into the kitchen. Are we getting drinks?" Murmurs of agreement. "Thank God." He pulled a handkerchief out of the discarded jacket to mop his forehead. "What brings you here today, Arthur?" he asked.

When Addy was younger, her father's tendency to barrel ahead and overtake any conversation had annoyed her. Today, she was grateful. She recalled the unpleasant face he had made when she broached the subject with him years before. He had said in a quiet, faraway voice, "Meek, indecisive men don't come back from the battlefield. I always like to make sure we are going somewhere, even if it's just in conversation." He had ended the statement with a wink, but she sensed the somber memories behind it. It had forced her to remember the ogre that dogged the older generation—the bloody, turbulent days of the Civil War, during which her father had begun his career as an army officer, which lasted until his retirement two years ago.

Arthur's reply dragged her thoughts back to the present. "Nothing particular. Just thought I was due to call on you all. My mother sends her regards."

"Of course. How is she?"

"She's well enough, thank you." Arthur's mother had been an invalid since a fall a few years before that had made it difficult for her to walk. "No better, no worse."

A rattle of cups and spoons announced Sally's return. After everyone had gratefully finished off the cold liquid in their glasses, Mrs. Cohart nudged her husband with her elbow. He made a show of standing and announcing, "Excuse me, I have some business to take care of." His wife picked up her needlework and followed him out.

Addy reluctantly set her empty glass on the small table beside her; without the distraction of the tea, she would be forced to engage Arthur. She already missed her father's ability to pull the conversation forward so easily. She folded her hands delicately in her lap and watched the smooth pale-blue silk of her skirt crumple with their weight as she dredged up something to say. "How is your job at the law firm going?"

"It's been wonderful. My uncle says I could really have a future in law." He made the remark with a stiff pride that said he expected Addy to be impressed.

"That's nice. What makes someone have a future in law? Besides an uncle who's already an established lawyer?" She felt the cruelty in her statement as soon as it left her mouth.

Arthur shifted in his seat, assuming a new position to counter her attack. "He got me the position, but that didn't mean I would be good at it. It requires a lot of attention to detail and logic."

"Well, I don't think anyone doubted you would do well," she said, trying to soften her words.

"Thank you." An awkward pause stretched between them. "What are you reading?" he asked finally.

Addy shrugged and held up the book. "The new Marie Corelli."

He sent his own sarcastic barb across. "Oh, yes, that literary great."

"My mother calls it trash, but what does she know." Her mother called it a lot worse things than that, actually: the devil's work, anti-Christian. And other hysterical accusations that Addy ignored.

"There are an awful lot of people reading trash, if that's the case," Arthur said.

Addy leaned forward, eager to delve into her favorite subject. The spiritualist craze was once again sweeping across both sides of the Atlantic, just as it had during her parents' childhoods, and Addy watched its progression with avid interest. "There's more to it than that, you know. What she writes about spiritualism is true. It happens."

"It sounds like the ghost stories we told as kids."

Addy set the book down next to her glass and wrapped her hands tightly in her lap again. "Wouldn't you like to speak with your father again? Tell him about your job as a lawyer?"

"Of course I would, but that's not possible. Not here on Earth, anyway."

"Yes, but why shouldn't we be able to talk to the dead now? If we went to a séance, you would see how true it is."

Arthur shook his head. "I'm going to have to take your word on that because I don't see either of our families agreeing to that sort of entertainment. But I can offer you a ticket to the theater. My uncle and I have an extra one for tomorrow night. Do you want to come?"

"Arthur, I just don't think it's right for us to keep going out together. When we were younger, it was fine, but now . . ."

"Now that you've turned me down, you mean? Don't worry, I'm not trying to change your mind."

"My mother certainly is."

"Ignore her. Come with us. Let's be friends again, really."

She felt the seconds tick by, wearing away at her resolve. "This one time," she said finally with a soft smile.

"Excellent. We'll call for you at seven o'clock."

He stood and offered his hand to her before he left. She didn't take it, and after a long moment he withdrew and walked out in silence. He had to understand how serious she was about the things she believed. She would let no one decry them, least of all Arthur.

The next morning her mother made no direct mention of Arthur's visit, but she pulled out her Bible at the breakfast table, her default action when she didn't know quite what to do or how to make her point.

Addy steeled herself for the upcoming exchange. Her father glanced up and then retreated into his newspaper. He would be no help, Addy knew.

Addy decided to head off the attack.

"Are you going to quote me the passage about a wife obeying her husband?"

"Honestly, Addy, I don't know what's wrong with you. I hope you aren't planning on skipping church again this week. Lord knows you need it." She cast her eyes up to the ceiling as if to emphasize that God was on her side.

"You know the Bible was also used to justify slavery in the South. Not everything it says is right."

"Well, just because politics have changed doesn't mean the Good Book is wrong."

Addy watched her mother carefully. Was she saying what Addy thought she was saying? Mrs. Cohart had come from over the Virginia line; her brothers had served and, in one case, died for the Confederacy. Addy's father, on the other hand, had served the Union faithfully his entire career. Addy moved her gaze to her father.

He peeked at her over the top of his paper. "For God's sake, Addy, stop trying to stir up shit."

Her mother reprimanded him for his language, but his sudden use of it made Addy think they had argued over her mother's loyalties before. Addy felt both vindicated and appalled that her mother could be so backward.

"Don't you want to have faith in something?" Addy's mother asked.

"I do. And now you know how it feels when you discount what I believe in."

"Honestly, that spiritualist nonsense hardly counts—"

"Stop it, both of you," her father broke in. "Addy, I hope you have something to entertain yourself with today besides bothering your mother."

"I'm going to the theater tonight with Arthur and Uncle Ted."

"Thank God," he muttered and returned to his paper.

Her mother daintily finished her breakfast while pointedly flipping through the pages of her battered family Bible. Addy scowled the entire time, then retreated upstairs to the company of Marie Corelli.

The family studiously avoided each other for the rest of the day. Mrs. Cohart took her dinner in her room, claiming a headache, and Mr. Cohart remained in his study, leaving

Addy the dining room all to herself. She sat at the head of the table as she ate, in her father's usual spot, just to see how it felt. Such a shame, she thought, that a woman so rarely got to officially preside over a room like this. That was true in her world, at least. But in the spiritualist one, most of the mediums were women. Addy yearned to watch one work in person or, better yet, to have powers herself. But as much as she tried, she had never felt any connection to the dead. Her feet were planted firmly in the material realm, though her head often drifted into the other one.

After dinner, she rushed to get ready since she had spent so much time daydreaming. Fortunately, Arthur and his Uncle Ted arrived a few minutes late. Addy met them at the door and hurried them outside, wanting to avoid socializing with her parents. She gathered the silver folds of her dress in one hand and stepped onto the bench seat inside the carriage.

"Shame your parents can't come out with us," Uncle Ted said cheerily after they had greeted one another.

Addy murmured her agreement, even though Arthur's earlier invitation had not been extended to her mother and father. Now that the omission had been pointed out to her, it left a sour taste in her mouth—not because she wanted her parents to come, but because it meant Arthur must be up to something. She shouldn't have trusted his "just friends" line. But she smiled and continued with the conversation. "My mother was supposed to be playing cards at the Bells', but she's not feeling well. And my father's shut up in the library with some scotch and a cigar, so, really, it's a perfect evening for both of them."

"Well, we're glad you could come, at least." Ted beamed through the dark curls oiled down over his forehead to hide his receding hairline. His collar pushed the flesh of his neck up into a little pouch under his chin. It was amazing that he and Arthur were related—one so dark and chubby, the other fair, trim, and handsome. Arthur's looks certainly weren't what kept Addy from accepting his proposal. Rather, it was a sense that their match would be one of convenience and comfort, while she yearned for love and drama. There was more to her than riding in a middling carriage to a middling theater with middling people she had known her whole life. A brighter future for her existed, tantalizing her, just out of reach, but she would reach it eventually.

Soon they were in the push of the crowd going into the theater. A man with a large mustache sneezed on Addy's shoulder and apologized profusely; Addy just scrunched her face at him and his red nose and kept walking up the stairs to the balcony. Arthur waved her into the seat beside him, as if Addy wouldn't have figured out where to sit if he hadn't shown her. She sat in the chair he had been planning to occupy instead so that she was sitting between the two men, just to prove her point. She daintily laid her gloved hands and her reticule in her lap without meeting Arthur's gaze.

She looked out at the swath of Washington society spread out before her. Couples bent toward each other in whispered conversation, old women peered through their opera glasses even though a curtain still covered the stage, and young women flirted their fans and their eyes at eligible men around the room. Dull, dull, dull—all of it.

The opera was pretty, but she found her attention diverting anyway. She always had a hard time concentrating on the singing when she couldn't understand the words. She doubted half the people there enjoyed it, either, but the theater was the place to see and be seen, so they all put themselves through three hours of torture on a Friday evening. She sighed and slumped back in her chair. Arthur touched her arm to make sure she was all right. She nodded and imagined her mother's sharp command to sit up straight and be polite. She smiled to herself at the thought, but Arthur seemed to take it as a reassurance meant for him and looked pleased.

During intermission, Addy was briefly left alone when Ted went to speak with someone he recognized and Arthur trekked to the lobby to purchase ice creams. She watched the streams of people file past. She caught the eye of a handsome young man, but he frowned and gripped the arm of his sweetheart as if afraid Addy would rip them apart. When Arthur reappeared, she was stifling a bored yawn with one hand. One ice cream had already melted onto Arthur's hand in slick yellowish drops. Embarrassed, he pulled out his handkerchief and wiped the mess off once Addy had taken her treat. They sat and ate in silence.

"Bored?" he asked after he had succeeded in licking back the drips.

Addy shrugged.

"I think it's a lovely opera."

"It might very well be, but that doesn't mean it's not boring."

Arthur frowned. Finally, without meeting her gaze, he said, "I don't know what else you're looking for, Addy. This"—he swung one arm around to indicate the bustling theater—"is what people do. They go to the opera. They make respectable marriages."

"Unlike me, you mean."

"I just think one day you'll regret treating us like we're all beneath you." He turned to face her. "I mean that sincerely. I worry about you, just like your parents do. We want to see you make wise decisions."

"No, you want me to accept the decisions that you all make for me. There's a difference."

He sighed and sagged in his chair. "Fine. I give up. But eventually we'll see who was right."

"I suppose we will." She sat with her spine straight, trying to seem imperious, but the ice cream in her hand made her feel small and childlike. She did the only thing she could think of to rectify the situation: she tossed the ice cream onto the floor and stormed off. She was not yet at a point in her life where she was able to discern the fine line between making a point and only making a mess.

On the ride home, the carriage seemed to jostle more than usual, as if shifting with the weight of the tension as it was thrown from one side of the vehicle to the other. It bumped off Addy's scowl, brushed against Ted's perplexed look, and alighted on Arthur's steady stare out the window, finding nowhere stable to land.

The uneven ride stopped sooner than expected. A glance out the window showed they were stuck one block down from the Coharts'.

As the passengers waited for a signal of what was wrong, a faint acrid scent weaved through the air. Smoke. Ted banged on the carriage wall to alert the driver, then stuck his head through the tiny floral curtain and out the window. "Oh, God," he gasped, and pulled himself back inside, dumbstruck.

Arthur was suddenly alert. "Is there a fire?" He, too, looked out, but what he saw drew him out onto the street, leaving the carriage door hanging open behind him as pedestrians darted around it. Addy started to get up. Ted grabbed her arm, but she was able to shake free. Arthur, captivated by the scene, did not notice in the first instant that Addy had run past him. When he did, he raced after her, navigating inelegantly through the gathering crowd, kicking up a swirl of dust in his wake. Halfway down the block he caught up to her, and she fell into his arms screaming as the flames consuming her family's home lit up the night sky behind her.

The room slowly coalesced around Addy as consciousness returned. Her head bubbled with ache, and the first thing she noticed was her raw and swollen bare feet, beat up by the delicate evening slippers that were never meant to be run in, now discarded by the door. She rolled onto her side and leaned over the edge of the sofa she lay on, fighting the urge to vomit. She was startled as a hand landed on her shoulder, gently pushing her onto her back again. The hand belonged to an elderly doctor who hovered over her, murmuring quiet, meaningless reassurances as he checked her condition. A thought prickled in the back of her mind as she took in the deep-green floral wallpaper of the small anteroom. There was some reason she was here, she knew, but her mind couldn't quite land on what it was.

She gazed around the room, her stomach calming as she sucked in slow, relaxing breaths. In the corner slightly behind her stood Arthur and his uncle, conferring quietly with a policeman.

Why is a policeman here? she wondered.

The doctor stepped away, satisfied, and Arthur immediately came to Addy's side like she were a homing beacon, grabbing her hand as he kneeled by the sofa. "Addy...," he said, his throat thick with phlegm as if he hadn't spoken for a long, long time. "Are you all right?"

"Better," she said, though the way Arthur craned his neck to hear told her that her voice did not sound as strong as she thought. The doctor passed her a glass of water. She sat up to drink it, though her head swam from the effort.

The four men collected around her exchanged worried glances, shared some secret message that she, the lone woman, was not privy to. Finally, Arthur broke the brotherhood. "I'll tell her," he said in a tone that showed he thought he was acting particularly bravely. When no one moved, he continued, "Can you give us a moment alone, please?"

The other three nodded and stepped into the hall.

This time Arthur sat on the edge of the sofa, the side of his body pressed against Addy's. She looked up at him and realized that her eyes were already cloudy with tears. She knew what he was about to reveal. "Addy," he said, repeating her name like a talisman he could call upon to keep the clouds at bay. "There was a fire. The house is destroyed, and... your parents didn't make it out. I'm sorry."

Addy grappled with him, shaking his shoulders, as if in wrestling him she were struggling with the truth. He embraced her, and for once she let him, propriety and all her resolutions be damned.

Chapter 2

Two Weeks Later

The black crinoline rustled around Addy's legs as she walked down the Simmonses' staircase, an audible reminder of her mourning. The smooth wood of the banister slid beneath the light touch of her fingertips. The housekeeper, a sturdy middle-aged woman with graying hair, waited in the foyer. "Mrs. Simmons is ready for her bath," Addy said to her.

"I'll send the maid right up, ma'am."

"Thank you," Addy said absently, relieved that her duty was over with for the day but not sure how else to pass the time. She had been staying with Arthur and his mother since the fire, helping out with the invalid Mrs. Simmons as a sort of repayment for their hospitality. Beyond that, her days were dull and bleak.

"Oh, and there's a letter for you on the hall table, ma'am," the housekeeper said.

Addy murmured a *thank you* and picked up the letter, taking it with her into the well-appointed parlor. After a quick glance at the signature, she set the letter aside. It was another missive from her older sister in Chicago, who, pregnant with her second child, hadn't been able to come to Washington, DC, for their parents' funeral. Trisha had also had plenty of excuses why she hadn't visited since her wedding five years ago, so Addy couldn't stand that Trisha acted like she cared now. Addy knew the letter would offer advice and platitudes, as if Trisha were presenting Addy with so many petit fours arrayed on a silver tray. Addy refused to take any, no matter how tempting they looked. Trisha had always been the practical, sensible one who dreamed only of marriage. She had wed at nineteen and moved to Chicago, leaving fifteen-year-old Addy at home with their parents and confining their relationship to occasional letters. Even though they were not particularly close, they looked remarkably similar; people had often asked if they were twins when they were younger. They both had the same pale skin; tall, slim figures; dark-auburn hair that shone fire red in certain lights; and light-green eyes.

Instead of reading the letter, Addy picked up the book she had left on the table the night before. It was another Marie Corelli, bought to replace the one she had left so carelessly on the end table at home that evening—now nothing more than ash. As much as reading was her only escape these days, the words still couldn't capture her attention this afternoon. She increasingly wanted *more*: to experience the things written in the books she typically devoured; to fall madly in love, no matter what society said or what the consequences would be; to travel to exotic places; to know that it was possible to bridge the gap between this world and the spirit realm.

And yet here she was, simply watching the dust motes float in a spot of sunlight in the Simmonses' front room, those dreams seemingly impossible to reach. It wasn't marriage necessarily that she objected to, only the type of marriage Arthur offered: constrained, dependent, predictable. She couldn't let him think her staying her meant otherwise. She had to force a change, and soon.

Arthur came home earlier than usual that night for dinner. He and Addy had to go to Uncle Ted's law office that evening for the reading of her father's will; in a seemingly innocuous mixing of friendship and business, Ted had been the Coharts' lawyer for many years. And now Arthur, of course, also worked for the firm. Addy watched him as they spooned soup into their mouths, wondering if he was already privilege to the contents of the will.

While Arthur hadn't brought up their marriage, Addy could sense that he was contemplating it during the uneasy domesticity they had established over the last two weeks. They had fallen into a routine, with Addy taking over the day-to-day running of the household, just as she would have if she were his wife. More reason for Addy to get away, though she still had no idea where she would go.

Mrs. Simmons usually took her meals in her room, which left Arthur and Addy on their own. Tonight a heavy silence joined the pair at the dinner table. Addy was engrossed in thoughts of what her life was missing and couldn't bother to make small talk. The first thing, she decided, was to actually do something rather than just read about it.

Once that decision was made, she knew what the first step should be. She would call on her old friend Mary Horace, with whom she had shared a French tutor when she was younger. Now married, Mary had been holding group séances in her home, hoping to reconnect with her young daughter, who had recently passed. Joining one of Mary's sessions would provide Addy the perfect entrée into that realm. She was toying with this pleasing idea and its ramifications when Arthur broke through her thoughts.

"Are you worried about hearing the will?" he asked. "Upset?"

It took her a moment to swing her thoughts around to the new topic of conversation. "What? No, I'll be fine," she said.

"It's understandable. It will be hard to hear his last words."

Addy gulped. She hadn't thought of it in those terms. "I wasn't upset about it until you put it like that."

He set his spoon in his soup bowl and leaned back in his chair. His blond hair was disheveled from the day's work, falling out of its oiled perfection. "What are you brooding about over there, then?"

Addy kept her eyes fixed on the tablecloth, tracing one of the tan lines along the red background with her finger. "I think I'm going to call on Mary Horace tomorrow."

"Why is that?"

"You know she's been holding séances."

"Yes, I do know that. That's why I asked." When Addy didn't respond, he continued, "It's not healthy. All of those spiritualists are fakes, taking advantage of people."

"Some of them are, sure, but that doesn't mean there aren't real ones. That's like saying because fool's gold exists that there's no such thing as real gold."

"You think Mary Horace has discovered real gold, then?"

"Perhaps. It's as good a place to start as any."

Arthur sighed. "I suppose there's no harm in you going once to see what it's like, but don't get too involved with it."

"I wasn't asking your permission."

Arthur stood, threw his napkin on the table, and got up without a word. Addy didn't follow him. Instead, she calmly continued eating her soup and tried to convince herself that his opinion meant nothing to her.

From the doorway he said, "You have to be ruled by somebody, Addy. Everybody does."

Addy fixed her gaze on him. "I will be ruled by myself."

He shook his head and walked out with an exasperated sigh.

Despite their argument, the always reliable Arthur was still ready half an hour later, waiting for Addy in the foyer, pacing in front of the oak door with his hands clasped behind his back.

They didn't speak as they climbed into the carriage. Still, Arthur rested his hand on top of hers on the red velvet seat between them. Addy moved her hand away. She would be strong on her own; she didn't need his support, even on a night like this. Especially not when she could sense the expectations of her that underlay his support. The carriage wheels clattered along amid the silence.

Once they arrived, a clerk showed them into the office, where Ted sat behind an imposing mahogany desk. A chipped tea set rested on one corner, and he offered his young companions lukewarm cups. Addy accepted hers but did not drink it.

Ted unfolded a few sheets of paper and spread them flat across the one empty space on the desk. "I'll read the will out to you, Addy, and of course write to your brother-in-law tomorrow to provide him with the details."

Addy grimaced at the need for a male relative to control the proceedings, especially when her father, whose final will they were supposedly enacting, had treated her as an equal. She had controlled her own allowance since she turned eighteen, no questions asked. And nothing the will said would surprise her, because Mr. Cohart had gone over all the final bequests with his daughter so she would know what to expect. In a way, Addy saw now, he had been preparing her for an impending life of spinsterhood. Addy bristled at the thought, then chastised herself for buying into—even for an instant—the common notion that an unmarried life was a negative. Her life would be her own from now on. She was ready for that.

At Addy's nod, Ted lifted the first page and began to read.

The words were a disappointment, not because of what they said, but because the dry legal jargon stripped all her father's garrulousness from the last words he'd left on Earth. Among the strand of empty sentences, she couldn't hear him at all.

It was over quickly. Both men looked to her for a reaction, but she had none to give; she simply set the still-full teacup down on the desk and folded her hands in her lap.

"That's good news, isn't it?" Arthur prompted her.

"It's nothing I didn't already know."

Arthur's eyebrows shot up in surprise.

In fact, with her focus on the sound of the words, Addy had lost all trace of the meaning as Ted read them. She worked from what her father had told her instead and hoped nothing had changed.

"If I understand correctly, the upshot is that my brother-in-law will receive the insurance money, but my father has left me the rest of his estate. Is that correct?"

"Exactly," Ted said cheerily, as if relieved she had done the expected thing and asked for his advice. "And I think it's safe to say your father had quite a good financial mind. It's a substantial sum of money. Certainly enough to keep you independent until you marry."

She stood, eager to escape the suddenly stuffy room. "Thank you. I expect you'll see to all the necessary arrangements."

"Of course." Ted stood and shook her hand.

She hesitated, holding his hand for a heartbeat longer than was strictly appropriate. "I'll meet with you again once I've decided what to do with the inheritance."

Ted nodded, seeming a little surprised at her forthrightness.

Addy turned and exited in a swirl of skirts before the men could ask her any more questions. Arthur followed after her, barely able to keep up with her frenzied step.

The following Friday afternoon Addy was waiting in Mary Horace's parlor. The house was small but neat, a row house right across the DC line in Maryland. It was not a neighborhood Addy had visited before, and she found nothing particularly interesting to recommend it. She hadn't seen Mary socially recently and was a bit anxious about reconnecting with her. Arthur's admonishments, too, repeated in her head even though she told herself not to put any value in them.

When Mary walked in, she was stunning in a deep-green dress that set off her dark hair, looking healthier and plumper than she had the last time Addy called on her. Something had healed the internal damage done by the death of her infant daughter, Addy could tell.

Mary had taken the conventional route that Addy had not—married at twenty to Frederick and a mother at twenty-one, though that joy had been taken from her so quickly. Comparatively, at twenty-two, Addy was an old maid. But that was how she wanted it. She couldn't imagine being permanently tied down to one person and one house at so young an age without experiencing the world first.

Addy stood to hug her friend, who, fortunately, didn't seem to mind the unannounced intrusion. "It's so good to see you, Addy. We barely got to speak to one another at the funeral." She sat on one sofa and waved Addy into the seat across from her. "I'm so sorry. How are you doing?" She crossed her wrists in her lap, one loose fist grasping a lace-edged handkerchief. Addy glanced up but did not see any indications of tears in her friend's eyes that would indicate a need for the handkerchief.

"As well as can be expected, I suppose. Just trying to go on with the day-to-day."

Mary gave a few emphatic nods. "That's all you can do. I found it's better to keep busy and fight the urge to stay in bed all day and weep."

"Yes," Addy replied, slightly disconcerted by the dismal turn the conversation had already taken. Hoping to shift topics, she said, "The Simmons have been very kind to me."

"Yes, I heard. How kind of them to let you stay there. Are things between you and Arthur . . . arranged properly now?"

Addy made a face. "No, they're not, though I'm sure that's what everyone thinks."

"And I take that to mean you don't want them to be arranged."

"No, I don't. That much hasn't changed."

Mary didn't press the matter further, and for that, Addy was grateful. "What's next, then? Off to Chicago to be with your sister?"

Addy sighed. "Of course, that's also what everyone thinks I should do."

Mary raised an eyebrow.

"My father left me quite a bit of money, you know."

The eyebrow dropped. Addy charged ahead.

"I think I might do some traveling." The idea hadn't really occurred to her until the words escaped her mouth, but once they were out, she knew it was the right plan.

"Really? On your own?" Mary let out a weak little laugh. "I'm sure you would enjoy that, but I don't think I would."

Addy smiled but used the pause to transition the conversation again, this time to the subject she had actually come to discuss. "I was wondering, if it isn't too bold, if I could join you at one of the séances you've been hosting."

Again, Mary's short tinkling laugh. "That's why you've come, is it? You could have just written." She smoothed the handkerchief across her lap and ran her fingers along the lace edges. "Of course you can come, if you're interested. Have you been to a séance before?"

"No, but I've read about them, and I'm fascinated. Of course, Arthur thinks it's awful." Addy scooted forward so she was perched on the edge of the seat, trying to get as close to Mary as possible. She asked, "It's helped you, hasn't it?"

"Oh, immensely. Getting to hear the voices of your loved ones and know they're safe and at peace . . . it's remarkable. Though, I have to say, the medium I have here isn't half as good as the one I saw in New York."

"When were you in New York?"

"Frederick had some business up there last month. You should visit her while you're on your travels. I can make an introduction."

"That would be wonderful." Addy could already picture herself careening through the streets of the metropolis and being feted in the foremost spiritualist circles. Though she had walked into the room without the faintest clue about her future, she knew now what she needed to do to give herself peace.

"But in the meantime," Mary continued, "you're welcome to come to the one I have going here tomorrow night. It will give you a taste for it."

Addy hadn't expected to join one so soon; the result was even better than she had hoped. She gratefully accepted. After a few more minutes of chatter, the pair embraced and Addy was out on the street again, tense with nervous excitement over the next day's adventure.

Rain finally broke the heat wave the next day. It seemed determined to make up for its long absence by letting loose three days' worth of downpour in one afternoon. The gutters filled, then overflowed, and umbrellas proved useless against the sky's torment. Addy spent the day sitting in the parlor window, dividing her attention between her book and the entertaining sight of people making mad dashes across the flooded street. She hadn't told Arthur or Ted about her plans for the evening, which she justified by reminding herself that she was now a woman of means and didn't need their approval. Still, waiting through the dull day as a guest in someone else's house certainly did not help her feel independent. She would have to solidify her plans and escape as soon as possible.

Later, Addy took her turn dashing through the rain from her door to the carriage and then back out at the Horaces'. Thunder crackled in the distance as the door closed behind her, signaling the sort of storm that might continue for days. She laughed it off and shook the water from her hat and coat. She was so looking forward to tonight that she wouldn't let anything spoil it for her, not the rain and certainly not Arthur's stern disapproval, which had emanated from him at dinner through his silence. Tonight, she was going to start the next stage of her life. She could feel it coming to greet her like a new friend.

A couple stepped inside right behind her, engaging in the same wet slapping and wringing of their clothes. Addy recognized them as Hope and Harry Mitchell, whom she had met a few times and whom she knew were regular attendees at these events. Once they had shaken the rain off sufficiently, Hope beamed and embraced Addy. "Addy, I thought that was you! How good of you to join us finally." Hope turned to her husband. "Harry, you've met Miss Cohart before, haven't you?"

"Yes, of course," he said, reaching forward to shake Addy's hand.

At that moment, Mary glided downstairs and greeted her guests. "Good, I see you've already seen our new member," she said to the Mitchells before leading the group into the parlor. "We'll have tea and coffee first so everyone can dry out."

The hot beverages were already displayed on the sideboard. The guests poured their own and then settled onto the sofas. Once everyone was seated, Mary said, "The Jensens are late as usual, I see."

Quiet murmurs of laughter drifted among the wisps of steam emanating from their cups. Addy noticed that Mary's husband was conspicuously absent from the gathering; from this, she surmised that he must have the same sort of objections Arthur did but that he was at least kind enough to let it take place in his house.

The night was still far from cool, and the wet coats left hanging in the corner were soon spouting a lazy haze of steam in the warm room. The wind picked up and whipped through an open window, sending a few china trinkets clinking together. Otherwise, the room was quiet, the mood already solemn in contemplation of what was to come.

Addy decided to break the silence. "Is the medium already here?" she asked, unsure how the evening usually went.

"Yes, she's upstairs preparing. We usually like to hold the séances in Margaret's old room," Mary responded, referring to the daughter she had lost.

"Is this your first one?" Harry asked Addy eagerly.

"Yes, my first one in the flesh. I've wanted to join for ever so long, though. I read about them constantly."

He leaned back in his chair and sipped his coffee with the air of a sage dispensing wisdom to his students. "Wonderful. It will change you, trust me."

"I hope so."

The front door opened, and soon Patty and Hugh Jensen stood in the entryway, peeking in at the other guests and waving as they removed their outer garments. They were both large, vibrant, and showy in their wealth—newly come by, something to do with a shipping company Hugh had invested in. Patty's dress was of bright-red silk, and Hugh wore gloves of the finest kid leather, with a cravat that matched his wife's dress. They clearly wanted to be seen. They could certainly afford higher-class entertainment on a Friday evening than a second-rate séance at the Horaces' now, and Addy figured their constant tardiness was probably a subtle reminder of the fact that they had many other places they could be.

The newly arrived couple stood and gulped down two of the now lukewarm cups of tea before they all moved upstairs. Addy hung at the back of the group, suddenly nervous about participating in the night's events, even though she had been so eager to before. The thought of connecting with her parents' souls, which seemed so innocent in the afternoon light with a book in her lap, seemed intimidating in the dark, candlelit room they now entered.

The medium introduced herself for Addy's benefit. She went by Madame Marsh, which seemed a bit extravagant to Addy, but Addy just smiled and shook Madame's hand without comment. The medium was a short woman with brittle brown hair and a warm smile. Once she began to speak, her easy manner chased away Addy's fears.

"You sit next to me, dear," Madame Marsh said, grabbing hold of Addy's upper arm and moving her toward the seat to the medium's right. She had no French accent; the title of *Madame* must have been one she gave herself.

The others picked their places at the round table. All the windows in the dim room were shut tight against the growing storm, lending a quiet, stuffy air to the room. "I'll go over the proceedings for the benefit of our new member," Madame Marsh said. The continued talk of membership made Addy slightly uneasy—she hadn't intended to join any club—but she was determined to press forward nonetheless. "First, I will slip into a trance to call the spirits to us and channel whoever comes forward. The spirits may choose to communicate by ringing the bell in the box, blowing out the candles, making noises, or moving an object. Then we will have a session with the Ouija board to get any specific messages." She turned to Addy; shadows cast by the flickering candlelight danced across her bulbous nose and dark eyes. "Any questions? Good. Then let's begin."

Addy couldn't help a little gasp of anticipation.

They joined hands around the circle, and Addy briefly observed the other participants; they all kept their gaze fixed on the medium, so she resolved to do that as well. Through their linked hands, Addy felt Madame Marsh begin to sway slightly. Madame also let out a low hum, like a small motor running.

"Spirits," the medium began, her voice booming across the room, "we call on you once again to cross over from beyond the grave and show yourselves to us. You may use me as a conduit—" She broke off to continue her monotonous humming. Goose bumps prickled along Addy's arms; she swore she felt the temperature in the room lower a few degrees.

The medium began humming again, then abruptly stopped. Her swaying halted as well, leaving her silent and stiff, eyes closed and mouth slightly opened. Just as abruptly, she opened her eyes and sucked in a huge breath, as if she had just emerged from under water. As she did so, a series of knocks sounded from beneath the table, and the candle flames wavered on their wicks. Addy saw Mary lick her lips in eagerness to hear what was to come next.

"Adalinda," Madame Marsh said without inflection. Addy choked out a shocked cry at the use of her full name and instinctually tried to tear her hands from her neighbors' grasps, but they resisted and held her firmly in place. "Adalinda," Madame Marsh repeated more slowly. But the voice that emerged from her mouth this time wasn't the one she had used before. Now it was deeper and broader. Addy's breath came in quick pants. It was a voice so known to her as to be unmistakable. Her father was speaking to her after death.

Tears of shock formed at the corner of Addy's eyes. She gripped Madame Marsh's hand tightly, anxious to hear what her father would say next. But after a few seconds of silence, Madame Marsh began humming again. Addy knew her father was gone. There would be no message for her tonight other than the knowledge that she was not alone.

The infant Margaret was channeled next, to talk to Mary. Addy closed her eyes and mentally withdrew from the rest of the session. She focused on each breath, trying to steady herself enough after the devastating blow of having her father taken from her so suddenly again. She was aware that Madame Marsh was taking turns, allowing everyone to hear from a loved one, but Addy didn't pay much attention to what was actually said in those otherworldly messages. Her own name, said by her own father, had been enough proof for her.

Eventually, Madame Marsh came out of her trance with a little jerk. Without commenting on what had just occurred, she asked everyone to lightly place their hands on the Ouija board, which sat in the center of the table. Addy had to rise out of her seat a few inches in order to reach it, though even then her fingertips mostly grazed the others' hands, giving her only the minutest feel of the ivory magnifying piece. The heavy drone of humming began again in earnest. She could feel the spirit energy in the room run up and down her arms like an electric current, then connect with the others and the board: the group was one channel communicating between this realm and the next.

The connection broke abruptly when Madame Marsh stopped humming and spoke. The energy stayed in Addy's fingertips, hovering over the board.

The medium's voice was even and flat, though still her own. "Give us the first initial of the person here whom you know." Immediately, the marker shot to a letter, taking everyone's hands on the same trajectory. Addy couldn't see where it landed but trusted Hope when she reported that the pointer had landed on *A*.

"It's your father again, Addy," Mary whispered. Addy quickly ran through everyone's names in her head: yes, she was the only *A* name. Whatever followed must be meant for her.

"What message do you have for us?" Madame Marsh asked.

Again, the pointer jumped to life. Addy stood and leaned over the table in order to see. The letters formed—painfully, slowly—into words, the tension building as the group called out the letters and guessed at the words. "D-O-N-O-T—*do not!*—M-A-R-R-Y—*marry!*" Addy waited for a heartbeat, expecting there to be more to the sentence—Arthur's name, perhaps, or some message about *when* she should not marry. But the pointer stilled, and everyone remained in reverent silence with their hands in place for a moment as the message sank in. The strangeness of it left little room for comment. Instead, the group reset themselves in their seats and prepared in a businesslike way for the next connection, smoothing their clothes and straightening their spines before they reached for the pointer again.

Addy followed the others' motions so it appeared she was participating in what followed, but her mind focused on solving the puzzle of the message she had just received. Why would either of her parents give her such an ominous command? Her mother—who in life had wanted nothing more than for her younger daughter to marry well—and her father had never once presumed to tell his daughter what she should do. It made no sense.

Finally, the séance came to an end. "There are no more spirits waiting to be heard tonight," the medium said. She released the hands of those beside her, and the others followed suit.

Harry laughed a little as he leaned back in his chair. Addy, too, relaxed, welcoming the loosening of the muscles she hadn't realized she had been tensing for the last hour. Suddenly, she felt like she could fall asleep in her chair. She watched as Madame Marsh stood, bowed, and exited the room without another word. The two couples began talking between themselves.

Addy shook herself awake as best she could as she caught Mary's gaze. Her friend was grinning, eyes sparking with pleasure. She slid over a seat so she was next to Addy. "I can't believe your father came through so strongly in your first séance. It took three times for Margaret to come through at all. He's strong. And now you know he doesn't want you to marry Arthur. Isn't that a relief?"

Addy chewed her lower lip. "Do you think that's what it means?"

"What else could it mean? Surely he couldn't mean that you should *never* marry? That would be ridiculous." She said this with an air of finality and certainty, her chin high in the air.

Addy shrugged, not entirely convinced. As the others stood and began to descend the stairs, Addy followed in a daze.

"Addy?"

She turned at the bottom of the stairs to find Harry behind her. She realized he must have been talking to her and she hadn't even noticed. "What did you think?"

Addy forced a smile. "It was remarkable. I'm exhausted now, though."

He patted her shoulder. "It does take a lot out of you. Go home and rest. I hope we see you here again soon."

"Me too."

Addy said the rest of her goodbyes and then waited on the front step for the Simmonses' carriage to arrive. On the way home, she looked out at the continuing rain without registering it, enjoying the swaying motion of the carriage ride as a comforting backdrop to her thoughts. By the time she arrived at her temporary home, she had resolved to tell the Simmons of her plans. It was time to start her new life. She wouldn't stay in faked domesticity with Arthur any longer. It wasn't what she wanted, and now she knew her parents agreed.

Chapter 3

Uncle Ted entered his parlor in just his shirtsleeves. His hair was hastily combed and lacked its usual regimented look. Clearly he had not been expecting visitors, even Addy, on a Saturday morning. She couldn't blame him. Showing up unannounced this early was not the done thing.

Addy stood as he came in. "I apologize for calling today, but once I've made my mind up on a thing, I can't wait on it."

"As well it should be," Ted replied, smiling blandly. "But to what in particular are you referring?" He waved her back into her seat and took his own across from her.

"Ever since my parents' deaths, I think everyone has been waiting for me to decide on the direction of my future, myself included. Now that the contents of my father's will have been made known to me, I've made up my mind."

Ted shifted in his chair, and Addy thought he clenched his teeth as well. "And what have you decided?" he asked.

"You know I'm ever grateful to you and your sister-in-law and nephew for your hospitality. But it's become time for me to move on, especially as I have never had the intention of accepting Arthur's proposal."

"I think we had all hoped you had reconsidered your position on that matter."

"While I have given the matter a great deal of thought, no, I haven't changed my mind. Instead, I'd like to use the inheritance to travel before I settle down."

"It might be best to use the inheritance to ensure your future."

"I don't plan on being extravagant, of course."

Ted sighed and rubbed his forehead. "The expected thing would be for you to go to your sister's, of course, but you always have avoided the expected."

Addy wasn't sure if this was meant to be derogatory or was simply an observation.

Ted shifted back into his role as concerned adult. "Surely you don't plan to travel alone."

Addy smiled. That point meant he was at least accepting of the idea. "I think it should be easy enough to secure a traveling companion." To sweeten the deal, she threw in, "I may go to my sister after, but I'd like to see a bit of the world first." Ted gave an approving nod, and Addy knew it was all now just a matter of ironing out the details.

"Have you given any thought as to where you might go?"

"Mary Horace has offered to introduce me to some of her connections in New York. From there I'll sail over to Europe." She neatly left out the *types* of connections Mary had in New York, and fortunately Ted didn't pry. Arthur must not have shared his concerns about Addy's pastimes with his uncle.

"Doesn't your mother have family in New York?"

Addy crossed her ankles and avoided Ted's gaze. She had hoped he wouldn't bring this up. She had a maiden great-aunt, a sister of Addy's mother's mother, living in New York. And Addy knew that if she was forced to stay with her great-aunt, all her plans for her new life in New York would come to naught.

"Yes. I will call on her while I'm there," Addy said.

"Surely she would let you stay with her."

"I wouldn't want to impose myself on such an elderly woman. It would be much more sensible to engage a companion closer to my own age."

Ted watched her closely for a moment, then a smile rose at one corner of his mouth. He gave a strong nod, indicating he had accepted her reasoning.

"I hope you're not planning on cutting all ties with us. I'm perfectly happy to arrange the trip for you. I can put an ad in the paper tomorrow to engage a traveling companion."

"Of course, I would appreciate any help you are able to provide. You know so much more about these things than I do." She almost gagged on the words, but she knew the best way to get a man on her side was to massage his ego. She smiled sweetly up at him as they stood and headed toward the front door, hoping she looked like the ignorant woman he must assume her to be. No, that wasn't quite fair to Ted. He did treat her equally, but still. The role must continue to be played.

At the door, his hand on the knob, Ted asked," Have you told Arthur yet?"

"No, I'll have to do that when I get home. I doubt he will take the news quite as well as you have."

"He's very fond of you, you know."

"I know." She glanced at Ted's hand, willing him to open the door and set her free. "But I can't be held responsible for that." Even she felt the way the words stung like a shock of static electricity.

After a pause, Ted finally opened the door, but he didn't move aside so she could pass. "Maybe a European suitor will be more to your taste."

Addy stepped around him and exited with a quiet "Thank you." How hard must it be for him to imagine that this trip was not just an excuse to go on a husband hunt? The previous night's message still lingered in her thoughts: *Do not marry.* She sighed, looked both ways up and down the street, then trod off toward the Simmonses' home and her dreaded conversation with Arthur.

Addy arrived just in time for lunch. From outside she could see Arthur pacing across the front rooms of the house, keeping the street in constant view.

He accosted her as soon as she walked in. "Where have you been? You didn't tell me you were going out."

"I don't need to tell you every time I go somewhere," she said in exasperation as she unpinned her hat and set it on a small table by the entrance. While her back was still to him, she reminded herself that all this would soon be behind her, and she fixed a pleasant smile on her face before turning around. "I went to see your uncle." She saw his shoulders relax and knew his anger had deflated. She rushed on before he could ask more questions. "Is it time to go in for lunch?"

He opened his mouth as if to press her further, but shook his head instead and turned to the dining room, waving her through. Addy walked haughtily ahead of him, a ruse to keep her courage up in advance of the conversation they were about to have.

Once they were cutting silently into the cold meat on their plates, Addy plunged ahead and broached the subject without preamble. "I'm leaving, Arthur," she said simply. "Your uncle is going to advertise for a traveling companion for me so I can go abroad." She reached across the table and set her hand gently on his, a gesture she had never dared before because of the hope it might have brought him. But now it would comfort him. "Of course, I'm so incredibly thankful for all you and your mother have done for me. But under the circumstances, I can't stay here forever as your guest. The inheritance gives me the freedom to do what I want, and I plan to use it." She paused, and a pleading look spread across her face. "Please don't make this harder than it needs to be."

Arthur leaned back in his chair and threw his fork onto his plate, but it was a movement of defeat rather than anger. Patches of red bloomed on his pale cheeks. "Of course, if it's what you want and my uncle supports it, there's nothing I can say. But I am disappointed. Not just for me but for you as well."

"I know, but I always said—"

"Yes, yes, I know. Like you said, let's not make this harder than we have to." He considered her for a long moment, then abruptly looked away, analyzing the tablecloth instead. "When will you leave?"

"All that is still to be decided."

He nodded and finally looked at her again. "You're welcome to stay here until you leave."

Addy was surprised that the statement even needed to be made; perhaps naively, she hadn't considered that Arthur might expect her to leave his house once she made a decision to abandon him. All the more reason to make the arrangements quickly. She skipped over all this and said only, "Thank you."

Arthur nodded, stood, bowed, and left the room without another word. He had never acted so cold and formal with her. She coughed, a bit of half-chewed meat caught in the back of her throat. She was sadder than she had anticipated over Arthur treating her in such a way, but she steeled herself against the thought and let it pass no further.

By the end of the week Ted had placed the ad, gathered the responses, and selected a few candidates to come in for interviews at his law office. It was at this point that he finally brought Addy into the process, which she resented only a little; best to let him do what he felt he needed to so things kept moving forward. By giving up a little control in some areas now, she hoped to gain ultimate control over her life.

She arrived at the appointed time on Friday afternoon. Three women waited in the hall leading to Ted's office, and Addy smiled nervously at them as she walked by. She was about to share the biggest adventure of her life with one of them. She cast a wish up to heaven that at least one would combine Ted's need for practicality with Addy's need for friendship. Traveling the world with a dour, disapproving governess type was hardly what she had in mind.

She stepped inside Ted's office and shut the door. He sat behind the desk as usual, pages fanned out in front of him. After they had exchanged greetings, she sat and gestured at the pages. "Are these their applications?"

"Yes, all ready to go."

She fixed her gaze on him for an instant too long, and it was another excruciating instant before he realized what her look meant. He leaped out of his chair, gathered the pages up out of their neat arrangement, and handed them across the wide desk. "Would you like to take a look at their qualifications before they come in?"

"Yes, I think it would be good if I knew the same amount as you, don't you think?" She skimmed the pages but took a bit longer than necessary going over them just to prove her point. Her father had never kept her in the dark like this about anything that concerned her own situation. She was beginning to realize how lucky she was to have been raised by such a man.

One of the women had traveled with an actual duchess—the old aristocrat's scrawl graced the character reference included with the letter. *Traveling with me, then, would be a step down,* Addy thought, and turned to the next candidate's pages. The other two had served as ladies' maids with some traveling involved, much smaller stuff. She thought she would rather have one of those than the other, who would be more likely to treat Addy with kid gloves.

She set down the pages on her side of the desk. "All right, why don't you bring the first one in?"

Ted ushered in Miss Smith, the duchess's companion. She was tall, thin, and middle-aged. She hardly looked like the sort of person Addy could picture spending months with.

Miss Smith first extolled her experience packing and keeping to a schedule. Ted nodded approvingly.

Then Miss Smith asked the question Addy was already learning to hate.

"Will we be seeking suitors while we're abroad? Making your debut in London, perhaps? We managed to get two of the duchess's three daughters married off during my tenure with her."

Addy made a sour face. "No. That's not the point of the trip."

Miss Smith exchanged a knowing glance with Ted. "Well, we can keep it in mind while we're out and about."

"Thank you so much for your time, Miss Smith." Addy stood and extended her hand, which the older woman shook weakly, as if it were not a gesture she was used to engaging in.

Once she had left, Ted said, "Addy, you can't dismiss someone just because they are practical."

"Is that what you want to call it?"

He sighed and shook his head, but went to the hall to bring in the second candidate.

Miss Garrison was an improvement. She was younger, at thirty-two, but very reserved. Addy couldn't tell if this was an affectation for the interview or if she really was so terribly shy. She stuttered her answers in a voice that barely carried the three feet between her and Addy. Either way, it didn't suit Addy at all. At least she didn't bring up suitors or marriage.

Finally, in came Miss Solder, wearing a dress that was practical but fashionable. Addy admired the way the deep blue of the dress complemented the pale-sky color of Miss Solder's eyes. She was the closest to Addy's own age, with a fine face and gloves that looked surprisingly expensive. She shook Addy's hand right away and did not shy away from answering any of Ted's questions.

After they had run through her qualifications to Ted's satisfaction, Addy asked, "What do you think the goal of this trip should be?"

Miss Solder looked taken aback but composed herself quickly. "I wouldn't presume to say, since it's your trip, ma'am. But there certainly are advantages to travel, in terms of broadening one's horizons and learning new things."

"First of all, please don't call me *ma'am*, Miss Solder," Addy said kindly.

"In that case, call me Tiffany, then, please."

"I hope that whomever I travel with will turn out to be more of a friend than a guardian."

"Again, I wouldn't presume to oversee your behavior, just your travel plans and your things."

Addy smiled. "That would be quite enough."

Ted looked between them. "I hope that you would still presume to maintain propriety on a trip with two young women alone."

"Of course."

The nature of the smile on her face, like she was trying to hold back laughter, made Addy think Tiffany saw the ridiculousness in Ted's worry just as much as Addy did. Addy beamed at her.

There was no question of Addy's choice, and she said so to Ted once Tiffany had left.

Ted ventured, "Miss Smith is by far the most qualified—"

"You can think of qualifications, and I can think of companionship. Traveling with Miss Smith would be fearfully dull. And likely to end in forced matrimony, which I do not want."

Ted smiled indulgently, as if he was about to present a child with a penny candy. "Miss Solder did have excellent character references, I must say. And I can tell you two would get on."

Addy couldn't disguise her pleasure. "It's decided, then?"

"I'll write to them with the decision tomorrow. That is, unless you want to wait and interview more candidates. There's no rush."

To you, there isn't, Addy thought grimly. But she shook her head and said she was content enough with the choice. "Thank you so much for your help," she said as she got up. Ted nodded and escorted her out into the hall with one hand placed tenderly on her shoulder.

Chapter 4

Two weeks later, Tiffany Solder had purchased train tickets to New York and turned the Simmonses' foyer into a staging area for trunks and packages. Planning had turned the days into such a flurry that Addy had barely had time to think about anything else, a welcome reprieve from the too-slow, too-thoughtful days that had preceded them.

Two days before their departure, Tiffany arrived at the Simmonses' with her own pile of suitcases, moving in temporarily to help with the final preparations. Addy was out when she arrived, making one last visit to Mary Horace to ensure everything was arranged for Addy to see the renowned medium whom Mary had raved about seeing in New York, Mrs. Alexi. This was the central purpose of the trip in Addy's mind, and she was pleased to hear that everything was in place for it.

When Addy got home, Tiffany was in an animated tête-à-tête with Arthur, laughter emerging from them both. Addy stood in the parlor door, trying to force the frown from her face, but she didn't quite succeed before they looked up and saw her. Seeing her new employer's expression, Tiffany quieted and pushed a loose lock of dark hair behind her ear.

"Have you checked on the status of the arrangements?" Addy asked coldly.

"Yes, everything seems to be on track." Tiffany glanced at Arthur while she talked, as if he had already succeeded in making her feel like she had to ask his permission for everything she did. The glance, coupled with the sudden cutoff of their conversation at her arrival, made Addy worry that they had been discussing her. She wondered what Arthur had told Tiffany—if he could have asked her specially to look after Addy for him or report back to him during their journey. There was no definite answer in either of their faces.

"Why don't you join us?" Arthur asked, indicating the empty spot beside him on the sofa.

Although she wanted to end his conversation with Tiffany, with her new suspicions circulating, she couldn't face making small talk with him right now. "I'll come down for tea." She added as an afterthought, "I'm tired." Then she turned abruptly and rushed up the stairs to her room.

By teatime, Arthur had left on some business, and Addy was relieved she didn't have to face him. She sat across from Tiffany at the small table in the breakfast room. Addy reached for the teapot, accustomed to pouring for Arthur and his mother, but Tiffany stayed her hand. "Let me," she said, and took over the duties. Her hands were steady and sure, and Addy admired the strength and calm of her demeanor. If only her loyalty to Addy could be assured of as well.

Trying to sound casual, Addy asked, "What were you and Arthur discussing this morning?"

"He was telling me some stories of you two as children."

Addy smiled. "We have had some adventures."

"You're lucky to have such a lifelong friend."

A nod only. "Did you talk about the trip as well?"

Tiffany blew on her tea, even though it had certainly cooled by now. She took a sip, then set it back down on the gold-rimmed saucer. "Are you and Arthur no longer friends?"

"How adept you are." Addy paused. "We were friends, but as one gets older, these things become more difficult. He asked me to marry him, you know."

"He didn't mention that."

"I refused him."

With a pointed look toward the piles in the entryway, Tiffany said, "I gathered that much."

Addy laughed, finally put somewhat at ease. "Yes, of course. I am glad we can be honest with each other, is all."

"As am I." She spun another lump of sugar into her tea with a spoon. "Have you been to New York before?"

"No. But you have, of course."

"Several times as a lady's maid. You'll enjoy it, I'm sure."

"I'll be glad to have you with me. You're far more worldly than me."

"That will change, I'm sure of it. You have an acquaintance to see there, I gather?"

Made sensitive by the reactions she had received about her interest in spiritualism, Addy hesitated to mention it, but she decided it was best to come out with it now, as Tiffany would find out soon anyway. She set down her cup and squared her chin. "Yes, a friend of mine here has secured me a meeting with Mrs. Alexi." She watched Tiffany's face and was surprised to see recognition cross it.

"The medium?" Tiffany asked. "I've read about her in the papers. Isn't it nearly impossible to get in to see her? She's the toast of New York society, I think."

"So I've heard. Which is why I'm lucky that Mrs. Horace knows her so well." Then, testing out the waters further, Addy asked, "You don't disapprove?"

Still mindful of her position, Tiffany said, "It's not my place to approve or disapprove, of course . . ."

Addy waved her off. "Let's not stand on formality, please."

"In that case, no, I don't. There are charlatans out there, of course, but as far as I know, no one has been able to prove Mrs. Alexi false." She sighed and bounced a little in her seat. "I would love to be able to have a session with her."

"Surely she can't object to my companion coming along, too."

"Really? That would be wonderful!"

Addy beamed. The two of them had even more in common than she had thought. She stayed with this idea a bit too long to keep the conversation going, but Tiffany rescued her.

"Mr. Simmons told me about your parents . . . I'm so sorry . . . Is that who you're trying to contact?"

Addy wondered which Mr. Simmons she referred to but decided it didn't matter. Her hand wrapped around the quickly cooling teacup, as if hoping to squeeze the last remnants of warmth from it. But she wouldn't let those memories darken her mood—not today. Instead, she pressed forward. "Is there someone on the other side for you?"

"Yes," Tiffany said quietly, as if speaking from the beyond herself. "Too many, really."

Addy nodded sympathetically but thought it best not to pry for now. She simply rested her hand over her companion's for comfort. Tiffany looked up at her with a gentle smile, but still moved her hand away.

It wasn't until she was back in her room that Addy realized how deftly Tiffany had moved the conversation away from talk of Arthur and honesty by engaging Addy in her favorite topics of the trip and spiritualism. Perhaps there was more going on between Tiffany and Arthur than she had realized, Addy mused. She would just have to wait to find out what exactly that was.

The next night was their last in the nation's capital. Ted joined them for dinner, and even Mrs. Simmons came down to join them, though she spent most of the evening groaning and rubbing her leg in what Addy could only guess was a grab at sympathy. After dinner, Addy said her farewells to Arthur's uncle and mother but escaped upstairs with the claim of unfinished packing before Arthur made his way around to her. As the evening continued, eventually she knew she could avoid the moment no longer. She had to say goodbye to him or risk bad blood between them forever. Even with her annoyance at so much of what he'd done, she didn't want that. Addy and Tiffany would leave early in the morning, and Addy had discouraged Arthur from getting up just to see them off. That made tonight her only chance.

She crept uneasily downstairs. The house, which had seen such a flurry of activity over the previous two weeks, had now fallen silent. The foyer felt like an empty tomb since all the trunks had already been sent ahead to the train station. She found Arthur in the study, a glass of brandy beside him and a cumbersome book open in his lap, though his attention was clearly focused elsewhere, an index finger rubbing his lower lip thoughtfully. She expected him to jump as she entered, but he just looked lazily up at her. She realized her steps on the stairs must have been obvious with everything else so quiet.

"Am I disturbing you?"

"Of course not. I was worried you weren't going to come down at all." He dragged a chair from its place on the opposite side of the end table so that it faced his own. Addy sat gingerly, her knees turned away at an angle, only inches from touching his. She worried the move showed too much familiarity, even still.

"I wouldn't do that to you."

"Everything is set for tomorrow?"

"Yes, I think so. Though something is bound to have been missed."

"Hopefully only small things."

"Yes." Silence stretched taut for long moments across the words waiting to be said. Finally, Addy sighed. "Arthur, I know this isn't how you wanted things to turn out."

He looked affronted. "No, it isn't. But I'm an adult. I'll be fine."

"I know you will—"

"I wish you the best, Addy. Though I will miss you."

"I'll miss you, too. You really are my oldest and dearest friend. I hate to think that has been ruined by all this." She reached across the small space between them, but he kept his hand planted firmly on the open page in his lap and made no move to help her bridge the gap. She withdrew her hand and folded it within the other in her own lap, hiding what had just happened. "We'll see each other again," she offered.

"Will we? You have no reason to come back here now. You'll travel the world having a wonderful time, maybe meeting some handsome European prince in the process. And even if you don't, you'll be off to Chicago to live with your sister. And I have no plans to leave Washington. So, you see, I think we probably won't."

"It's hardly as dramatic as that, is it?"

He didn't answer.

To try to relax the atmosphere, she added, "Besides, I hardly think I'm princess material."

Arthur gazed at her with a new coldness. "You'll write, I presume?"

She, too, left a question unanswered. She stood, instead, and said, "I wish the best for you, Arthur. Good night." She realized how absurd the last phrase sounded, but for some reason she couldn't bring herself to say goodbye. She turned and left without any answering closing from her old friend.

Back in her room, she recalled the time before she and Arthur began school, when all they had to do was play in the back garden and daydream. They used to play a game, shared just between the two of them. In it, they would go to the future. Not their own futures like many children did, pretending to keep house or tend children. No, Addy and Arthur would travel to other ages, lingering with aliens and watching spaceships burst into the sky. Sometimes, the people they would encounter on these adventures would tell them some story about how an Arthur Simmons or Addy Cohart from long ago had invented or written or believed something so incredible that it had helped create that new miraculous world and were always remembered fondly.

Addy brushed a few tears off her cheeks at the memory of Arthur's eager blond head joining in so much dreaming with her own.

What had happened?

She felt the hard reality of life had drained something from all of them, and that the idyllic future she had believed in so dearly as a child would never come to pass.

But she would do her best to make it so. To make some change that even just one person years from now would remember fondly as the thing that Adalinda Cohart did.

Chapter 5

The next morning passed in a half-awake haze of whispered instructions and muffled clanging of boots and bags as Addy and Tiffany tried not to wake the ones who were staying behind. Addy was silent throughout the carriage ride to the train station, trying to take in the final views of her hometown through the strange shapes of early dawn. She could feel each passing minute build momentum, taking her closer to her destination. She glanced at Tiffany, dozing across from her, but let her rest. There would be plenty of time for conversation later. Besides, Addy would have to get used to being alone with her own thoughts since independence was what she had claimed to want so defiantly.

During the train ride, the two women switched roles, with Tiffany watching the scenery intently as it passed and Addy resting with her eyes closed, sometimes drifting off and other times wrapped in her thoughts. She kept running over everything that would have to be done when they got to New York, as if worrying over it in advance would help it get done more effectively: find the hotel, unpack, write to Mrs. Alexi to confirm their meeting. While Addy's body ached with tiredness, her mind would not let it rest.

When the train pulled with a final puff into the New York station, Addy felt like she had been awake for days. After a jumble of identifying their trunks and sending them ahead to the hotel, Addy and Tiffany walked out to the street, giving Addy her first view of the city she had dreamed about.

Even from her own small vantage point, she could feel its gargantuan difference from Washington, already a backwater in her mind. Around them, the city moved at a determined, noisy pace and seemed to stretch up to the sky. The closest city to it Addy had seen was when she had visited Chicago after Trisha's wedding, but that city had felt newer and more eager. New York, in contrast, felt more settled in its ways, accepting of its superiority. Addy let Tiffany lead her by the hand to the waiting cab so she could keep her eyes on all that was going on around her.

She continued her watch out the window of the carriage as they inched through the crowded streets. People and horses mixed together, unbothered by each other.

"It's a bit overwhelming, seeing it for the first time," Tiffany said.

"No, not overwhelming. It's invigorating, don't you think?" She looked back out the window without waiting for Tiffany's response.

Tiffany laughed. "I suppose it is. It's hard to be unlively in New York."

Addy only half heard the words. She was engrossed in crafting stories for all the people they passed along the street, imagining the great friendships she was bound to make among such a vast number of people.

"Have you thought about what you'd like to do today?"

Addy dragged herself from her reverie. She had been so busy earlier thinking about all the things she *had* to do she hadn't given much thought to what she *wanted* to do. "What do you suggest? Though, to be honest, I don't know that I will be up for much."

"I think a ride around Central Park would be just the thing for a day like that."

"Hm? Oh, yes, that sounds lovely. I've seen engravings of it."

"It's much more impressive in person."

Addy sighed and twisted her mouth into a pout. "How is it that I feel like the living dead and you don't even seem tired?"

Again, Tiffany laughed quietly and sweetly. "I'm used to getting up and working at all hours, I suppose. And I've traveled enough that I can sleep well even the night before a big event."

Addy frowned, feeling keenly her lack of work and of *living*, though she knew Tiffany didn't mean to reproach her.

Their conversation was interrupted by a sudden jolt of the carriage. Both women peered out the window. They had stopped along the curb in front of a hotel. *Their* hotel, Addy thought, excitement bubbling in her stomach.

The coachman helped Addy and Tiffany down onto the sidewalk. The brick building they landed in front of was imposing but homey enough. Addy was pleased. Mary had recommended the hotel, and her friend did not disappoint. Tiffany checked them in with a middle-aged desk clerk, who then ushered them upstairs to their suite. It was bright and tastefully furnished, if a decade or so out of date. That only made it feel more like a home with old, familiar furniture.

Addy explored all the nooks and crannies of the rooms, opening every drawer and cabinet and peeking out every window. It would, after all, be their home for the foreseeable future, so she might as well get accustomed to it now. Addy had preferred to leave her departure date open to see how her time in New York went before she decided to leave.

The luggage arrived shortly from the station. Tiffany called down for a light lunch to fortify them before they began to unpack. Addy could see already that Tiffany would be the sensible one throughout their journey, and she resolved not to do anything to make Tiffany feel like she had to corral her mistress too much. It wouldn't do to be seen as flighty or unwise just as she was trying to make her own way in the world. Especially if it turned out Tiffany was reporting back to Arthur and Ted.

The sandwiches and coffee perked up Addy's spirits and sent her mind whirling another million miles a minute. Tiffany puttered around, checking the trunks and strategizing the unpacking. Addy leaned beside the window that looked out over the street and watched the passersby. An elegant couple walked sedately past, followed by a much poorer family rushing down the street. A group of young men stopped across the road, talking, with one waving an elaborately carved walking stick to emphasize his words. A child wandered by on his own, looking purposeful rather than lost. She wanted to build pasts for all of them, but they were too many and too fleeting. She gave up and instead sat at the small writing desk to compose a letter to Mrs. Alexi, the woman on whom she had pinned all her hopes of New York.

Addy and Tiffany went downstairs once their respective tasks were complete. Addy dropped off her letter to be couriered to Mrs. Alexi. Then they ventured out into their first New York afternoon. Tiffany directed the cab driver to Central Park. When they got there, Addy wanted to be in the middle of the scene instead of just watching it pass by, so she suggested they walk instead of continuing the carriage ride.

They went at a slow pace along the paths of the park. Tiffany let Addy take in her surroundings largely in silence. It was dreadfully hot, and Addy began to regret her decision to walk. She spied a pond a ways off and was determined to rest on its banks once they reached it.

As they rounded a corner, they nearly bumped into a young man wearing a brightly colored vest and cravat. He tipped his hat to them. "So sorry, ladies," he said. "I'm just in a bit of a hurry." He took a step to move around them but then hesitated. "Actually, I wonder if you could help me." He peered off into the distance. "I was trying to chase down a street urchin who stole my wallet, but it looks like I've lost him now."

"Oh! Should we get a policeman?" Addy asked.

Tiffany gripped Addy's elbow tightly.

"No, there's nothing they could do. These blasted boys are everywhere." He held a finger to his lips. "But I don't suppose you could loan a fellow a few cents for the cab ride home, could you? I can send the money to your hotel once I am able to get some more cash from my bank tomorrow. You are touring the city, I assume?"

Addy opened her mouth to speak, but Tiffany jumped in. "I'm sorry, but we don't have any cash, either." She pushed Addy by the elbow to guide her away.

"But—" Addy began.

Tiffany continued to move them away from the man. Addy glanced back. He was already moving on—probably, she thought, in hopes of still finding the boy.

Once they were out of earshot, Tiffany stopped and faced Addy. "Are you really so innocent that you nearly fell for that?"

"What do you mean? He needed help."

Tiffany rolled her eyes. "He was conning you. He saw right away we were tourists and was trying to get some money out of us. I guarantee he's moved on to his next victim by now."

Addy frowned as she ran through the scene again; then she laughed. "My God, what would I do without you?"

Tiffany's smile was weak and watery. "It's good that you learned over a few cents and not a more serious amount. Just keep your wits about you."

They spent the cents they had saved from theft on lemonades and sat on the grass by the water. Even among the hubbub of so many conversations and yelling children, it was the most peaceful Addy had felt in a long time.

As they walked back into the hotel after leaving the park, Tiffany stopped in the lobby to discuss their playgoing options with the concierge. Addy begged off and went back their rooms. Once there, she changed out of her walking clothes and was glad to be alone to do it, not liking to admit how much she had sweated during their excursion. The damp spots in her dress and the slicks of moisture caught under her corset didn't make her feel very ladylike. While New York didn't feel as humid as Washington, she was certain it was hotter.

She wanted nothing more than to collapse on the sofa, but she knew she wouldn't get up for the rest of the day if she did. Instead, she gulped a glass of water to refresh herself and did nothing more than rest her fingertips against the floral arm of the couch. She remembered she hadn't asked for messages at the front desk when they came in. There might be a reply from Mrs. Alexi. The thought was important enough to drive her back downstairs, taking the ornate iron elevator down to the broad lobby.

Tiffany was still talking to the concierge, now holding a couple of leaflets he had given her. Addy approached the front desk and before she could say anything, the clerk said, "Ah, Miss Cohart. Perfect. I was about to send someone up. You've just had a guest arrive."

"A guest?" she asked, stopping in her tracks a few feet short of the desk.

"Yes, that gentleman over there." He gestured to a youngish man standing in the center of the lobby, waiting with a rare stillness and patience. To Addy, he seemed to be the only person in New York not in constant motion. Immediately, she sensed something was special about this mysterious visitor. She walked toward him, trying not to look too eager. Based on his prideful smile, she guessed she had only partially succeeded.

The man stayed in the same spot as she neared. When she was close enough, he stuck out his hand. "Miss Cohart, I assume?" His manner was brusque and unpretentious.

"May I know whose hand I have the honor of shaking?"

He inclined his head, sending thick dark curls shaking around his clean-shaven face. "Of course. My name is William Fairley. Mrs. Alexi asked me to come see you."

Addy couldn't suppress the little "Oh!" of pleased surprised. "I certainly wasn't expecting an in-person reply."

"Yes, well, she often doesn't have time to write letters. And she has to find ways to keep me busy as well." He said this last with a wink.

"You work with her?"

"Yes. I like to say I'm one of her protégés. But I make quite a good errand boy, too."

Addy laughed politely. "Are you a medium?"

He bowed again. "Not nearly as good of a one as she is."

"I've heard she's the best." At that moment, Tiffany appeared at her elbow.

"Tiffany, this is Mr. Fairley. Mrs. Alexi sent him." She indicated Tiffany to introduce her. "Miss Solder is my traveling companion."

"A pleasure. You must be the one who will be joining us at the séance."

Tiffany nodded. "I hope that won't be a problem."

"Of course not. We're available tomorrow night. Why don't you both join us then?"

Tiffany bit her lip and glanced at Addy. "I've just booked us two tickets at a play tomorrow night."

"Come after, it will be fine," Mr. Fairley broke in. "We start late anyway, for obvious reasons." He slipped a card out of his pocket and handed it to Tiffany. "Here is our address. She looks forward to meeting you." He nodded to each of them in turn and then took his leave.

Addy was enraptured as she watched him walk away. The cut of his coat perfectly accented his narrow hips.

"Who is he?" Tiffany asked. "He seems too well dressed to be a servant."

"He's one of her protégés. Another medium."

"Paying his dues by running errands and calling on her potential guests, I see." She leaned in conspiratorially. "And he's quite handsome, too."

Addy blushed unexpectedly. "I suppose he is."

"'Suppose'! You know it."

"Well, yes." Recovering herself, she continued, "It's no surprise she sends him to call on young ladies. But we're going there to see Mrs. Alexi tomorrow night, not him."

"If you say so."

Tiffany took Addy's elbow and guided back her back to the elevator. Neither woman could help taking one last glance after Mr. Fairley, even though he had already disappeared onto the street.

***

The next night, Addy gasped as she stepped out of the carriage in front of the playhouse. The humidity had finally given way to rain earlier in the day. It had ended as they left the hotel, leaving behind a fine mist that transformed the light from the streetlamps into something soft and strange. It bathed the theatergoers near Addy in halos and highlighted the sequins on their fine clothes and the diamonds on their fingers. And yet everything more than four feet away was blurry, so when the people walked up the steps to the entrance, they disintegrated slowly from view. Addy felt they had entered a magical world, cut off from the rest of the city.

After the surreal atmosphere outside, the elegant lobby in its garish brilliance was a letdown. But still, Addy forced herself to look around and take it all in. As she gazed around the room, she touched Tiffany's arm lightly. "Isn't that Mr. Fairley?"

Tiffany craned her neck to see where Addy was looking. Finally, she noticed him in the movement of the crowd, once again standing stoically and unbothered by what was going on around him. "It is him, I think."

Addy gave a tentative wave to catch his eye. When he saw them, he sprang into motion like a wind-up toy, navigating through the crowd to reach them. "Excellent! I've found you," he said in triumph once he was in front of them.

"You were waiting for us?" Addy fingered the neckline of her dress as she spoke.

"Yes, forgive me for being forward, but I thought I'd accompany you so I can escort you to Mrs. Alexi's after the play." He winked and leaned in closer. "They can't get started without me there, so you know you won't be late."

Tiffany looked perplexed. "But how did you know which play we were seeing?"

He winked again, and already it was starting to feel a bit like a tic rather than the charming affectation it had seemed at first. "I am a psychic medium, after all." He laughed at the ladies' surprised faces. "I asked the concierge which tickets you had purchased before I left the hotel."

The tension went out of the interaction as they all shared a laugh. Mr. Fairley extended his arm to show the way. "Shall we?"

The play was a comedy, and Addy enjoyed it immensely. Mr. Fairley's presence between her and Tiffany certainly didn't hinder her enjoyment, either. At one point he leaned over, tapped her arm and pointed out something onstage, and she thought she might swoon beneath his gaze. For the first time she was close enough to see his eyes were blue, and their brightness drew her in.

Even though it felt late to Addy, when they emerged back onto the street, New York nightlife still flashed hectically by. The mist had dissipated, and the buildings and gaslights shone forth in brightened glory. Mr. Fairley waved a cab down, and soon they were on their way to Mrs. Alexi's.

"Tell us about yourself, Mr. Fairley," Tiffany prodded.

"I am a New York native. My father was a bookseller, and I ran his shop up until six years ago, when I met Mrs. Alexi and she recognized my talents for what they were."

"You never knew before then that you could . . ."

He smiled indulgently. "I never knew how to control it or what name to give it. She helped me with all of that." He neatly shifted the conversation. "This is the first stop on your travels, isn't it? Where to next?"

"Europe," Addy answered. "I'd like to see London and Paris. And Rome. But none of that is set in stone quite yet."

"You're not ready to rush off from New York anytime soon?"

"No, we haven't set any departure date yet."

"Well, I wish I could go with you. It sounds lovely. I've never been to Europe myself."

Addy started to speak, but the carriage ground to a halt, and Mr. Fairley announced their arrival. He jumped down first, then helped the two ladies down. The street here, more residential, was quieter than the one they had left. The house in front of them appeared unlit, as if no one was inside. Undeterred, their host ushered them inside.

The front hall they entered was dimly lit with a few candles. The formal front rooms on either side were dark, but a faint glow came from the back rooms. Addy peered into the dark room to her left to try to see the furnishings but could only make out shapes. Her attention was redirected as a woman came down the stairs. Addy knew instantly that it was Mrs. Alexi. Her steps were slow, her spine straight—a pace and pose designed to draw attention.

She was of average height, middle-aged, plump, and dark complexioned. Her dress was deep blue, trimmed with black lace. At the bottom of the stairs, she extended a hand to her guests, and they both in turn took it and curtsied to her as if she were a duchess.

"Now, which of you is Miss Cohart and which is Miss Solder?"

They made the introductions, and Addy was impressed that Mrs. Alexi had recalled both of their names, when she must have so many guests.

"Thank you so much for meeting with us."

Mrs. Alexi waved Addy's comment away. "Of course. I will always be available to Mrs. Horace's friends." She led them into the back sitting room, from which Addy had noticed the emanating light. "Has Mr. Fairley given you the background on what I do?"

Addy and Tiffany shook their heads as they sat on a low sofa. The room was tastefully furnished—elegant without being overly ornate.

"Ah, he was too busy enjoying himself with two beautiful young ladies to think about work, I presume," she said with a sour look at her protégé. "Let's have some tea while we chat, shall we?" She went over to a silver contraption in a corner of the room and began to heat the water. Without turning around to see their reactions, she continued,

"It's a samovar. My parents were from Russia, and it's still the only way I like to take my tea." The other three sat in silence until she returned with a tray of steaming cups. Then, settling back into her seat, she once again began to hold court. It was clearly a speech she had given many times.

"I discovered my gift when I was very young, though I didn't entirely understand it then. It wasn't until we began hearing about the Fox sisters all those years ago that I began to understand what it was that I was experiencing. Since then I have spent my life honing my skills and helping people connect with their loved ones who have crossed over. Because it is true that they have only crossed over to another place. They are not gone." She paused to take a sip of her tea. "Some of my clients also see Mr. Fairley when I am booked. He has been under my tutelage for several years now." She let her gaze travel over each of the other three, checking that they were paying attention. "I prefer not to use the usual trappings that many mediums do, especially with small groups like this. As you are true believers, I feel safe in thinking you are not here just to see a show."

It wasn't worded as a question, but Addy nodded anyway.

"There won't be bells or candles or moving objects, just messages to you from those you miss. Shall we begin?"

The two young ladies nodded eagerly, and Addy grasped Tiffany's hand in anticipation. Addy had expected more of an organized event like she had seen at Mary's, but now that she saw what Mrs. Alexi was about to do, she thought it couldn't be more perfect.

Mrs. Alexi set down her teacup and closed her eyes. Mr. Fairley continued sipping his tea, legs crossed, relaxed, as if nothing remarkable were about to happen. Addy felt his demeanor a bit disrespectful, but of course there was nothing she could say. She focused instead on the medium she had actually come to see. She knew she would never treat a session like this as if it were commonplace, no matter how many times she had seen it.

Mrs. Alexi rocked back and forth gently, then jerked her head to the side so she was facing Tiffany directly. "Tiffany," she said suddenly, her voice a pitch higher and her eyes still closed. "There are so many of us here for you." Her head jerked oddly again. "You have the necklace?"

Tiffany nodded furiously and fondled a gold chain around her neck that Addy had never noticed before.

"I do."

"Good. Give it to us."

Tiffany looked around, unsure, but after an instant's hesitation, she unclasped it and placed it in Mrs. Alexi's open palm. As soon as the necklace landed in her hand, Mrs. Alexi opened her eyes and reappeared as her old self. She licked her lips before speaking.

"They want to write a letter to you. I'll use this to connect with them again to channel their words. I'll give it back to you once the letter is ready, of course."

"Of course," Tiffany said, but a quick squirm in her chair showed Addy that she wasn't entirely comfortable leaving the treasured item behind.

Mrs. Alexi closed her eyes again but shook her head and reopened them after a moment. "That's all, I'm afraid. I can't control who chooses to appear, unfortunately." She smiled sweetly at the disappointed Addy.

Addy had hoped so desperately for an explanation of her parents' last message. The whole session had been so quick. Was that really all they had come to see?

Before Addy could ask any one of the jumble of questions within her, Mr. Fairley rose as if responding to a silent cue. "I'll show you ladies out." He helped them up into the same waiting cab, then sent them on their way.

Both women sat in stunned silence for the first half of the ride. Finally, Addy said, "What did you think?"

"We'll see what the letter says, I suppose." She looked warily at Addy. "I am sorry no one appeared for you."

"That can't be helped. Like she said, she can't control it." But her voice trembled just enough to give away her disappointment. "She wasn't quite what I expected."

"I suppose people rarely are."

Addy wanted desperately to ask who the person was and what the necklace meant. Tiffany avoided Addy's gaze, and Addy guessed such questions wouldn't be welcome. At least not until they got to know each other better.

"I wonder if she'll see us again," Addy said.

Tiffany shrugged. Addy joined her in watching the night pass by out the carriage window.

Two days later letters arrived from Mr. Fairley for both Addy and Tiffany. They opened them together in their sitting room.

"Is it the letter she promised?" Addy asked before even looking at her own.

Tiffany scanned the page, then nodded.

"What does it say?"

Tiffany looked up, and by the startled look in her friend's eyes, Addy could tell she had asked the wrong question. Of course it was none of her business.

"I'm sorry. I shouldn't have asked. I'm just excitable, that's all."

"May I . . . ?" Tiffany inclined her head in the direction of her small bedroom, which was really no more than a closet off Addy's room. Addy nodded, and Tiffany rushed away to read her missive in private.

That left Addy alone to read hers, which she couldn't imagine would be nearly as thrilling as Tiffany's. She was still a bit put out at how the reading had gone, but there was nothing she could do about it now. She would just have to finagle another invitation to Mrs. Alexi's, that was all.

Mr. Fairley was all business, enclosing the bill for the session. It was becoming clear that Mr. Fairley did all his benefactress's dirty work. Addy sighed. Practical matters had to be dealt with, she supposed.

But on a page separate from the bill, he had written a note to her.

I am sorry no one came through for you the other night. Why don't you come by one night this week, and I'll hold a session for you? I realize I am not quite as illustrious as Mrs. Alexi, but I think you will find my skills satisfactory. No charge, of course—consider it an extension of the previous session. Write with the night you would like to come by. I look forward to seeing both of you again.

Well, that was a nice surprise. Even if she couldn't get another meeting with Mrs. Alexi, this at least was something. She wrote a quick note saying they would come by the following Thursday, then rang down for a porter to retrieve the message and send it off.

She waited for Tiffany to come out so she could share the news, but her companion didn't emerge again until dinnertime, and when she did, it was clear she had been crying. Not sure how to comfort her, Addy let it be, and waited until after they had eaten in the sitting room to tell her about Mr. Fairley's offer.

"That's very kind of him," Tiffany said. "But you won't mind going on your own, will you? Unless you think he means it to be just the two of you there, then I'm happy to chaperone."

"I doubt that will be necessary. I'm sure Mrs. Alexi must be booked up all the time and always has people coming and going. But don't you want to go?"

"I heard everything I need to hear in that letter from Mrs. Alexi."

"It was that accurate, then?"

Tiffany hesitated. "Yes."

"You know I don't want to pry, but—"

"It's fine. It's only fair I tell you since I know why you sought her out . . ." Tiffany drew in a shaky breath. "The short version of the story is, my mother and brother died of typhoid when I was thirteen. My father was a drunk but had been respectable earlier in life, so I was able to get a place as a companion. I hated him so much . . ." She paused and tried to sound brighter, but Addy knew there was a lot still lurking beneath the surface. "They've all been gone for a long time, so it hardly matters anymore. But, still, it was nice to hear from them."

Addy reached across the table and covered Tiffany's hand with her own. "Of course it matters. I'm glad Mrs. Alexi was finally able to give you some peace."

Tiffany looked up into Addy's eyes. "Thank you. I'm not sure *peace* is quite the right word . . . but I hope Mr. Fairley is able to do the same for you."

They sat in silence, the night hanging heavy over them, until Tiffany excused herself to turn in early and left Addy alone with her thoughts. She pondered Tiffany's statement. Was peace really not possible? Then what was the right word for what she was trying to achieve? If she didn't know what she was reaching for, how would she know when she grasped it? The answerless questions turned into dark dreams that lay with her until the morning.

Chapter 6

On Wednesday, Addy gave in to propriety and left her spiritualist connections behind her for a day. Instead, she went to have tea with her maiden great-aunt Gerty, whom Addy hadn't seen since she was a child. Tiffany, still somewhat moody from the letter she had received from Mrs. Alexi, elected to stay behind since it was a family visit. That left Addy to take her first solo carriage ride across the city. Being let loose in the city on her own was exhilarating, even from the confines of a carriage. Finally, she had achieved her freedom, even though she was sure a well-intentioned lecture waited for her on the other end.

Her aunt Gerty lived in a large apartment she had bought decades ago, before the war. It took up two floors of a townhouse on a tree-lined street. The maid showed her into the parlor, where Gerty waited. Gerty stood, leaning on a cane and looking incredibly frail. When Addy had last seen her, she had already seemed old but at least was sturdy. Now Addy hugged her gingerly, afraid the old woman might shatter with too much pressure.

"It's good to see you, Aunt Gerty. It's been too many years."

Gerty eased herself back down onto the sofa. "I'm afraid it's been too many years for a great many things when you get to be my age. I'm surprised you even remember me. Please, dear girl, sit. Rachel," she said, addressing the maid, "please bring in the tea things. And take Addy's hat. Why didn't you do that in the hall?" She continued talking as Rachel took Addy's hat and gloves and exited. "I heard, of course, about your poor parents. Terrible thing. How are you coping? No, dear, don't rearrange the cushions. How have you been enjoying New York?"

Addy already suspected that there were not many questions Gerty actually wanted the answer to, so she didn't bother to respond.

Rachel reentered with the tea tray.

"Ah, here we are. Help yourself, dear." Gerty waved Rachel away, who left without having said a single word. Living with Gerty, Rachel probably didn't get much practice ever getting a word in, Addy thought, and had to lift a hand to cover her mouth and hide a smile.

Addy scooted over slightly to avoid the cushion Gerty hadn't want her to move. She poured tea for herself and her aunt, then followed Gerty's lead in selecting tea cakes to put on her own plate. The food occupied the older woman, and there was finally a moment of silence, which Addy jumped in to fill.

"I've been enjoying New York immensely. It's quite a change from Washington."

"I'm glad to hear it. A lady should travel before she settles down." Gerty didn't look up from her plate as she spoke, talking around bits of cake. "I traveled quite a bit in my day, you know. How is that girl you hired working out?"

"We get along quite well, actually."

"Yes, but is she a proper lady's maid?"

"I don't call her that, but yes, she's quite proper and helpful. She's done this sort of thing before."

"There's no need to call things anything other than what they are. That's the problem nowadays." She reached to grab another sweet. "You know I've had a letter from that man of yours."

Addy was genuinely confused. "What man?"

"That man you were supposed to marry. Mr. Simmons."

"I was never supposed to—"

"Well, he certainly thinks you were, and that's what matters. And your mother certainly thought you were, too, if it comes to that."

While Addy had written a few times to Arthur and Uncle Ted for form's sake since she had been away, her life in Washington already seemed hazy and long lost. As far as Addy knew, the Simmonses had never met Gerty, but Addy wasn't surprised that they had taken it upon themselves to correspond with her now that Addy was in New York. "I never—"

"He's still quite concerned about you—though, really, a man should admit when he's vanquished, you know."

For an instant, Addy thought she and Gerty might get along. They were both independent women who didn't put too much stock into the necessity of marriage, it seemed. Gerty herself had never married, and nothing in her tone now suggested she regretted the decision.

Then Gerty suddenly tore her attention from the cakes and sat up ramrod straight. Addy knew she was not going to like what was coming next. Her imagined friendship with the older woman fizzled away.

"Now, what's this about you getting mixed up with all this spiritualist nonsense?" Gerty asked.

"I would hardly say it's *nonsense*—"

"Don't try to pull the wool over my eyes, dearie. Young people like to think they find everything new under the sun, but all that has been going on since I was young, too, you know. It was nonsense then, and it's nonsense now. Frauds and swindlers, the lot of them."

"While there certainly are some fakes out there, the woman I've come to see was recommended by a friend. She's not a fraud."

"And you've given her money, I suppose?"

"Yes, of course . . ."

"And you know how to sort out all the frauds from the real ones, do you?"

"What we've seen so far proves—"

Gerty waved a hand dismissively. "I don't want to hear about it. Just make sure you don't waste all that money your father left you on nonsense. He's probably already turning over in his grave."

"My father always trusted me—"

"Yes, he indulged you, Adalinda. That's all. I, for one, do not indulge unnecessarily." She reached for her teacup.

Addy took the brief opportunity to interrupt her aunt's diatribe.

"I assure you, I am quite capable of managing my own affairs, and the amount I have given Mrs. Alexi—the medium—is hardly the whole of my inheritance. Arthur shouldn't have interfered and brought you into this."

"Oh, it's 'Arthur,' is it? I think *Mr. Simmons* was quite right to inform me of what was going on. I do hope you won't get in over your head. I can always have a room made ready for you and your girl at a moment's notice."

"I do appreciate that, Aunt, truly." Addy was tired of the conversation, but she found she wasn't as angry as she thought she had a right to be. The old lady meant well, at the very least, but surely even she could see that everyone constantly telling Addy not to do something would only ensure that she went through with it. Addy wouldn't be swayed by pressure from others who thought differently than she did.

She stood abruptly. "I best be going. I'll be sure to call on you again before I leave the city."

"But you've hardly eaten your cakes!"

"They were lovely, but I'm afraid that's all I can manage. Thank you again." Addy turned in a swish of skirts and walked out without notifying Rachel of her departure. The front door was heavy, and Addy had to wrestle with it for an instant longer than expected. When she had squeezed out through the narrow gap she had created, she felt that she had accomplished something and was one step closer to nobody telling her what to do.

But she hadn't quite reached that point yet. When she got back to the hotel, Tiffany asked her how the meeting with Gerty had gone. Addy expected Tiffany to laugh along with her story of Gerty's talkativeness, but instead, from her seat on the sofa, Tiffany frowned and nodded. Addy felt the disapproval hanging between them like a veil.

"Out with it, then," Addy said. When Tiffany didn't respond, she clarified, "Tell me what you're really thinking."

Tiffany sighed and tilted her head a little, considering.

"I've just been thinking since the session with Mrs. Alexi," she said finally. "About this whole movement and what it's really given people . . . and if some people aren't taking advantage of it."

"So you agree with my aunt and Arthur. Have they said anything to you?"

Tiffany clenched a hand in her lap. "I am capable of making up my own mind, believe it or not."

Addy shook her head. "I'm sorry. I didn't mean that. I just don't understand. You got your answers and now you want to begrudge me mine?"

"No, that's not it." She looked away. "Just go ahead and enjoy the session with Mr. Fairley. I'm sure it will be fine."

"Of course it will," Addy said, but it came out sounding more petulant than she would have liked.

She couldn't fathom why everyone seemed to be against her in this. Tiffany had given up her interest in spiritual matters since receiving her letter, while the one communication Addy had received from her own parents had only whetted her appetite for more. But she knew having to fight for what she believed in would make the answers she found all the more valuable.

Two days later, Tiffany, always professional, saw Addy off to her meeting pleasantly enough. When Addy arrived at Mrs. Alexi's, the house was dark and quiet once again. The butler showed her into the same back parlor where they had held their previous session. Once Addy's eyes had adjusted to the dim light, she recognized Mr. Fairley standing beside a large circular table, waiting for her. He always seemed to be waiting and always managed to do it patiently, she thought. As for herself, she hated having to stand around, a slave to someone else's schedule.

Mr. Fairley left whatever reverie he had been in and jumped into action as soon as their eyes met, bounding toward her with an outstretched hand. "Miss Cohart! Thank you for coming."

"Thank you for the invitation." She looked around nervously, trying to pick up on any sounds coming from upstairs. "Will we be alone?"

"Yes. Mrs. Alexi is at a client's home, holding a séance. We won't have to worry about being interrupted."

"How nice," she said, forcing a smile. Strictly speaking, it was hardly appropriate to stay. But, strictly speaking, she hardly cared. This was her chance to connect with her parents. She wouldn't give it up.

Having sensed her reluctance, Mr. Fairley said, "It will all be aboveboard, I promise." He waved her to a seat, and she sat with a sense of finality. The decision had been made. It would hardly reflect well on her to back out now.

"I have a few techniques I'd like to try with you tonight," he continued, sitting across from her.

The facing sofas felt like they had been scooted closer together since her last visit, the space tighter, her knees practically grazing Mr. Fairley's, who, even so, insisted on perching on the edge of his seat like an excited schoolboy.

"Mrs. Alexi likes to keep things simple, but I think there is also a place for manifestation and other things that are a little more convincing for people."

"I hope you don't think I'm a skeptic who needs convincing."

He smiled mildly, as if she had said exactly what he had expected. "Of course not. But it's always nice to get justification for one's beliefs." He stood and crossed the small space to her side in one step. "May I?" he asked and sat beside her without waiting for an answer. He closed his eyes and drew in a few deep breaths, and Addy followed suit.

A knock sounded at the door. Their eyes flew open.

There was a pause before Mr. Fairley said anything, causing the knock to come again.

"My apologies. I suppose I must get that." He hurried off toward the front door.

Addy heard an unfamiliar male voice drift in from the foyer, followed by Mr. Fairley's. She was starting to wonder whether she should get up and introduce herself when their conversation ceased and she heard footsteps heading toward her. She stood to greet the new visitor. Strangely, she already resented whoever it was for interrupting her time with Mr. Fairley. She forced another smile as a heavyset older gentleman walked in, with their host close behind.

"Allow me to introduce Mr. Belk," Mr. Fairley said. "One of my most devoted clients. And this is Miss Cohart, one of Mrs. Alexi's clients that I have taken the opportunity to steal." He said this last with a winning smile and a slight shake of his curls.

Mr. Belk bowed and looked Addy up and down. "I can see why you would want to steal this one," he said as an aside between men, then spoke to Addy. "How lovely to meet you."

"You as well," Addy replied, though his leering look and comment made her want to smack him across the face.

"I hope you don't mind terribly if he joins us," Mr. Fairley said. "I had told him to come by whenever he would like."

She wasn't sure if another male guest in attendance made the situation better or worse. "Of course not," she said after only a moment's hesitation.

Addy took her same seat. Mr. Belk rushed to sit next to her, and his thick thigh pressed against hers unnecessarily. Mr. Fairley sat across from them, but she could tell by his glance that he saw the impropriety of Mr. Belk's behavior. Addy wished Mr. Fairley would suggest they switch places, but he seemed unwilling to say anything against his "most devoted client."

"Let's sing a hymn to begin," Mr. Fairley suggested once they had all settled in and joined hands, and the trio went through a quiet, off-key rendition of "Nearer My God to Thee." When they finished, Mr. Fairley closed his eyes and squeezed Addy's hand. "I ask the spirits to make themselves known," he commanded in a deep, booming voice she hadn't known he possessed. Addy jumped as a sudden series of raps sounded under the table and a china vase floated off a nearby shelf before setting itself neatly down again.

After the sounds and movements subsided, the silence that reigned seemed complete, like the silence of the dead. Only, if she listened closely, she could hear the rise and fall of the others' breaths, reminding her she was indeed still alive.

Finally, Mr. Fairley said, quite unnecessarily, "They're here."

Another tensely quiet moment passed. "Adalinda, it's your father."

The voice wasn't her father's like it had been at Madam Marsh's, but Addy was surprised by the use of her full name, which so few people knew. "We love you." The words were slow and drawn out, distorted. "What questions do you have for us?"

She hadn't expected to be asked such a direct question, and it took her long enough to formulate one that she was afraid the spirits may have slipped away in the meantime. "What of your last message?" she finally ventured.

The pause was long, but then the slow speech started up again. "You have acted on it."

"Yes," she said, though she wasn't sure if it had been a question.

"Then it is done."

Addy nodded, satisfied. There was her answer. It had been a warning only against marrying Arthur, after all.

After a few more moments, Mr. Fairley shook himself out of his trance. She panicked, realizing she had thought to ask only about herself and not about how her parents fared on the other side. She suddenly didn't want them to go. She was desperate to ask more! But Mr. Fairley turned his same mild smile to her, and she knew they were gone. He gazed at her, and she was struck again by how handsome he was. How strange to think he was a bachelor.

Mr. Belk shifted in his seat, the fabric of his trousers scratching against Addy's dress.

Mr. Fairley returned to himself and immediately moved on to the next thing. "Come," he said in his normal tone of voice. "I want to try something new with you." He ushered her to an armchair placed in a more open part of the room. "Mr. Belk has seen this before, so I won't put him through it again."

"I'm always happy to observe new initiates."

Mr. Fairley nodded in his direction, then returned his focus to Addy. Under his close watch, she felt like she was the only person in the room—perhaps even the only person in New York.

It startled her when he spoke, breaking the enchantment.

"I'm sure you know that spirits have the ability to manifest in photographs even when we can't see them with the naked eye," he said. "I've had some good results taking photographs of clients, and your parents came through so strongly, I feel almost certain they'll make an appearance this way."

Addy settled into the chair and followed his directions on how to sit, still and silent, while he pulled out the camera and took the shot. Her forehead itched the entire time, but she didn't dare move to scratch it.

"Wonderful," he said when it was done. "I'll bring the image to you in a few days, once I've had a chance to expose the plate."

"Thank you," she said, and stood to leave. She sensed that more time had passed than it seemed and that it was probably growing late. It was best to extricate herself now, before things got any more improper. "I should go. But thank you so much for the attention. I can't wait to see if the camera has captured anything."

"I'm sure it did." He showed her to the door without letting her say goodbye to Mr. Belk. For that, she was grateful. Mr. Fairley kissed her hand a heartbeat longer than was strictly necessary. She blushed the entire carriage ride home.

Three days later Mr. Fairley called at the hotel, clutching a package to his chest, which Addy assumed contained her otherworldly photograph. His eyes were bright and eager as he entered their sitting room. He greeted Addy and then Tiffany, who sat mending a hem and barely acknowledged him. Addy stiffened at her friend's rudeness but said nothing.

Mr. Fairley, too, ignored her manner. "Miss Solder, I'm sorry you couldn't join us the other night."

"Thank you for the invitation, but that was Miss Cohart's time, and I didn't want to interfere. Tell me," she continued, her voice tight, "have you brought me my necklace in that package you're waving around?"

The question slammed into Addy. She had forgotten all about the borrowed item. "Oh, Tiffany, is that why you've been so sour? You should have told me, and I would have gotten it on Thursday. I'm sure it was just overlooked."

"Yes, I'm sure it was a mistake," Mr. Fairley replied. "Mrs. Alexi must have thought she had included it with the letter. I'll get it as soon as I return home and send it back by messenger. I certainly don't want you to think you've been treated badly."

"Of course not. It's just that it's never normally away from me, and to have it taken . . ."

"I understand. You'll have it by the end of today, I assure you."

"There, you see? It's settled," Addy said. "Please, sit, Mr. Fairley. Have you brought the image?"

"Yes," he said, maneuvering onto the sofa. "I think you'll be quite amazed." He unwrapped the brown paper and presented her with an already framed photograph.

The centerpiece of the photograph was her seated in the chair, but behind her floated a faint form. She leaned in close to see it better and gasped. It was her mother, appearing quite like she did in Addy's favorite photograph of her, the one that had been used in her obituary. "My God. It worked just like you said it would. Look, Tiffany," she said, passing it over.

Tiffany examined it for a moment. "This is your mother?" she asked hesitantly.

"Yes, without a doubt!" Addy had never thought she would see her mother again, but here was proof that she was still present, looking over her daughter.

"That's amazing," Tiffany said with much less enthusiasm than her employer, and handed the photograph back.

"I'm so glad you're pleased with the result," Mr. Fairley said. "As I said, this is a new method of channeling for me. Now, I'll take my leave so I can make sure that necklace is retrieved."

All three stood, and Addy ignored propriety and embraced him. "Thank you, Mr. Fairley. Truly."

He seemed unfazed by the unexpected hug. "Of course. I'm always glad to help people connect with their loved ones. I hope you'll be by to see us again. Good day, ladies." He bowed and showed himself out.

❦

Addy and Tiffany had just returned from dinner that night when a knock sounded at the door. Tiffany answered it and held a quick conference with the visitor. Curiosity piqued, Addy called, "Who is it?" Tiffany stepped aside, and their visitor from that morning walked in. "Mr. Fairley, a second visit today?" Addy asked.

"I came to personally deliver Miss Solder's necklace and reassure her it was just an oversight. And offer my deepest apologies for the error."

Addy glanced at the gold chain dangling from Tiffany's fingers. He at least was a man of his word. "How kind of you. Since you're here, will you stay for a drink?"

"Only if it wouldn't be an intrusion."

"Of course not. Please, come in. Tiffany, do we have any sherry?"

"I believe so." She walked over to a cabinet and returned with two glasses brimming with the crimson liquid.

"Won't you join us, Miss Solder?" Mr. Fairley asked with an inviting lift of his glass.

"I'm quite tired, so I'll go to my room, if that's all right," she said, addressing Addy instead.

Addy assumed Tiffany's sudden tiredness had something to do with the return of the necklace, just as she had begged to be excused when her letter had arrived. Tiffany's continued reluctance to engage with Mr. Fairley made her a bit uneasy, but Addy didn't dare say anything about it now. "Of course. We'll call you if we need anything." She determined to be extra pleasant to Mr. Fairley to make up for Tiffany's determination to shut him out.

Once Tiffany left, Addy said, "We're quite flattered by the attention you and Mrs. Alexi have paid us, I assure you. It hardly seems necessary."

"Don't mention it. We always like to make sure our clients are well taken care of. Though, if I may be so bold, there are some clients that are more of a pleasure to work with than others."

Addy suppressed a grin but passed over the compliment. "All the same, we're grateful. Tell me, if *I* may be so bold, how did you go from being a bookseller to being a medium?"

"It's a question I get asked often, at least by those who know something of my past life." He paused to take a sip of sherry and collect his thoughts. "I was married," he began simply, enunciating each syllable as if he were reciting a rehearsed history. "My wife, sadly, passed away in childbirth."

"Oh, I'm so sorry."

He inclined his head in acceptance of her sympathy. One forefinger traced a ring around the base of his sherry glass. "That was eight years ago now. I began to attend séances with Mrs. Alexi to try to reach out to my wife. She drew me out of my grief; then she helped me develop my own gifts. Eventually, I sold my shop and began working with her full-time here."

"How wonderful that she encouraged you like that. It must have taken a certain amount of bravery to make that leap, though." Addy, too, paused to drink. "May I ask what happened to the child?"

"My daughter lives with my sister, Jane, and her husband and children in Boston. It's better for her to live with a family than be raised by a bachelor father."

"Of course, you must do what you think is best for her." Addy wasn't sure that was what was best, but who was she to judge, childless as she was? "What's her name?"

"Harriet."

"How lovely."

"And you, Miss Cohart? We all come to Mrs. Alexi to seek guidance in our grief. How are you dealing with yours?"

Addy contemplated the question, resolving to give a real answer rather than the usual canned response that was required for most conversations in good society. It wouldn't do to talk about crying oneself to sleep at a dinner party.

"I suppose," she began, "as is to be expected, it changes from day to day. I think about my parents always, but sometimes it is a sad thought, or a regret, and sometimes it is a good memory. But it is so comforting to know that are still with me in a different form."

"Yes, we all feel that. I wish we could convince all the skeptics so they would know the same peace we do."

Addy nodded. "What a lovely thought. I know plenty of people who could use that kind of comfort."

"We all do." He cleared his throat, holding a fist in front of his mouth as he did so. "Miss Cohart, I wondered if I might call on you again."

"You're always welcome here. Please forgive Miss Solder. She was just tired this evening, having been a bit anxious about her necklace."

"Oh, I took no notice of that at all," he replied quickly. "What I meant was, might I call on you in a personal capacity?" He swallowed. "You have no other attachments, I assume?"

Addy hesitated, watching him closely, wanting to be sure she understood his meaning. "No, I have no attachments at this time, though I have to say, I haven't been seeking any. But, yes, you may call."

He relaxed and beamed, causing a shallow dimple to appear in one cheek. "Excellent. I'll be off now, but I look forward to our next meeting." He stood. "Thank you for the sherry."

"You're welcome." Addy walked him to the door. He leaned over to kiss her hand, and she squeezed his fingers lightly in return. Once the door closed behind him, she hugged herself out of newfound happiness. She suddenly felt more like the young twenty-three-year-old woman in the bloom of life that she actually was than the grieving old maid she had been living as recently. She very much looked forward to Mr. Fairley's next visit.

The next morning Addy and Tiffany discussed Mr. Fairley's visit over breakfast in their hotel room as they scraped butter onto their toast.

"Will we be seeing more of him, do you think?" Tiffany asked as she took her first crunchy bite.

Addy peered across the table at her. "Are you teasing me?" She laughed. "What did you hear?"

"It's not a very large suite, you know."

Addy tossed her napkin onto the table in feigned anger. "Well, aren't you the little eavesdropper?" She could tell Tiffany was not fooled by her display. She relaxed back into her chair. "Yes, I think we shall."

"My, my, do we have a suitor?"

"We'll have to see how it goes before it comes to that."

"Still, it's exciting. He is handsome."

"I'm surprised you noticed. I'd gotten the impression that you didn't want anything else to do with him."

"It's not that. I've just had the message from my family that I needed, and I didn't feel the need to participate further. And now that he's returned my necklace, I feel much better. But . . ." She wavered, chewing her lower lip. "Doesn't he seem a bit too . . . suave to you?"

Addy bellowed out a laugh. "What on earth does that mean? How can someone be too suave?"

"I don't know. It was just an observation." Tiffany looked away, then dragged herself back. "Ignore me. It's so exciting. Whatever will your Mr. Simmons say?"

"There's no reason he needs to know at this point. I'd rather save myself the lecture."

"The distance certainly makes that easier. Sometimes it's good to cut ties."

"I don't know that I'll ever cut them completely, but it is so nice to be away." She picked a piece of fruit out from the bowl in the center of the table, using the movement to give her time to consider her next statement. Should she let Tiffany know she had heard her talking with Arthur in the hallway the night before they left and ask her about it, or keep that knowledge in her back pocket?

"Everything all right?"

Out with it, then. "Have you been in touch with Arthur since we left?"

"Why would I . . . ?" When she saw Addy's look, Tiffany sighed. "I write to him. But no secrets have been divulged, I promise. I won't say anything to him about Mr. Fairley's attentions if you don't want me to."

"Please don't. I don't want people talking about me behind my back. And you know Arthur will have an opinion about it. Besides, I don't know if it's fair to him, to shove it in his face that I have moved on to another suitor . . . Though nothing has even happened yet. Let's not get ahead of ourselves."

Tiffany nodded almost sadly. "I won't say anything to him. But he only wants to check up on you out of love, you know."

"Please don't say that nonsense to me. He wants to possess me, that's all."

Tiffany cracked a smile. "I think that could be said about any man and anything."

Addy laughed, relieved to have the tension crack. "Well, let's not give them the pleasure of talking about them any longer than we have to," she said. "What are we ladies doing today?"

Suddenly, the days ahead seemed full of hope.

Chapter 7

Mr. Fairley called at the hotel a few days later, brandishing a bouquet of lilies that the ladies had no vase for. Tiffany went down to the front desk to see if she could find anything to put them in while Addy and her guest waited awkwardly in the sitting room. Addy waved Mr. Fairley onto the sofa. He sat clutching the flowers between his knees.

"They're lovely, thank you."

"I don't know why I thought you would have packed a vase in your luggage."

Addy laughed. "I'm sure there are women that have packed more than that."

He also laughed and released one hand's grip on the stems. "I didn't want to say anything, but if you've ever watched a lady's trunks be carried in, you wouldn't be surprised by anything that was in there."

"I'm sure not. But we're not quite that high class, Tiffany and I."

The smile in his eyes bored into her soul. "I wouldn't have it any other way."

Addy blushed just as Tiffany swept back into the room. She lifted a glass vase to show it off. "Success!"

Addy stood. "You're amazing."

Tiffany sloshed some water into the vase and reached for the flowers. As she dropped them in, a few drops of water splashed onto the coffee table, and Mr. Fairley stood and wiped up the wet spots with his handkerchief.

"What a team," Addy said.

Mr. Fairley looked at her so intensely she felt sure he was about to embrace her or do something even more embarrassing, but he caught himself and sat on the sofa again without any outburst.

Tiffany set the pretty arrangement of purple and white flowers in the center of the coffee table. Then she settled herself in an armchair on the other side of the room with some needlework. Addy knew she was trying to be inconspicuous, but it was hard not to feel that she and Mr. Fairley were being chaperoned all the same.

The conversation was mundane at first. She told him about her parents and sister, her old life in Washington. He talked about his clients and his work, darting around any mention of his personal life. Awash in his attention, Addy hardly noticed the omission. Instead, she explained how she had come to be interested in spiritualism and her experiences with it so far.

"Can I ask a personal question?" Mr. Fairley asked her.

"Of course."

"During our session, you asked about the last message from your parents. You seemed very much preoccupied by it. May I ask what that message was? Of course, you don't have to answer, but it may help me connect with them again."

"They don't tell you that when you're channeling them?"

William brushed a curl out of his eye. "No, unfortunately, I only know what they say in the moment. There's no time to explain the backstory since the spirits' presence is so fleeting."

"That makes sense." Addy rubbed a forefinger around her palm. "They had told me not to marry my suitor back home. A childhood friend who wouldn't take no for an answer to his suit."

"That's very practical advice for a spirit to give."

Addy smiled. "I suppose so. It was odd, though, because in life my mother was so keen for me to marry Arthur."

"It's Arthur, then?" He raised one eyebrow. "That seems quite familiar."

Addy shook her head. "Like I said, he was a childhood friend. We were practically family."

"I was only teasing." He cleared his throat. "Anyway, I think that spirits can change their opinions from those they held in the physical world. They have a different perspective in their new state, obviously."

Addy was about to respond, but Mr. Fairley stood.

"I best be going. I'm sure Mrs. Alexi has some task for me to attend to."

Addy stood as well.

"Thank you so much for the flowers."

He nodded. In the doorway, he took her hand and kissed it.

"Please," he said, "call me William."

Addy couldn't help the beaming smile that crossed her face.

"Then you must call me Addy."

He released her hand with a smile and left. Addy watched his back recede down the hallway with a kind of reverential awe.

Over the next few weeks, Addy saw William frequently socially and at home. She found herself growing more and more fond of him as they shared meals, went to the theater, and walked around the city. He was suave, as Tiffany had said, but Addy relished rather than derided that quality in him. Being charming and convincing was necessary for his profession, and, after all, it was her and William's shared interest in spiritualism that had brought and kept them together.

She eagerly accepted an invitation to join a group séance he was leading one weekend. It would be her first time seeing him give a full performance. She even managed to convince Tiffany to accompany her, now that more time had passed since the meeting with Mrs. Alexi and the return of the necklace.

Addy also brought two new friends, Lauren and Christopher Martin, to the séance, whom she and Tiffany had met while out riding in the park one day. There was an embarrassing incident with chasing a hat blown away by the wind, and Christopher had gamely rescued it for them. The couple had recently moved to New York from Toronto and were eager to establish new connections, just as Addy and Tiffany were.

Addy knew the Martins had agreed to attend the séance as an entertaining evening rather than as true believers, but Addy was happy for any reason to get them through the door. Once there, she hoped that William's gifts would convince—though at the very least she was happy to have them meet William, since she had kept her new friends up to date on her blossoming courtship.

Addy and Tiffany dined with the Martins at a small restaurant by the Martins' apartment before heading to the séance. On the way to Mrs. Alexi's, Addy had to rein herself in like a runaway horse to keep from gushing too much about William and all the wonders that were certainly in store for the group that night. But a short while into the ride, as she described her most recent conversation with William, Addy caught Tiffany covering her mouth to try to smother a laugh. Addy realized she had not been very successful in keeping her flow of words under control. She forced herself to switch to mundane topics and feigned interest in the Martins' trials with decorating their new home, though her mind was elsewhere.

"You'll be dealing with all this soon, I think," Lauren teased Addy, inadvertently drawing the conversation back to the topic Addy had been avoiding for all their sakes.

"Me? I think that's a little premature to say."

"Only a little?" Christopher joined in the teasing.

Addy laughed but felt her face redden. She brought her fingertips to one cheek to try to hide it, scratching a nonexistent itch.

"We still have to approve of this Mr. Fairley first, Christopher, so don't get too far ahead of yourself," Lauren said.

"I really hope you both do approve of him, but please let's change the subject." She wasn't sure why the lighthearted comment bothered her, but she sensed that it tapped a secret hope in her heart that she wasn't yet ready to admit existed. She had tried so hard to stay away from the trappings of domesticity, but lately she felt it beckoning. Perhaps her nature wasn't quite as contrary to social convention as she—and everyone else—had thought.

Addy was relieved when they arrived at Mrs. Alexi's house without further mention of her marriage prospects. The group was a little late, leaving time only for introductions and none for small talk. To make up for it, William clasped Christopher's hand and kissed the ladies' cheeks when they were introduced, paying them extra attention.

The group—eight in all—went into the back drawing room. The round table had been moved to the center of the room, with chairs circling it. Addy was disappointed to be seated away from William. Lauren sat on his right while another guest, a Mrs. Gregory, whom Addy had just met, sat on his left. A sour mix of jealously stirred in Addy's stomach, but she tamped it down, knowing she was being ridiculous. Proximity to the action was necessary to make Lauren believe. Addy no longer needed any kind of proof. She took comfort in the fact that Tiffany was beside her and Mr. Belk was on the opposite side of the table, where Addy wouldn't be subject to his leers.

The séance began with a song, as usual. They all held hands on top of the table as a level of proof against anyone making fraudulent noises or movements. Addy saw Lauren glance nervously at her husband, and Addy sent a reassuring smile in their direction.

Soon William was in a trance, quiet, his breath slow and steady. And then came the first series of knocks. Mrs. Gregory, instructed beforehand on her role, interrogated the spirit while William was in his trance.

"Do you know anyone here?" she asked.

One knock: yes.

"Is it a woman?"

One knock.

Addy hoped that the spirit was once again for her, but further questioning divined that the spirit was Mrs. Gregory's late husband, with whom she had communicated at previous séances. She seemed unflustered by his presence, as if he had just come home from work on a regular day.

"Give us a sign of your presence," she commanded, in the same voice she had probably used to tell him to take off his muddy boots in life.

On cue, items began to rattle on shelves, and a stream of piano music floated in from an unknown location. Then a gaseous mist began to form between William and Lauren. Addy and some of the others gasped as they recognized facial features in the vapor. Addy squeezed the hands of her neighbors in excitement. Even with the fuzziness of the face, Addy knew it had to be Mr. Gregory. His widow was unfazed enough that Addy wondered if Mrs. Gregory couldn't see the miraculous manifestation from her seat. It would be a travesty if Mrs. Gregory had lost her awe for such miracles.

"Thank you, Henry," was all Mrs. Gregory said. "We are glad to know you're with us."

The activity stopped.

"Is there anyone else?" she asked.

Silence dragged on, drip by drip.

Then William opened his eyes. It was over.

William shook the hands of his guests as they filed out. Mr. Belk fluttered around the back, trying to find a way to be helpful. Addy managed a small smile at him, but fortunately William sent him back into the séance room to tidy up before Mr. Belk could come over to talk to her.

William came over to Addy and her friends. "Mr. and Mrs. Martin, thank you for coming. I hope you enjoyed yourselves."

"Oh, yes," Christopher replied. "It was very entertaining."

"And spooky," Lauren added, raising her eyebrows in a manner that showed Addy her friend was still not quite taking this seriously.

William let her flippancy slide. "I'm glad. We'll have to all have lunch one day so we can get to know each other properly."

"That sounds lovely."

He turned to Addy. "All right, darling, good night." He kissed her cheek and let his hand graze her back as she turned to leave.

Addy smiled and touched his arm affectionately.

He leaned and whispered into her ear, "I hope you will be friendlier to Mr. Belk next time."

Addy frowned, startled. "I hardly had the chance—"

But William had already moved on, shaking Tiffany's hand without notice or further comment, and in a moment they were off.

Once they were back in the carriage, Addy regathered herself after the reprimand from William. To keep her mind off it, she quizzed her guests about their reaction to the event.

"I'm not sure you couldn't explain it all away," Christopher said, "but it was a good show."

"Really?" Addy asked, disappointed that she had not made firm believers of her new friends. "What about when he appeared?"

Christopher looked over at his wife, slightly exasperated. "In that dark room, you could see whatever you wanted to in that smoke."

"It was a face clear as day to me. Didn't you think so, Tiffany?"

"It did look rather like a face."

"A resounding endorsement." Christopher laughed. "I'm looking forward to lunch, though. We hardly had a chance to speak with your 'darling' tonight."

Addy grimaced at his teasing. "*I* called him nothing of the sort."

"He certainly is handsome," Lauren said in a gossipy tone.

"That's just what I said." Tiffany rolled her eyes. "And she didn't like it then, either."

They all laughed, and Addy gave up and joined in.

A few days later Addy, Tiffany, the Martins, and William gathered for lunch at an upscale café overlooking Central Park. Outside, the day was hot and threatened rain, but the atmosphere inside was pleasant and cool. By the time they were halfway through the meal, Addy was thrilled. Everyone seemed taken with William and his lighthearted but deferential manner. She felt like her choice of suitor had been approved, and somehow that justified all the recent decisions she had made about her life. It was satisfying and exhilarating.

When William stepped away for a moment, Lauren leaned toward Addy and whispered, as if to reassure Addy of her approval, "Addy, he's perfect. Has he said anything final yet?"

"No, of course not. It's still so early." Though, really, she didn't know if it was early or not. Arthur's was the only proposal she had ever received, and that had come after what had been in reality a lifelong courtship.

Lauren shook her head. "He obviously cares for you. You need to push him to make a declaration. A woman can't wait around forever."

Tiffany hushed them both as William returned to the table. Addy, unsure whether the advice was sound, would have to discuss it with Tiffany later. She didn't want to do anything to ruin her relationship with William. She had never been in any hurry to get married before, so why rush now?

After lunch, the Martins caught a cab home, leaving the others in front of the restaurant. William took Addy's arm. "Can I walk you home?"

Addy looked up at the thickening gray clouds. "It might rain at any moment!"

"If it does, I think you'll find that we don't actually melt in the rain."

Addy laughed. William had a wonderful way of keeping things in perspective.

"I'm not going to risk it," Tiffany said. "I'll take the omnibus home."

"Are you sure?" Addy asked. "At least let us get you a cab."

"I think you'll find I can survive a bus ride, too. I'll see you at home."

Addy nodded and smiled, realizing how much their New York hotel suite had already come to feel like home. She also sensed that Tiffany was purposefully trying to give her and William some space. Tiffany rushed off to catch the omnibus, and the remaining pair started slowly on their way, in no rush to part, even if it meant being caught in the rain.

"Your friends are lovely," William said. He sidestepped another passing couple, pressing closer against Addy as he did so.

"I'm lucky to have met them. And I'm so glad you all got along."

"Why wouldn't we, when we all love you so?"

Addy blushed under the force of his adoring smile. "Mutual friendships don't always mean people will get along."

He nudged her with his elbow. "Come now, I hope you know I'm not a friend."

Addy laughed lightly but felt the pressure to navigate the moment deftly. If only she could have gotten more of Lauren's advice before having this conversation. "I think friendship is included in the other thing, don't you?"

He chuckled. "Yes, I suppose so, if 'the other thing' is what you want to call it." He paused to look up and down the street before leading them across it. "So, friend, what are your plans?"

"What do you mean?"

"You had meant to move to Europe at some point, hadn't you?"

"Yes, I'd like to travel some more."

"And your funds will permit it?"

"Yes, my inheritance should last me a good while as long as I'm not extravagant." She shook her head. "Really, William, what a curious thing to ask."

He looked down at her reassuringly. "I just want to make sure you are comfortably situated, is all." They walked a bit in silence. "I don't suppose you could be persuaded to stay in New York?"

"At the moment I have no plans to leave." It wasn't really an answer to his question, but it was the best she could do. Until she knew his intentions, she couldn't put all her own plans on hold.

"You know," he said as they came to the corner of the block the hotel was on, "I wish I could speak with some of your family members." The first fat raindrops began to fall, and, with their destination in sight, they picked up the pace.

"I wish you could, too."

He squeezed her arm. "I didn't mean to bring up your parents. I just meant, what about your aunt that lives here?"

They ran through the hotel's double doors just as the storm broke behind them. It took Addy a moment to catch her breath and speak again. "I don't think that's a good idea. While she may like you personally, she's very disapproving of spiritualists. And I don't want to hear that lecture again."

"Perhaps I could write to your uncle?"

It took her a moment to think who he could mean, but then it struck her as obvious: she did still refer to Ted Simmons as Uncle Ted out of habit. "He's not actually my uncle, though to his credit he has acted in that capacity much more than he had to." She considered. If William wrote to Ted, surely Arthur would hear of it, but that couldn't be helped, not really. If she wanted things settled, the men would have to get involved. "Yes, I suppose that would be okay."

"Wonderful."

"Are you going back in the rain?"

"I'll join the line for a cab." He pointed to a line forming near the entrance by all those who had given up on walking anywhere that day.

"I'll send you a note with his address."

He beamed and they bid each other goodbye. Addy ran upstairs, excited to tell Tiffany of the conversation.

A week later Addy received a letter from Ted saying that William had inquired about her financial state and, ultimately, her hand. It was odd to hear it from Ted when William had made no direct mention of it himself. She told herself that was just how things were done: the men must always decide things among themselves first, or they would never be satisfied. She perused the rest of the letter to find Ted's response.

While it is not my proper place to give or deny permission in this matter, I urge you to consider carefully what you are about to do. I do not say this because of my close connection with Arthur. I say this because of my love for you and for your parents. Do not rush into anything headlong. I know you are a smart girl and unlikely to have your head turned, but the nature of his profession does concern me, mostly because it will affect his ability to take care of you and any children that may come of your union. I also know of your previous aversion to the idea of marriage, which made the proposal somewhat of a surprise to me. But if, after careful consideration, you decide this is what you want to do, I wish you all the happiness in the world, and I pray you invite us to the wedding.

Addy folded the letter carefully and held it in her lap as she considered its contents. It wasn't a rousing approval by any means, but at least he wouldn't stand in the way. And he had made no mention of discussing the matter with his nephew. That, perhaps, would come later, when the marriage was certain.

Noticing her pensive expression, Tiffany asked what was wrong.

"A letter from Uncle Ted. William wrote to him to ask for my hand."

"That's wonderful!" She hesitated when Addy didn't share in her excitement. "Isn't that what you wanted?"

Addy pursed her lips and crossed her legs, still clasping the letter. "Of course it is. I just wish he could approve of it without reservations. I wish someone in my family—or almost family—could be as happy for me as you are. It just . . ." She shook off her doubts. "Never mind. I can't let it get to me."

"You're right. He hasn't said no. And you can't let it keep you from being happy. When do you think William will ask you?"

"I don't know. He's hinted before. Maybe he will now that he's had an answer from Ted."

"I, for one, am very happy for you." Tiffany really did seem to have given up on her reservations about William, and for that, Addy was glad.

She stood and hugged her friend. "You don't know how much I appreciate that."

The next time Addy saw her potential fiancé was at a séance hosted by Mrs. Alexi. She arrived early, hoping to catch a word privately with William, but found him engaged with other clients. After the session, his goodbye at the door seemed almost perfunctory. Addy worried that something in Uncle Ted's letter had put William off his intention.

She wrote to her sister explaining the situation anyway, hoping that by the time she received a reply she would be officially engaged. Though if William didn't come through . . . She refused to think about it. If that happened, Trisha would snatch her back to Chicago, dashing all Addy's dreams of freedom. Addy considered leaving any mention of William's profession out of the letter, since that seemed to be the sticking point with everyone, but ultimately decided the truth must be told. She also refused to be shamed for her beliefs. Besides, Ted and Gerty had probably already written her sister—they were always discussing Addy behind her back—so Addy could be caught in a lie of omission.

Addy knew Trisha would be full of sisterly advice—Trisha loved being the expert—and Addy knew she would get the handwritten equivalent of an earful in her sister's response. Though considering how much Addy had wanted some relationship advice earlier, perhaps not everything her sister would say would be a waste of time. Trisha and her husband were happy enough, it seemed, so Addy could do worse for a source of advice.

Addy wrote carefully, taking three drafts to make it neat and thoughtful, thinking through her description of William, of how much praise would seem too much. She didn't want to sound like her head had been turned, as Ted had said, but also wanted to appear firm in her resolution that this was the right path for her. Everyone's doubts had only made her more determined, and she wanted her determination to be clear. When she finally posted the letter, she felt relieved that it was done. Now she only had to wait for William's proposal, which she reassured herself must come soon.

William called at the hotel for tea a few days later, bringing news of Mrs. Alexi's latest success—passing tests posed by a journalist meant to catch frauds in front of an audience of hundreds. It was a triumph for the spiritualist cause.

"How wonderful!" Addy said, folding the newspaper containing the article and passing it back to William over the table. "I wish I had been there to see it. Surely people must believe now."

"People only believe what they want to believe," William replied evenly. "We can't make it our mission to convert everyone, because we'd never succeed."

"You must have more faith. Few by few, we can get there," Addy insisted.

William just smiled and sipped his tea as if slightly amused by her unwavering devotion to the cause. "A few devotees are more useful than a thousand people who come for the amusement. Like your friends, the Martins."

Addy frowned. "It was their first experience. Everyone has to start somewhere."

He looked at her as if assessing something. "You know, with your fervor and my gifts, we could make quite a team."

Addy perked up at this comment. Perhaps now he would make himself clear . . .

But instead, he shoved the paper under his arm and stood. "Until next time, the lovely Miss Cohart." He tipped his hat to her and walked out.

She watched his back retreat, feeling deflated and useless, waiting so anxiously for declaration of a suit that might never come.

To keep her mind off all this, Addy began to plan travel out of New York City. The end of summer had declared itself in a final surge of stifling heat, and she longed to breathe some country air. She left the logistics to Tiffany; she was adept at it, and Addy was grateful to have her in her employ. Addy would simply show up and go where Tiffany told her, which made Addy feel quite the woman of leisure.

The first three-week trip would be a progress through the state to Buffalo and Niagara Falls, then onward to Toronto to visit the Martins, who had returned home for a cousin's wedding. After returning to New York City, Addy hoped to journey to Boston through the fall foliage.

She knew the time away would do her good and help clear her mind of the constant worrying over William's intentions. Sometimes, as she lay in bed, she thought that perhaps she should have continued to deny all suitors; life had been so much less complicated when she had. She gulped when she thought about all the ways her life had been much less complicated just a few short months before, at the start of the summer. But she had shown she could handle these changes. Now she just needed to restore some balance back to her life.

Her willingness to leave New York showed she would not put her life on hold while William made up his mind. She wanted this to be clear to him as well. Her family—both blood and not—seemed relieved by this decision when she wrote them about it, since it showed she still had her independence and her own mind.

William appeared ambivalent about the proposed absence; he was pleased for Addy but hinted that perhaps it would be more proper for her to stay in New York City, where she had more connections than just Miss Solder. Addy dismissed the notion as a ploy to get her to stay and continue hanging on his every word. She hated herself every time she found herself doing it, but when he spoke, she couldn't tear herself away. It created a tug-of-war between them as they walked in the warm air the evening before she was set to leave, each of them trying to prod the other to say what was really meant but neither giving in.

Addy eventually tried a different tack, bringing up another topic that they always avoided. "Maybe when I go to Boston in the fall, I could visit your sister and meet your daughter. Bring them your good wishes."

William reacted immediately. He released his hold on her arm and stopped walking. His nostrils flared. "Why on earth would you want to do that?" he asked, loud enough that passersby turned and looked.

"I'd like to meet her. And surely she'd like to hear a personal message from you."

"What makes you think she doesn't get plenty of messages from me as it is?"

Addy started walking again, quickly enough that he had to dash to catch up. When he had, she said, "I don't know, William. You never mention her. I thought it would be a nice gesture, that's all." She turned and glared at him but didn't slow down. "But clearly you don't."

He darted in front of her so she had to stop, and he placed his hands on her shoulders to hold her in place. His eyes were intense but not unfriendly.

"I'm sorry. It just surprised me, is all. Of course you can see her if you would like. But there's no point in worrying about it now. We can arrange it all when the time gets closer."

She twisted out of his grip but didn't run off again. Finally, she was ready to plunge into what was really bothering them both. "What do you want from me, anyway, William? You ask my uncle for my hand and then never ask me for it. I don't understand you."

"I'm not the one running off to all different places. I don't even know if you plan on staying in New York."

She tried to keep her voice low so that it wasn't obvious they were having an argument on the sidewalk. There were some moments when even she cared about appearances. "I'm only 'running off,' as you call it, because I'm not going to sit around waiting for you forever. If I had a reason to stay in New York, I would."

There was a heartbeat of a pause, during which Addy waited anxiously for his response. Suddenly, he threw his head back with a laugh. "Now, why did it take so long to say what was on your mind? I had asked before, you know."

She squirmed a bit and said quietly, "Well, at the time, I didn't know what you planned to do . . ."

He grabbed her hand. "So don't go. Stay in New York and marry me. We can get married right away. I never want you to sit around and wait for me."

Addy's heart soared as he finally said the words she had been waiting so long to hear. In that moment, she floated for both an instant and centuries in his arms, an expanse of time passing that she could not quite grasp. "Yes," she said, and still the magic of the moment was not broken. Emboldened by the dark, they embraced and kissed.

Tiffany looked appalled when Addy came home and told her that the trip Tiffany had worked so hard to plan was canceled.

"I have to stay and plan the wedding. We'll get married right away, he said."

"Surely it can wait three weeks."

Frustrated, Addy said, "Just do what I say, Tiffany."

Tiffany stood rooted in place, the fire on her face growing. Then she took in a shaky breath. "I have to go send a telegram to the Martins. And the hotels. And everyone else." She dashed out of the room.

Addy collapsed onto the sofa. With the rush of adrenaline passing, she found herself close to tears for a reason she couldn't find words for.

Tiffany remained rather aloof over the next few weeks as the wedding plans progressed. Addy sensed her disapproval but ignored it, and Tiffany withdrew from their friendship somewhat, staying strictly professional in their interactions. Addy knew she had at least partially caused this with how she had spoken to her, but she refused to apologize for asserting her will.

The Martins, Ted, and Trisha all hid finely veiled judgment between the lines of their letters, never having guessed that Addy would bend so quickly to her fiancé's will. But there would be time to visit Toronto later, Addy reasoned, and time to visit her sister. For now, William needed her in New York; his reputation as a medium was flourishing, and he had intimated that after their wedding, she could serve a prominent role assisting him. She couldn't wait to be part of something so grand and meaningful.

The wedding would be small, especially considering their lack of family and Addy's few friends in New York. Arthur and Ted insisted on coming up, which Addy accepted, though she was not looking forward to the moment when she saw them again.

Though Addy had never been one to obsess over finery, she found herself delighting in choosing the dress and dinner menu and other accoutrements for the big day. Her life was turning a corner, and the fact that she couldn't quite see what was around it made it all the more exciting.

One night in the middle of all this, she made up the eighth member of a circle at Mrs. Alexi's séance. The medium had agreed to engage in automatic writing in front of everyone rather than doing it on her own away from prying eyes, as she had when she penned Tiffany's letter.

Once Mrs. Alexi had entered her trance, she said, "I have a message for you, Addy." Like a flower perking up at the touch of the sun, Addy sat up straighter, thrilled that her parents would come through to congratulate her on her impeding nuptials. A slight cock to the medium's head as she listened to the spirits, however, quickly flattened Addy's elation as she sensed that something was not quite as expected. Mrs. Alexi hesitated, but continued scribbling with her eyes closed, her face flushed. When she finished, she set the pen down and held the paper in front of her with her eyes still closed. The other guests passed the paper around the table to Addy.

The words tilted at odd angles across the page, but the message was still legible.

You haven't listened to us, it said.

Addy's heart skipped a painful beat, and she coughed to cover up her shock. She had almost entirely forgotten about her parents' warning during that first spirit session, since she considered its meaning now void. Surely they couldn't mean for her to *never* marry? Why would they insist on that? She mustered a smile, thanked Mrs. Alexi, and tucked away the sheet of paper without showing it to anyone. The message unnerved her, but there was no way she could back out on William now. He was her destiny, she felt now more than ever. And Mrs. Alexi's hesitation as she wrote the message must have meant she didn't take much heed of it, either. Addy would keep the message to herself, a secret she promised would have no power over her.

Chapter 8

Arthur and Ted arrived in New York two days before the wedding, ostensibly to help with the final preparations, but Addy knew they also wanted to see her and sense her state of mind in advance of the ceremony. She had Tiffany meet them at the train station, and Addy readied a nice spread for them all to enjoy once they got to the hotel. She would show them how happy she was—and how determined.

There were hugs all around when they arrived, of course, and Addy was surprised at how good it felt to see them again. It was like an old part of herself returning. Since she had been away, she had relegated them to a hidden place as ogres of her past, but when they walked in the room, she saw they were just Arthur and Ted Simmons, who had seen her through the best and worst times of her life.

She asked how their journey had been, and they replied with the usual formalities. They admired the hotel suite, and the loveliness and bustle of the neighborhood, even though they had both been to New York many times and had probably stayed in much nicer places. She appreciated the pleasantries nonetheless.

"When shall we meet the famous Mr. Fairley?" Arthur asked once they were seated and partaking of the sandwiches and cakes.

Addy wasn't sure whether a hint of bitter sarcasm lay beneath his words or if she only imagined it, but she knew she had to play nice either way. "He'll join us for dinner," she said.

"Quite right," Ted said. "We want you to ourselves as much as possible before he takes ownership of you."

Addy bristled at the idea of being owned by anyone but, not wanting to start the visit off on the wrong foot, stayed silent. She knew her marriage would be one of equals, and that knowledge was all that mattered. Tiffany filled the awkward moment by serving everyone again, topping off their tea or coffee and making sure they had what they needed. Addy welcomed the distraction and the switch in everyone's attention.

"So, Miss Solder," Ted said as he chomped on a tartlet. "You've been our man on the ground here. What do you think of Mr. Fairley?"

So, not as much of a change of attention as Addy had hoped.

"It's hardly my place—"

"Nonsense. You've been a great friend to Addy. I know she would expect you to have an opinion."

Tiffany smoothed the lap of her dress. Despite her reservations about William, Addy knew she could trust Tiffany to support her in front of the guests. "Mr. Fairley has been very kind to us ever since we got here. He's quite the gentleman. And good looking, to boot."

"Oh, a handsome chap! Perhaps Addy has had her pretty little head turned after all."

Addy knew Ted was just being jovial, but she scowled and felt her cheeks burn beneath his teasing. Somehow these two always managed to make her feel like a silly girl. William and Tiffany—and her other new friends—treated her like the woman she was.

Arthur, too, seemed uncomfortable, and he moved the conversation along. "Where will you two honeymoon?"

"Niagara," Addy said, collecting herself again. "Tiffany and I canceled our trip there before the engagement, so we simply changed the dates."

"And the purpose, it seems like," Ted said with a wink.

Addy forced herself to smile back at him.

"Will you go to Toronto, too?" Arthur asked.

"No, not this time. The Martins are back in New York, so they can attend the wedding, and we were really only going to see them."

"Now, why all the rush? Is there a reason to hurry?" He gave Addy a meaningful look.

Addy gasped while Tiffany stifled a laugh.

"Uncle, I don't know what you're implying, but we're getting married quickly because there's no reason to wait."

Ted shrugged and feigned innocence. "I meant no offense. It's just a modern world now, is all. I don't know what goes on in it."

"Really, Uncle, leave off," Arthur said. The redness of his cheeks showed he was as shocked at the turn the conversation had taken as Addy was.

She wondered if Ted was getting to that age where one didn't have quite as much control over what one said. He was very gray, and practically bald. A question to pose to Arthur privately, perhaps. Still, she couldn't help but stew over the comment. Was that really what he thought she had been doing in the city? Being independent did not mean she was no longer respectable. Though, to many of the old school, the two things were one and the same, she realized.

"How about a walk?" Tiffany asked. She began to collect the plates to give no reason to object. "The weather's fine."

Relieved at the chance to end the conversation, everyone agreed, and they headed out into the steamy afternoon.

William joined Addy, Arthur, and Ted for dinner in the hotel restaurant that evening, looking particularly dapper in his best suit and freshly trimmed curls. Tiffany had elected to stay upstairs so as not to impose on the family gathering. The men shook hands before sitting, seeming friendly enough, but everyone's actions were guarded, ready to go on the defensive if necessary. Addy noticed Arthur looking William over closely, assessing the man who'd been chosen over him.

Addy smiled and forced cheerful chatter about the Simmonses' trip from DC and the upcoming nuptials. Everyone followed her lead politely, and Ted made no more unfortunate comments. His mind couldn't be that bad, then, Addy reasoned. Perhaps she had jumped to conclusions earlier. He did, however, unknowingly slip into territory Addy had learned was sacrosanct to William.

"Will your daughter be living with you once you're married?"

William pressed his lips together and moved his fork around his plate without picking anything up. "We hadn't really discussed it. My feeling, though, is that at this point it's best to leave her where she is. It would be difficult for her to leave Boston and the only home she's ever known."

"Yes, I suppose that's true," Ted said, though he still looked unconvinced, watching William out of the corner of his eye.

Sensing an opportunity to press the point safely, since William would be loath to object in front of the others, Addy asked, "But she'll come to visit, won't she? Or we can go to Boston after the honeymoon?"

"Of course," William said with a tight smile. Addy accepted his response but doubted this would be the final word on the matter. There was some reason he wanted to keep his bride and daughter apart. But whatever it was, she reassured herself, it had to be a good one. Perhaps, like Addy, he was simply trying to start over without the baggage of the past.

Ted interrupted her thoughts with the next item of business.

"Tiffany will move on, I assume?"

"Yes," William answered before Addy could even open her mouth.

Arthur caught the glare in Addy's eye.

"It's for the best, Addy. You won't need a companion anymore," Arthur said.

Addy couldn't find the words to respond. How did she end up encircled by men's decisions again? Especially with these men, who barely knew each other yet so easily agreed on the path her life should take?

"Have you written her a character?" Ted asked. "I can do it, if you prefer."

Addy had to clench the edges of her chair to keep her eyes from rolling or an exasperated sigh from escaping her lips. Instead, she threw him a crumb, as she had learned to do.

"Yes, Uncle, please write it. I hardly have time now, with planning the wedding."

Ted beamed, but Addy took no pleasure from his contentedness.

William sat a hand on her shoulder, but his touch was cold, and she shook him off.

Arthur watched her carefully but said nothing for the rest of the meal.

The night before the wedding, a knock came at the hotel-room door long after everyone had left for their own beds. Addy and Tiffany wrapped their robes tightly around themselves, and Tiffany opened the door a crack and peered carefully around it.

"Let me in, dear," a familiar voice floated in.

Addy neared the door as Mrs. Alexi pushed her way in. She looked Addy up and down before she spoke.

"I sensed you wanted to talk to me after the last message you received, but I am so busy, you know. But here I am now, just in time. Tell me." She sat on the sofa and awaited Addy's reply as if she were a queen holding court.

Addy stood in front of Mrs. Alexi and glanced at Tiffany. "I'm not sure..."

Mrs. Alexi waved her hand at Addy. "Oh, out with it, girl. Let's not stand on ceremony here. It was not the message you were expecting, was it?"

Addy remembered the feeling of the crumpled note scratching against her bosom. "No," she said quietly. "No, it wasn't."

Mrs. Alexi tapped the seat beside her. "Sit here."

Addy obeyed.

"I hope you know that even though I spend my life connecting with spirits, I do not let them guide my own actions. They are not God, you know."

Addy nodded. "Yes, yes, I know—"

"Of course, they have insights that we on Earth may not have. But they still carry their life's prejudices with them as well."

Warming to the subject, Addy sat forward. "That's just the thing. In life, they would have been so eager for me to wed. Why this message now?"

Tiffany, hovering over the pair, started to ask a question, but Mrs. Alexi breezed over her.

"It is not for us to know everything. Consider it, but do what you think is best." She stood abruptly. "I will leave you now." But instead of walking out, she gazed at Addy and set one hand against the younger woman's cheek. "Good luck, my dear girl," she said, then turned and left.

Addy sensed there was something that Mrs. Alexi had left out, but she was determined to be comforted by the conversation anyway. Her parents were not omniscient. They did not understand everything about what was happening here on Earth. Addy had not let her parents dictate her decisions while they were alive, so why let them now that they were dead?

She looked across the room at Tiffany, who watched Addy with an expression close to disgust. When she caught Addy's eye, her face relaxed, and she said simply, "Let's go to bed, shall we?"

But Addy stayed where she was. This was the last moment she had to talk to Tiffany about the thing she had been putting off since yesterday's dinner. Sensing something needed to be said, Tiffany hung back and waited for Addy's words.

"There is the matter of your . . . employment that we need to discuss."

Tiffany's face went cold. "You're letting me go, I assume."

"I'm so sorry, Tiffany. I have to. William can't justify the extra expense."

"Of course he can't." She sniffed, but it was haughty instead of tearful. "I'll go pack." Tiffany started to walk away.

Addy called after her, "I'll give you two weeks' extra pay."

Tiffany paused but didn't turn, then continued into her bedroom.

Addy suddenly felt she had just lost her best friend. And she was afraid a best friend would be just what she would need in the next stage of her life.

Tiffany treated her civilly in the morning and didn't let the previous night's declaration affect the way she helped Addy prepare for her big day. The excitement pushed out any uneasy thoughts Addy had harbored about her parents' warning or William's inexplicable reaction to the idea of Addy meeting his daughter. The conversation with Mrs. Alexi had eased Addy's mind somewhat, and for once, Addy was determined to focus solely on the world of the living.

It was easy enough to do. There was the ritual of putting on the white dress, the ordeal of getting the train and veil to fit in the carriage, the clatter of the ride to the church. While her reading material had never gravitated toward fairy tales, she felt like an enchanted princess, and she was satisfied. For this one day, a wedding felt like everything she had ever wanted. Happily ever after approached.

Uncle Ted waited in the foyer of the church to give Addy away. He beamed as he took her arm, and if he still had any hesitation about the circumstances of her wedding, he didn't let it show. She was immensely grateful for it.

Addy walked down the aisle with a proud, strong step. She found herself so distracted by having everyone's faces turned toward her that she didn't actually look at William until the last three feet of her walk. When she did, she saw that his gaze, too, was turned toward their audience. Finally, their eyes met, and they both smiled.

Ted released his hold on her arm. Addy glanced back at the front row as Ted sat. Arthur shot Addy his best grin. Addy wondered how much that joyful front had cost him. From the other side of the aisle, Addy caught Mrs. Alexi watching everything with an intense expression, but she would say nothing to neither bride nor groom all day.

The rest of the ceremony passed by in a blur punctuated only by the sight of William's beaming face as they said their vows, a burst of Tiffany's and Lauren's laughter on the church steps, the snag of the lace hem of her dress catching on her heel as she stepped into the carriage. And at the end of it, she was no longer Miss Cohart, as she had been all her life, but Mrs. Fairley. A new woman with the entire future open to her.

Shut up in the carriage after, William kissed her in a way he never had been able to before. As they pulled apart, she felt like she was arriving in another world, one she had gained entry to by becoming a full-fledged grownup. She snuggled up against her new husband's side and felt no need for words.

They arrived at Addy's hotel. Tiffany waited out front. The sight of her face through the carriage window made Addy nostalgic already. Tiffany helped Addy down, but William stayed inside.

"I have to finalize some things," he explained. "I'll see you tonight."

Addy waited a heartbeat for him to lean down and kiss her, but it didn't come. There would be time enough for that, she reassured herself. Instead, she let Tiffany help her corral her dress so she could make it back to their room. Once there, she changed, then joined Tiffany in their final packing arrangements—her to leave for her honeymoon, Tiffany to return to Washington.

Addy hovered in the doorway of Tiffany's bedroom for several minutes before deciding to speak. "I'm sorry I waited so long to tell you. I suppose I knew what the decision would be, but I waited until William said it so I wouldn't have to."

Tiffany sighed and turned to face Addy. "It's fine, really. I'm not surprised at the decision. You needed a chaperone and now, as a married woman, you don't. It's that simple."

Addy embraced the employee who had become her friend. "It's never that simple." Addy released her. "Please write. It will be nice to hear from you. And if you're available when we go abroad, I may be able to convince William to rehire you then."

"Of course. I want to hear all about the honeymoon. And I really do wish all the best for you in your married life."

The words were kindly meant, Addy knew, but something in the angle of Tiffany's chin and the nervous tapping of her fingertips against each other hinted at an uncertainty that her well wishes would come true. Or she was more annoyed at the abrupt end to her employment than she let on. But Addy used her own joy to brush away the negative thoughts.

"Thank you for everything. I couldn't have navigated this city without you. And I hope that William and Mrs. Alexi helped you come to terms with the losses in your family."

"Think nothing of it," Tiffany replied as she turned to place a few more things in her trunk, leaving a question as to which part of Addy's speech she was responding to.

"Will you be all right on your own in the morning?"

"The Simmonses have kindly offered to escort me back to Washington."

By the time Addy replied, "Good," Tiffany's back was to her again.

It was time to go.

Addy took a last look around the suite that had served as her home through the hot and messy summer. Satisfied, she turned her back on it and shut the door behind her as she left.

Addy and William had reserved their own hotel room close to the train station for that night. In the morning they would have a farewell wedding breakfast at Aunt Gerty's, then leave for Niagara. When they returned from the trip, Mrs. Alexi would have transformed a few upstairs rooms for their use. At first, Addy had had reservations about her and William lacking their own household, but it made sense professionally and financially—plus, it meant she would have unparalleled access to the two mediums' gifts. In that sense, even though her path had strayed from what she had planned, she hadn't completely abandoned her true purpose in coming to New York.

Addy arrived at the hotel before William. The front desk clerk handed her a note saying William was finalizing a few things at Mrs. Alexi's and would be arriving late. Addy sighed and went upstairs alone. She puttered around aimlessly for a few minutes, knowing there was no point in unpacking for just one night, but as the adrenaline from the day left her system, exhaustion gathered around her like a flurry of dust blown by the wind. As soon as she lay down on the bed to wait for her husband, she fell into a deep sleep unbroken by dreams.

Addy awoke with a start, surprised to find the night had passed without her knowledge. She still lay in her dress on top of the covers. She stretched and rubbed her eyes. Her right side ached where her corset had dug between the ribs as she'd slept. A low snore interrupted her thoughts, and she turned to find William sleeping beside her. She kissed his cheek, but he didn't stir. *What an un-wedding night,* she thought dryly. But it was probably for the best. Now they would be well rested, and the first night in Niagara would be that much more special. She checked the clock. They still had one hour until breakfast, so she would let him sleep a bit longer. She spent the intervening time freshening up and admiring the plain gold ring now circling her finger. She got so caught up in her daydreams that she woke William late, and they had to rush to make it out the door in time.

Fortunately, Addy and William made it to Aunt Gerty's only a bit late. Arthur, Ted, and Aunt Gerty were already seated around the dining room table, a mahogany monstrosity that took up too much of the room. Tiffany had left the family to celebrate this last meal together. Addy's joy from the previous day had dissipated, and she didn't feel much like celebrating. In fact, with the impending separation looming over the meal, Addy felt rather solemn and had found herself blinking back tears on the carriage ride over, though she couldn't quite put into words why they had come.

Once the bride and groom walked in, there were hugs and handshakes all around, with William staying by Aunt Gerty for an extra moment, forcing pleasantries with her in a quiet voice. Gerty had begged off the wedding, citing her age and how long the day would be, but Addy knew she had probably just wanted to make her disapproval plain. Gerty had, however, offered to host the wedding breakfast because she couldn't toss away propriety—or her few remaining family members—completely.

Addy settled into her seat and accepted a tray of bread as it was passed around.

Gerty began a long monologue describing everything laid out on the table, and for once Addy was happy to have the silence erased so completely by someone else. She kept her gaze directed at her plate, not feeling strong enough to look into Arthur's or Ted's eyes.

Eventually, the virtues of the food were sufficiently extolled, and Gerty moved on to what she felt was the matter at hand.

"Tell me, young man," she said to William, her fork poised over her plate. "You don't really plan to continue this spiritualist nonsense now that you'll have a family to think of, do you?"

"Actually, I do, ma'am."

"Besides," Arthur cut in. "Mr. Fairley is already a family man, isn't that right?"

Addy snapped to attention. How dare Arthur meddle like this?

"What's this?" Gerty asked, looking between the two young men.

William spread one of his long arms across the table in a languid gesture that somehow gave him complete control of the conversation. "It's true, Aunt. I have a daughter who lives in Boston with my sister."

"Why on earth isn't she here? Adalinda, did you know about this? Ted, did you? Who is this child's mother?"

"Once we're settled, I may send for her," William said, bypassing the string of questions.

It was the first time he had acquiesced to this, but after a moment of looking into his eyes and seeing nothing solid, Addy guessed that this was simply a statement to placate the family. She said nothing.

"Childbed death, I suppose?" Aunt Gerty looked her niece up and down. "Well, let us hope Addy is strong enough."

"We still have at least nine months before we have to worry about that," Ted said. Addy knew he meant it as a joke, but it clattered awkwardly onto the table.

Gerty frowned. "It is never too early to worry about the youth of this country. Honestly, I never thought I'd see the likes . . ." She continued to expound on the ills of youth today, and Addy was glad to have the subject changed.

The life seemed to have gone out of everyone but Gerty. They ate and didn't have much to say. Each was absorbed in his or her own world, with the old woman's constant chatter as the backdrop.

Then the meal was over. The final embraces were exchanged, the last touch of Addy's old life. Finally, she took William's hand, and they turned their backs on the rest of the party. The pair of them made it to the station and into their train car. Addy and her husband settled into the vibration of the train's movement as it pulled away, marking the initiation of something yet unseen.

***

They chugged through the hours, their minds heavy with the weight of waiting for the future to begin—or at least, Addy's was. William gave no indication to her of what his thoughts carried. The pair leaned against each other, still tired from the previous day's festivities with nothing to reenergize them. Addy felt the press of his thigh against hers as a tangible presence in the train compartment with them—another person she couldn't quite take her mind off.

Always reliable, Tiffany had packed sandwiches for them before she left, and a few hours into the journey, they unwrapped them in their laps, licking crumbs off their fingers as they watched the scenery pass. It was a hot, dry day, and the greenery outside shone vibrant in the sun. After they finished eating, the air in the compartment felt more relaxed, and Addy leaned back in her seat, a lazy smile on her face.

William must have felt it, too, because he cleared his throat and began to speak. "Addy, you've asked a lot about my daughter."

Addy frowned. She was surprised at the topic he had chosen but didn't want to back down from her position. "It's not a strange thing to ask about."

He grasped her hand. "I'm not saying it is. It's just a very... tender subject for me. But now that we're married, it's right you should know the truth."

Her frown deepened, the corners of her lips tugging themselves down toward her chin. If "the truth" needed to be told, it probably wasn't something she wanted to hear. Instantly, their physical connection was broken, her hand leaving his.

William forged ahead. "It's not as bad as all that, really. It's just that... she's Jane's child now."

"What does that mean?"

He sighed and shifted. "The truth is, she hasn't answered my letters in years."

"What? Why?"

William shushed her and put a hand on her shoulder. "After my wife—my first wife—died, I was not in a fit state to raise a child. What do I know about infants? My sister had just had a son, so she agreed to take in Harriet. But she's very devout, and once I started working as a medium, she cut off contact—for Harriet's sake, she said."

"But how can she do that? Keep you from your own child?"

He turned his gaze away from her. "I signed her over to my sister and her husband. Legally, I have no rights over her. It seemed the best course of action at the time. I was a mess then."

"Surely you can fight it."

"I decided long ago that it's best to let it be. Let Harriet live her life undisturbed. She thinks Jane is her mother, and there's no reason to confuse her. And it means that now the two of us can have a fresh start together."

Addy crossed her arms over her chest. She had never yearned for children like most women, but she couldn't fathom willingly giving up her own flesh and blood so easily—especially how a man, with so many legal advantages, could do so when women so often had to fight tooth and nail for the same rights. But, still, it was William, and he had his reasons. She understood what he faced with his profession in the eyes of the world, but that his family would completely cut him out of their lives shocked her. Her own family's doubts suddenly seemed mild in comparison.

It was time to go.

Addy took a last look around the suite that had served as her home through the hot and messy summer. Satisfied, she turned her back on it and shut the door behind her as she left.

Addy and William had reserved their own hotel room close to the train station for that night. In the morning they would have a farewell wedding breakfast at Aunt Gerty's, then leave for Niagara. When they returned from the trip, Mrs. Alexi would have transformed a few upstairs rooms for their use. At first, Addy had had reservations about her and William lacking their own household, but it made sense professionally and financially—plus, it meant she would have unparalleled access to the two mediums' gifts. In that sense, even though her path had strayed from what she had planned, she hadn't completely abandoned her true purpose in coming to New York.

Addy arrived at the hotel before William. The front desk clerk handed her a note saying William was finalizing a few things at Mrs. Alexi's and would be arriving late. Addy sighed and went upstairs alone. She puttered around aimlessly for a few minutes, knowing there was no point in unpacking for just one night, but as the adrenaline from the day left her system, exhaustion gathered around her like a flurry of dust blown by the wind. As soon as she lay down on the bed to wait for her husband, she fell into a deep sleep unbroken by dreams.

Addy awoke with a start, surprised to find the night had passed without her knowledge. She still lay in her dress on top of the covers. She stretched and rubbed her eyes. Her right side ached where her corset had dug between the ribs as she'd slept. A low snore interrupted her thoughts, and she turned to find William sleeping beside her. She kissed his cheek, but he didn't stir. *What an un-wedding night,* she thought dryly. But it was probably for the best. Now they would be well rested, and the first night in Niagara would be that much more special. She checked the clock. They still had one hour until breakfast, so she would let him sleep a bit longer. She spent the intervening time freshening up and admiring the plain gold ring now circling her finger. She got so caught up in her daydreams that she woke William late, and they had to rush to make it out the door in time.

Fortunately, Addy and William made it to Aunt Gerty's only a bit late. Arthur, Ted, and Aunt Gerty were already seated around the dining room table, a mahogany monstrosity that took up too much of the room. Tiffany had left the family to celebrate this last meal together. Addy's joy from the previous day had dissipated, and she didn't feel much like celebrating. In fact, with the impending separation looming over the meal, Addy felt rather solemn and had found herself blinking back tears on the carriage ride over, though she couldn't quite put into words why they had come.

Once the bride and groom walked in, there were hugs and handshakes all around, with William staying by Aunt Gerty for an extra moment, forcing pleasantries with her in a quiet voice. Gerty had begged off the wedding, citing her age and how long the day would be, but Addy knew she had probably just wanted to make her disapproval plain. Gerty had, however, offered to host the wedding breakfast because she couldn't toss away propriety—or her few remaining family members—completely.

Addy settled into her seat and accepted a tray of bread as it was passed around.

Gerty began a long monologue describing everything laid out on the table, and for once Addy was happy to have the silence erased so completely by someone else. She kept her gaze directed at her plate, not feeling strong enough to look into Arthur's or Ted's eyes.

Eventually, the virtues of the food were sufficiently extolled, and Gerty moved on to what she felt was the matter at hand.

"Tell me, young man," she said to William, her fork poised over her plate. "You don't really plan to continue this spiritualist nonsense now that you'll have a family to think of, do you?"

"Actually, I do, ma'am."

"Besides," Arthur cut in. "Mr. Fairley is already a family man, isn't that right?"

Addy snapped to attention. How dare Arthur meddle like this?

"What's this?" Gerty asked, looking between the two young men.

William spread one of his long arms across the table in a languid gesture that somehow gave him complete control of the conversation. "It's true, Aunt. I have a daughter who lives in Boston with my sister."

"Why on earth isn't she here? Adalinda, did you know about this? Ted, did you? Who is this child's mother?"

"I just wish you had told me," she said, "instead of letting me keep bringing it up and looking like a fool."

"I'm sorry," he said.

She waited for an explanation of why he hadn't told her but saw quickly that it wouldn't come.

"I'll write and explain it to the Simmonses, since it seems to bother Arthur so much," he offered.

"Leave Arthur out of it. Let him think what he wants."

"If that's what you prefer."

William set a hand on her knee, but she brushed it off. The last thing she had wanted was to talk about Arthur and the past on her honeymoon. She and William were meant to be starting a new life, and constantly bringing out their old baggage would only drag them down.

A distance remained between them for the rest of the day. When they finally arrived in Buffalo and made it to their hotel room, their lovemaking was stilted and awkward, not at all like Addy had hoped it would be or felt promised by the earlier press of her husband's thigh.

The next day, better rested and awash in the romantic beauty of Niagara, their moods improved, and they fell more easily into step with each other. Addy leaned into William's arm as they walked along the falls, proud of the handsome couple they made.

"What do you think?" he asked as they paused to watch the roar of the water and feel its spray.

"I think all of it's wonderful."

He laughed. "All of what, exactly?"

"Being here, in this place, with you."

He leaned down and kissed her. When Addy looked up, she saw a middle-aged couple watching them, but for once she did not blush. She just squeezed her husband's arm tighter.

In the evening they sat by the fire, even though the weather didn't call for it. The heat from the fire condensed the room to just their two bodies, wrapping them in its blanketing comfort and forcing all awkwardness to leave.

They lay in bed, too hot with the fire crackling, but unwilling to move.

"We'll go far, you and I, if we stick together," William said.

Addy ran her finger along the edge of his brow, memorizing the way the curls lay plastered against his forehead with sweat. "Of course we'll be together."

He shifted onto his side to face her. One finger traced the curve of her hip. "Yes, but I want you to promise me you will always be on my side, no matter what happens."

She gazed him an instant too long, sensing that something lurked beneath this seemingly silly request. When she saw him open his mouth to speak again, she put a finger to his lips. "We only have one side now. Our side. Nothing can split us."

He kissed her long and deep. "I'm glad we understand each other," he said, once they had caught their breath again.

Addy wasn't actually sure she understood him at all, but the mystery he presented intrigued her, and she had the rest of her life to solve it.

By the end of the five days of their honeymoon, Addy felt absorbed by her new husband, like she was a loose collection of atoms called to action only when he walked into the room. It was a feeling an earlier version of herself would have hated, but now she felt power in the devotion, the commitment to his happiness and success.

They emerged from the final puff of the train back onto the platform in New York City. Even though the streets were packed with people and vehicles, the city seemed empty to Addy, waiting to be filled with memories of her and William. She squeezed his hand, and he smiled, but she could tell his smile did not encompass the myriad hopes she held. It spoke instead to his practicality and determination, traits she could not fault. She knew that when he looked around the city, he saw places waiting to be conquered, to be brought to heel. Together, the couple would ensure that happened.

The rooms Mrs. Alexi had set aside for them on the third floor of her house were small and comfortable—a parlor, a small kitchen and dining room, and a bedroom that looked over the street, with a bathroom down the hall. Almost everything they could need had been stocked in the cupboards as well.

"This will be more than enough for us, don't you think?" William asked as he slipped off his gloves.

"Oh, yes," Addy said as she unpinned her hat, with more conviction than she felt. All the rooms together were smaller than her hotel suite had been all those months, but she had to focus on how beneficial the arrangement would be for William's career and for her own connections with the dead. "It's so kind of Mrs. Alexi to provide this for us."

William gave a little snort. "Well, she owes me quite a bit. A few months' free rent is a nice gesture, but it hardly covers everything."

"What on earth does that mean?"

"You know I've done a lot for her because of how she saved me."

"Saved you how, exactly?"

He shrugged.

"Please, William, tell me something."

He sighed and, for once, relented. "I was not in my right mind after my first wife died. In fact, I tried rather half-heartedly to kill myself in Mrs. Alexi's bathroom after a séance where my wife didn't come through. Instead of throwing me out, she healed me, offered me a job, gave me the opportunity to help her and, therefore, others like me who are desperate. We owe each other quite a lot, actually."

Addy stared at him for a long moment. She was shocked, of course, but also felt a pity she knew he wouldn't want. The story, however, encapsulated much for her about why the spiritualist cause was so important. And it began to illuminate the depths of William's soul, for which she was grateful. But instead of saying all this, she said nothing.

"How about some tea?" he asked.

The distraction was a relief. "That sounds like just the thing." Addy forced a brightness into her voice. She paused, for one instant wondering who she should call up to prepare it, then, in the next, realizing it was up to her. It certainly wouldn't do to enlist Mrs. Alexi's servants without permission. Perhaps she could convince William to hire a daytime serving girl—it would be cheaper than having Tiffany live in with them.

But for now, she drew on her experience helping with the Simmonses' household. She certainly wasn't afraid of a little work. She opened the cupboards, found a teapot, filled it with tea leaves and water, and stoked the stove with coal. She looked through the cupboards for teacups as she waited for the stove to heat up.

William settled down at the kitchen table. "I'll go to the bank tomorrow so I can get money for your allowance," he said.

She opened a cupboard door, closed it again without registering what was inside. She looked back at him over her shoulder. "What allowance?"

"Your allowance," he said again, with no further elaboration. "Do you want it weekly or monthly?"

Ire moved up her spine like a physical thing until it reached her mouth, making her words clipped and tense. "I want to use my money as I see fit."

"My dear," he said, extending a hand slightly toward her along the table in mimicry of his supplicating tone, "you know that's not possible. We must keep a financially strong household. I assure you, the allowance will be quite enough for your needs."

She glowered and poured the barely warm water into the teacups. Forgetting the strainer, the liquid came out a dark, cloudy mess. She slammed down the teapot, disgusted at her mistake. "You discussed this with my uncle, I suppose?"

"Of course."

"No one thought to tell me."

He stood and came over to her, pouring the useless tea neatly down the drain. "You must know that now that we're married, there is no such thing as what you call 'your money.' I didn't think it needed to be said."

"Of course it needs to be said. I thought you respected me more than that."

"I do. Of course I do. Forgive me for my lapse in judgment in not telling you earlier."

His words rang hollow. Forgiveness was all well and good, but it didn't change what he had decided for her. She looked down at the mess darkening the sink and felt her strength for fighting drain away with the liquid. She dropped the teapot and the subject. She looked up into his handsome face. "Could we get some tea from downstairs, do you think?"

He left in search of it. Addy stayed behind with a few tears on her cheeks, which she wiped away furiously once she heard his footsteps returning on the stairs.

Part II

Chapter 9

The letter arrived late one afternoon as the daylight weakened and the first snowflakes of the season drifted from sky to ground, mingling as they landed, caught unaware of the momentariness of their lives. Addy set the envelope on the table without daring to open it. She would wait for her husband to discover whether it brought the good news they hoped for after a month's exchanges across the Atlantic.

William opened the letter as he and Addy sat around the table that evening. A spiritualist organization in London had offered to sponsor Mrs. Alexi to visit them. Mrs. Alexi, claiming she was too old for the journey, recommended William instead. Even though his reputation had grown both in the United States and abroad, at first it had seemed as if the Brits would not accept the substitution. However, Mr. Belk, who often traveled to London on business and knew several people in the spiritualist arena there, had swayed a few key members on his last trip. Addy felt confident the letter contained a formal invitation.

"They have secured sufficient donations to fund our travel," William announced proudly once his eyes had scanned the page.

"How wonderful!" Addy climbed into his lap, kissed him, and ran her fingers through his curls. "When do we leave?"

"Two weeks' time."

"Goodness, that's soon."

"See? You'll get to travel Europe after all."

"Do you mean we can go to the continent while we're there?"

William set the letter on the table. "Let's not get ahead of ourselves. The funds they've raised are barely enough to cover our expenses in England."

"Yes, but it won't cost much more to go across the Channel. We can use some of my money for that, surely."

A hint of displeasure twitched across William's face. Seeing it, Addy let the subject drop into silence; money was still the one topic that always divided them, though their marriage was harmonious otherwise.

"Perhaps Tiffany can come as my companion?"

His countenance turned even more sour. "You'll be accompanied. By me. And I'm sure the ladies there will keep you company and take you out."

Addy frowned and looked down to analyze the stitching in her slippers. "I suppose."

"Let's talk about what we *are* going to do," William declared, encircling her waist with his arms. "We'll get the steamer on the fifteenth, and five days later we'll be in merry old England. To see the sights and, more importantly, recapture the country's interest in the spirits."

This turned Addy's frown into a beaming smile. "Spending the holidays abroad. I can't wait," she said, looking forward with a childish impatience to leaving the city she had once so desperately longed to arrive in.

"And we owe Mr. Belk a debt of gratitude for making these connections for us."

Addy still had her own thoughts about that man and the leering way he looked at her—or any other young woman that crossed his path. But she had to admit that he had not failed them in this instance. Perhaps he had some redeeming qualities after all.

She got up and poured two small glasses of wine.

"To Mr. Belk," she announced as she lifted hers in the air.

William mimicked her motion. "To the brightness of our future."

Once again, there was a flurry of days as they prepared for departure. Since her parents' deaths, Addy felt she was always preparing to leave someplace. Each journey took her farther from where and who she had been. But the movement was good for her; it was stasis she feared.

Mrs. Alexi had been a constant backdrop to Addy and William's relationship thus far, and Addy cried when they said goodbye to her before leaving for the dock. Addy hated to admit it, but Mrs. Alexi filled a motherly role Addy missed having in her life. Mrs. Alexi understood Addy more than her own mother ever had. Now she and William would truly be on their own for the first time, motherless again, and in a strange place, no less.

Addy and William stood on the deck as the ship pulled away, bundled against the chilled morning air while they watched the New York skyline shrink, as if the city were a dream they were slowly waking up from. Addy closed her eyes and held her breath, and when she opened them again the city was gone, its immensity no more than a myth. Her breath came back quick and steady in the cold.

"I've never been on the open sea before," she said, though she felt the banality of the statement as soon as the words left her lips.

"You can watch it if you want, but I'm going inside where it's warm," William said, heading toward the door. Addy watched the gray sea for an instant, then followed quickly behind her husband. He didn't wait for her to catch up.

On the first day of the voyage, the sea broke against the vessel cold and choppy. Addy holed up in the warm cocoon of the cabin, wrapping gratefully around William whenever he joined her. He was already off making new connections among the other passengers, but as evening wore on, he stayed with her.

The second morning, feeling less seasick and more prepared to engage with the world beyond her husband, Addy dragged herself out of the cabin to socialize. The sun was out, but from the shivers of those she saw on the deck, she could tell the air was still bitingly cold, and she didn't dare venture into it.

When she arrived in the dining room, William was already holding court at a central table, half a dozen fellow passengers leaning forward to hang on his every word. She had to stand next to him for several seconds before he stopped talking and looked up to introduce her. She smiled through the awkwardness and shook hands with all the eager potential patrons—Mr. and Mrs. Klein; Mr. Watt; the misses Edwards (Lacy, the older, and Patricia, the younger) and their chaperone, a silent, elderly Aunt May, who appeared to be the complete opposite of garrulous Aunt Gerty.

"A pleasure," Addy said to the group, and cast her gaze around the table for a seat. No one moved to let her sit next to her husband, so she took a spot on the opposite side and accepted the waiter's offer of tea. Everyone's gaze remained fixed on William.

"I think in two nights' time, I should be ready," he was saying.

"Ready for what?" Addy asked.

No one responded to her for a moment, until Aunt May turned and said gently to her, "He's holding a séance for all of us." She grinned, and decades of age fell away from her face. "I've never been to one before, but I've heard so much."

Addy smiled. "That's wonderful. I'm sure you'll enjoy it."

The aunt nodded and turned her attention back to William.

Addy sighed and picked at her breakfast, using her fork to take a couple of stewed tomatoes on a ride past the scrambled eggs. She was happy to recruit new believers, of course, but if that was William's entire focus, it was going to make her trip incredibly dull. So far, his early promise of making her his assistant and an integral part of his work hadn't materialized. Maybe now that they were out of New York and away from Mrs. Alexi's support, that would change. She perked up at the thought.

In the meantime, Addy entertained herself with observing her neighbors. The young Edwards girls dripped with diamonds, even at breakfast. She supposed it was normal to show off one's wealth at that age, when appearance matters so much. Addy inadvertently found herself looking down at her own wrists and fingers, bare except for the plain wedding ring. Her mother had never seen much sense in wasting money on jewelry, so Addy had never received any, and William, of course, worried constantly about money.

She shook her head to clear it. It didn't matter at all. Nothing mattered except the work of converting people into believers. It was William's work, and hers, even though so far she moved it forward only by supporting him and not complaining.

Two nights later Addy and William approached the Edwardses' cabin, which had been selected to host the séance since it was the largest of the group's. The girls had clearly enjoyed decorating, Addy observed as she walked in. Veils were strung atmospherically across the walls, and so many candles lit every surface it mimicked daylight.

As first-timers, the participants held no automatic distrust of William's methods. They clearly hadn't let the discouraging opinions in the papers about fraudulent mediums influence them. The group let William take his seat and Addy hers next to him without any searches or pointed hints that the couple might be in cahoots to pull off a scam—objections Addy had heard far too often. It was refreshing, and Addy beamed in the warmth of their trust. If only everyone could lay their hesitations aside like these people could, the cause would grow exponentially.

The circle fell into silence. Addy could feel the spirits near them; it was like a touch left lingering an inch from your skin, making the hairs on the back of your neck stand up. For her, that was all the proof needed. She hoped the others let themselves feel it, too.

The session began well enough. Mr. Watt seemed pleased to hear from his mother, and Mr. Klein received a message from a long-departed brother.

Then it was the Edwardses' turn. Addy could sense that William would give everyone a message; he wanted to impress here, a practice round before his big debut abroad. But she also felt that goal was a stretch. There was rarely a séance where everyone came through. Whoever showed up was out of mortals' control, even those mortals with a gift like William's.

But he persisted in his plan. Addy could feel a delicate sheen of sweat collecting in the center of his hand, held palm up under hers.

His voice, though, remained steady. "There are parental figures for you on the other side. They want to thank your aunt for watching over you."

Addy cracked one eye open in time to see the sisters exchange incredulous glances.

Patricia, the younger one, said, "But our parents are still alive in New York. We're just traveling without them since mother is ill."

Beside her, Addy felt Aunt May shift in her seat.

William didn't miss a beat, but his words sped up to a more natural tone rather than the drawl he usually used while channeling. "Spirits sometimes come through in their role. A parental figure could be anyone who filled that role for you. Grandparents, perhaps?"

Addy sneaked another peek. The sisters were nodding, their perfectly placed curls bobbing. "Yes, our grandparents are dead," Patricia said.

"They're glad your aunt was able to step in and chaperone you on this trip."

"Do my parents have any message for me?" Aunt May asked.

William paused. Addy almost laughed. Rarely were the séance members this chatty. And William had backed himself into the corner with that one, focusing too much on the girls and forgetting how the grandparents must also be related to May.

"That's all, I'm afraid," William said. "You may release the circle."

Hands dropped into laps. Eyes opened. Everyone looked around at their companions. Addy glanced at William, but he did not meet her gaze, preferring to fiddle with the tablecloth instead.

The sisters clapped their hands. "That was so much fun!"

William looked at them out of the corner of his eye but said nothing, so Addy stepped in.

"I hope you realize it's more than just fun."

"Oh, yes," Lacy said, looking at her younger sister. They both burst into giggles.

Addy bristled at being the object of whatever joke they had between them. Clearly she had misjudged their lack of prejudice against spiritualism.

"Perhaps we had better clean up," Addy suggested.

"We can do that," May said. She stood and began showing the guests out, though William paused to talk to the Kleins, leaning one hand on the girls' vanity, which was strewn with the jewelry and ribbons that the girls hadn't selected for that evening's ensembles.

Addy waited for him outside the entrance to the suite. When he emerged, he looked enraged.

"Don't say anything about it," he said and hurried ahead of her.

By the time the others exited the suite, William had already disappeared down the hall. Addy walked slowly back to her cabin with the Kleins. She asked Mr. Klein innocuous questions about his brother and avoided the topic of the awkwardness that had just transpired with the Edwardses. When Addy shut the door to her and William's room behind her, she felt a surge of relief.

By morning William had calmed. When he and Addy arrived at breakfast, he greeted their tablemates affably.

The Edwardses, however, were stony. Patricia looked particularly distraught.

"Has something happened?" Addy asked as she settled into her chair.

Aunt May sighed. "One of the girls' diamond necklaces is missing."

Mr. Watt took over, telling the remainder. Addy assumed the Edwardses had already been forced to share the story several times this morning. "They searched the staff, but nothing has been found so far. I would hate to think one of the passengers is a thief."

"God, no," William said before he sipped his coffee. "But you're sure it's not just lost?"

"We looked everywhere. The porter did, too," Lacy said. She placed a hand over her sister's.

"I hope they find whoever took it. They can't have gone far on a ship," Addy said.

"Did you leave the cabin at all last night?" William asked.

"We went out for a bit of air after the séance," May said.

"What they need to do is find out if anyone saw someone go into your cabin during that time."

"I suppose that would help," Lacy said. "We'll suggest it to the porter."

William raised the cup held before his face an inch in acknowledgment, then downed the rest of his coffee. "Addy, what do you think about taking the air?"

She looked down at her half-eaten breakfast. But William was already up, and in the next instant he wrapped a hand loosely around her upper arm.

"Forgive us," he said to the others. "My wife's been feeling a bit ill, and I think the morning air would do her good."

"Good luck with the search," Addy said as they walked abruptly away.

"I have not been ill!" Addy hissed at her husband as they made their way along the deck. At least, she hadn't been since the first day.

"I know, but I needed to get away from that table and all their stupid prattle about diamonds. Wear one of your other fifty diamond necklaces, for God's sake."

Addy remembered the glittering vanity from last night. "Yes, I doubt they will really miss it much. But, still, a theft on this ship . . ."

"It's probably the maid or something. Or it fell under a dresser when the ship moved. Somebody's bound to lose something on a trip like this. It's almost expected."

"Really?"

William didn't respond. Instead, he guided her back inside and down to their cabin.

"Now I think I don't feel so well," he said once they were there.

He lay back on the bed. Addy sat beside him and rubbed his temples. Once he had dozed off, Addy settled into the armchair with a book. Not a Marie Corelli this time, but a good, familiar Jane Austen. She was soon off in the world of nearly a hundred years ago and forgot all about the Edwardses' problems and her husband's slipup the night before. By the time William awoke from his nap, Addy's concerns had faded away with the promise of reading a well-scripted happy ending.

They spent the last day and a half of the voyage in the warmth of the cabin. They talked of their dreams for William's success in England, made love, read, napped. They took meals in their cabin and saw nothing of their dining companions. The time was a swirl of coziness that Addy didn't want to leave. It shocked her when the time came to emerge from their cocoon and out into the noise and dirt of the Southampton wharf.

But once her feet landed firmly on the wooden dock, she knew they had arrived, and she readied herself to conquer this new land.

Chapter 10

The day they landed bled fog, blurring the motions of people hastening through the streets. Addy pulled her coat collar tight around her neck, and beside her she felt William do the same. It was an invigorating gesture, announcing that one was about to plunge forth into the elements and *do something*. Except they did not quite know what to do. Fortunately, an English couple they had met on the ship walked past and told Addy and William to follow them to the train station. They moved forward.

Once they arrived in London, one of the spiritualists who had raised funds for their trip met them at the station. He was eager, thin, and red haired, and he introduced himself as Mr. Pierce. "Welcome," he said, pumping both their hands, William's first, then Addy's. "We're thrilled to have you."

"We're thrilled to be here," William said.

Satisfied with these pleasantries, Mr. Pierce waved them on, leading them to a cab station outside. Addy trailed behind, struggling through the crowd and holding on to the back of William's coat, overwhelmed by the hubbub after the insulated calm of the voyage. She was grateful when she finally collapsed, exhausted, onto the carriage seat.

Mr. Pierce began talking even before he was comfortably in his seat across from them. "I think you'll find the hotel to your satisfaction," he said. "It's in a nice area, not too far from all the things you'll want to visit. And close to the Dowager Countess Greeley's London residence. She's most anxious to meet you."

"Yes, you'd written us about her," William said. "She has a long interest in spirits, doesn't she?"

"Oh, yes. Unfortunately, many of the mediums now working in London have been caught in various acts of fraud. Our golden age of spiritualism seems to be fading away. The countess is very anxious to find the genuine article again. She was close with Mr. Home, you know, before he retired. One of the greats."

He paused, but it was clear it was a pause to gather his thoughts only and that he had no intention of surrendering control of the conversation, something Addy guessed he did only rarely. She thought, with a little smile, of Auntie Gerty.

"We've heard great things about what you've been doing in the States," Mr. Pierce continued. "Mrs. Alexi recommends you most highly." He sniffed, glanced at his pocket watch. "Shame she couldn't come as well."

"She of course sends her regrets."

"Yes, yes." Mr. Pierce turned his ginger mustachio toward Addy. "Well, Mrs. Fairley, you're quite lovely, even at the end of such a trip. Travel must suit you."

"You're very kind," Addy mumbled, disconcerted by the depth of his appreciative gaze.

Mr. Pierce continued looking at her as if he had not heard her. But in her exhausted state, Addy refused to repeat herself.

William shifted in his seat and apologized for her. "We're both quite tired by the journey." The carriage jolted and pulled to the left, trying to avoid something. The driver's angry shout carried back to his passengers. Addy tensed, but Mr. Pierce looked unconcerned, so she forced herself to relax.

"Of course, of course," Mr. Pierce said. "I'll drop you off at the hotel so you can rest. Tomorrow night the countess will host a reception for you with all the donors."

"That sounds wonderful," Addy said, more confident now that their host's gaze had left her, though exhaustion still weighed down her words, making her response barely audible above the roar of the city outside. "It will be so nice to meet everyone," she said a bit louder.

"Yes, so we can thank them personally," William agreed.

"We'll need to work out a schedule for your readings and séances. Everyone will want some time from you. That's your most precious commodity, and one we must manage carefully." He held up one forefinger to emphasize his point.

"I'm more than happy to oblige everyone I can."

The carriage halted, and they stepped out in front of their hotel. A chilled breeze caressed their faces like a living thing, heavy with the grime of the city. Addy felt it depositing a film of dust on her face. She had to stop herself from wiping it off with her new white gloves she had purposefully donned that morning to make a good impression on the new city.

The building they stood in front of was stone—whitewashed once, perhaps, but now gray. It was stately, older than anything she had seen in New York. She squeezed William's bicep in anticipation. Mr. Pierce waved them in.

Inside, the air was calmer and more pleasant, indicative of a sealed-off world. The only sounds were the shuffle of feet across marble, the rustle of a newspaper, the informative whisper of the concierge. Addy found herself standing straighter, proud to be part of such a formalized space. She stayed silent as they checked in and followed the bellhop upstairs to their room. It wasn't a suite, but it was large, with a living area set around the fireplace; a small, round table by the window; and an imposing four-poster bed pushed up against the far wall.

"What do you think, dear?" William asked, trying to jar his wife back into conversation.

"It's lovely," she said, going to peer out the window, which overlooked a small courtyard behind the building.

Satisfied, Mr. Pierce took his leave, promising to call on them in the morning.

Once he was gone, Addy sat heavily on the bed, peeled off her hat, gloves, and coat, and tossed them beside her. "I feel like I finally know what they mean when they say 'sleep like the dead.' I think I could sleep for days."

"I know. Me too. But we can't yet." William lay on his back on the bed, his legs hanging over the edge. "I was afraid he would never leave."

"Or stop talking." Addy laughed.

"He's very nice."

"I didn't say he wasn't."

William cracked a smile in response but remained his serious self. "We're very lucky to have him. Let's not make this into another Mr. Belk situation."

Addy shook her head and turned away. "When do you think the trunks will get here?" she asked.

"I have no idea. Are you really worried about unpacking now?"

"It's something to keep me occupied so I don't fall asleep."

William pulled out his watch. "We missed lunch. Why don't we call down for something to eat?"

Addy nodded and went into the bathroom to freshen up while he ordered.

Soon a knock came at the door. William answered and jumped aside as the same bellhop rolled in their trunks. "I'm sorry, I thought you were our lunch," he said to explain his surprise.

"No, sir, just me," the bellhop said, with a banal expression that Addy knew was meant to be uninterpretable to the guests. He stacked the trunks in one corner of the room, and, when he was done, William fumbled in his pockets with the unfamiliar change. He handed a few coins to the bellhop, who left looking satisfied.

As the door closed, William shook his head. "I have no idea what I gave him."

Addy came over and investigated the coins remaining in his palm. She picked one up, looked at it, and set it back down. "Don't ask me. Someone on the ship tried to explain the system to me, and I still don't understand it at all. Too many things going into other things in different amounts."

"We'll have to ask Mr. Pierce tomorrow."

"I'm sure he'll have plenty to say about it."

"Addy, be nice to him. He's the reason why we're here."

"I have been perfectly nice to him."

"You hardly said a word."

"I'm tired." She lifted the lid on the topmost trunk, one of William's she hadn't packed herself. Its new, uncracked leather had a blue silk lining that rippled smoothly beneath her fingers. Incredibly handsome and poised, just like William. "What's this?" she asked, lifting out a few items to show him before setting them back in their places: some photography plates, a lace veil, a packet of some powder she couldn't identify.

William came up behind her and closed the lid, leaving her barely enough time to extricate her fingers. "They're materials for the séances. I'll unpack it."

"Won't they have all that here?"

"I like to have my own supplies, just in case." His voice was flat, cold, a verbal *No Trespassing* sign.

Addy frowned but didn't have the energy to push him further. During their time in New York, she had participated in William's séances and entertained the guests, but she had never helped him set up. That was something he and Mrs. Alexi liked to do together as much as possible. It seemed there was still a lot she didn't know about the process, and it hurt that William wouldn't show her, but she told herself he would share his secrets eventually, just like he had with the truth about his daughter.

Without another word, William dragged the top trunk off so Addy could unpack the one beneath. Lunch arrived, so they took a break and busied themselves over the tea, sandwiches, and fruit. After they unpacked, even though London beckoned outside, they stayed in, lulled to an early sleep by the quickly falling night.

Mr. Pierce arrived after breakfast the next morning, ready to show his charges around the city before that evening's reception. A fine drizzle hazed over the cold day but didn't lessen Addy's excitement. They took a carriage down to the main sites along the Thames, Mr. Pierce and William spending the ride going over the schedule for the next two weeks. Addy craned her neck, trying to take in as much as she could through the small carriage window, which kept the tops of the buildings they passed just out of view. Instead, she saw mostly a vista of blue and tan facades, fronted by sidewalks teeming with Londoners.

They pulled into the entrance to a large bustling square. "Here, we get out," Mr. Pierce announced. "Sorry for the rain—but this is London, you know, chaps."

Addy should have heeded his warning, because when she stepped down out of the carriage, she slipped on a wet paving stone and steadied herself on Mr. Pierce's arm. Stable again, she looked up and gasped at the view. Off to her right stood an imposing stone cathedral, half-hidden by the morning crowds. Across the way was a long brownish building. She tilted her head back to take in the clock tower. "Is that Parliament?"

"Let's worry about getting out of the road first." William laughed and grabbed her elbow to guide her onto the sidewalk. She *tsked* at him but didn't complain.

"Yes, Westminster Abbey and Parliament, with Big Ben. We can tour one but not the other." Mr. Pierce sounded like an announcer she had seen at the circus as a child, only Mr. Pierce was corralling his guests instead of animals.

They walked to the Abbey and purchased their tickets. Once inside, she wandered around trying to look everywhere at once, starting to touch famous inscriptions but then pulling her finger away at the last instant when she realized what she was doing. In her focus, William and Mr. Pierce were lost to her.

However, once some of the awe had faded, she became aware of the crowds traipsing over the gravestones of the country's most famous figures, and she felt some of the seriousness of the lives and deaths of these people escape her. After all, at the end even the most illustrious figures were nothing more than anyone else, just words marking a piece of ground that the living thought nothing of walking over. Still, she found herself dreaming of holding a séance here and connecting with these spirits. She almost mentioned it but caught herself just in time. It was a ridiculous thought, she knew. But, still, she wanted to know these people who had lived, to hear what they had to say about the modern world.

She squeezed her husband's hand. "William, do you feel anything when you're in a place like this?"

William stopped his conversation with their companion and looked at her quizzically. "Whatever do you mean? It's quite impressive, certainly."

She shook her head firmly. "No, I mean, do you *sense* anything? There must be so many spirits around."

He smiled, but his look hinted that he was humoring her somehow. "Nothing like that." He turned away and pulled her along to the next marker along the wall. "That's why we go through the rituals of the séance—to call the spirits to us."

"That makes sense," she said, and let her attention be drawn to a quote on Dickens's tomb.

They toured the rest of the building, and once they had circled back around to the entrance, Mr. Pierce said, "How about a spot of lunch?"

They assented, and he led them to a small café on a narrow street nearby. It was still raining, but not so hard that anyone thought to open an umbrella. However, once they sat inside, runnels of water glided down Addy's mint green silk dress and formed a puddle around her feet. When William removed his coat, it flung droplets of water over her and the table. She laughed and played with the tiny globes of water until they soaked into the tablecloth.

Mr. Pierce watched her from across the table. "I know many a lady who would be much more bothered by the rain than you are, Mrs. Fairley."

She shrugged. "It will always dry."

"What a practical way of thinking. It brings to mind the ultimate message of spiritualism: that we may die, but there is always the chance to reconnect. We needn't worry too much about it, in that case."

"Hear, hear," Addy said as she lifted a spoonful of soup to her mouth. After she had swallowed, she continued, "I hope that William is able to convince many people of just that fact. It is so freeing once one realizes it." She looked over at William, but he added nothing.

They ate slowly, savoring being out of the rain and watching London pass by through the trails of water sliding down the window as the rain grew heavier. Mr. Pierce covered the bill, and William made no effort to contradict him. She frowned at his lack of manners but let herself be swept back into the London afternoon. Mr. Pierce was their sponsor, after all. She waited under an awning as the men went to fetch a cab, though the overhang couldn't keep the raindrops from splashing up onto the hem of her dress, creating a dark ring around the bottom.

A small boy came up to her, thin and ragged. "Spare a penny, mum?" he asked, extending a filthy palm.

Addy pulled out her reticule and placed a bronze coin into his hand. "Are you alone?" she started to ask, but the carriage pulled up and the boy ran off, prize clutched close.

William reached an arm out of the carriage door to help her up. "Did you just give that boy money?"

"Of course I did." She plopped onto the seat beside him. "He was pathetic."

"You'll have every beggar in London after you now," Mr. Pierce said.

"Surely you don't expect me to turn him away?"

The men just exchanged a look that shut her out completely.

"There are other methods to assist the poor," Mr. Pierce said. "If you keep on like that, I'm afraid we may have to tighten your purse strings."

Addy stared at him, shocked that he felt he controlled her.

William said nothing to defend her.

She crossed her arms and looked out the window, not even registering the sights on the way back to the hotel.

Once Mr. Pierce had left Addy and William to rest and prepare for that night's reception, Addy pulled out her hairpins and furiously brushed through the still-damp knots. "Do you think we can see Buckingham Palace tomorrow?"

"I can't hear you when you talk to me upside down through your hair." William laughed, coming over to lean down beside her.

Addy flung herself back upright, nearly knocking into William's chin in the process. "Can we see Buckingham Palace tomorrow?"

"Let's see what Mr. Pierce has planned for us."

"Is he going to manage all of our time while we're here? I mean, it's nice to have a local guide, but . . ."

"I have my first séance tomorrow evening with the countess. If she approves of me tonight, at least, it will be the first. I'll need time tomorrow to show you how to help me set up, too."

Addy beamed, all thoughts of Mr. Pierce instantly forgotten. "I'm so glad you're finally going to let me help!"

He kissed the top of her head. "But you must do exactly as I say."

"Of course." She pulled a lavender dress out of her trunk, which was still only half-unpacked. "Do you think this will do? It's my nicest dress, but even so, I don't know if it's good enough for London society. Especially with a countess to impress."

"It's the dowager countess, and she's eighty-five years old. I doubt she's on top of the latest fashion trends."

Addy smiled, fondling the ivory lace around the dress's collar, feeling it scratch against the tender skin of her fingertips. "Yes, but you don't want everyone to think we're some poor provincial Americans, do you?"

William shook his head in exasperation. "Just put on the dress."

"That's funny you think it's that simple. I'm a mess from the rain."

She peeled down to her underclothes and went into the bathroom to freshen up. William called after her, "They're going to think we're provincial *because* we're Americans, no matter what you wear."

Night had fallen by the time the carriage arrived to pick them up. The weather had cleared, bright spots of starlit hope visible through the clouds for the first time since they arrived. Sitting in the countess's carriage, Addy felt like Cinderella going to the ball, though her prince was already with her. She squeezed William's hand and grinned the whole way there.

The ride was short, as Mr. Pierce had promised, and brought them to a whitewashed town house with a small green lawn setting it off from the square. The entrance was vivid with people arriving. Gas lamps in the entranceway cast shadows on their faces, hid secrets in the folds of their coats. Addy was suddenly nervous, brutally aware of her foreignness in this place. William, unperturbed, hopped down from his seat and set off proudly for the doorway. Addy took a deep breath, reminded herself that they were the guests of honor, and forced herself to hold her head high as they walked to the door.

In the next instant they crossed the threshold into their new world.

The parlor swirled with unfamiliar faces and a cacophony of chatter laced with the thin strands of a quartet playing in an alcove at the far end of the room. Mr. Pierce emerged from the crowd. "Excellent! The guests of honor have arrived. Let me take you to meet your hostess."

They sidled through the other guests, who were reluctant to move out of anyone's way, even though Addy caught whispers identifying her and William as the Americans. They came to a corner with an elegant pink floral armchair. An old woman weighed down with jewelry sat in it, presided over by a number of hangers-on. Beside her sat a middle-aged blonde woman in a much less opulent chair, who seemed to make a point of looking disinterested in the proceedings. This group parted as the trio approached.

Their red-haired leader bowed. "Countess Greeley, allow me to present Mr. and Mrs. William Fairley."

The countess held her wineglass a touch higher in greeting. "I'm very pleased to finally meet you, Mr. Fairley. You are growing renowned for your talents. And Mrs. Fairley, of course."

Addy curtsied but felt she was periphery to the exchange. Her husband bowed deeply. "Countess Greeley, what an honor. We so greatly appreciate your hospitality. I look forward to working with you."

"Yes, yes. Well, enjoy meeting everyone. Dinner will be in an hour."

Mr. Pierce turned back to his charges to confirm that they were in fact dismissed. "She has a lot of other guests to see to."

"Yes, of course," William said as Mr. Pierce guided them away from the countess's corner. "I just hope we didn't give a bad impression."

"Not at all. That's just the way those kind of people are. Can't appear to like anyone too much, you know."

This made Addy think of the other woman they had not been introduced to. "Who was that blonde woman beside the countess?"

Mr. Pierce swiveled around to check. "Ah, yes. That's the countess's spinster daughter. Lady Agatha."

He turned his attention back to identifying people in the crowd—another unimportant woman successfully dismissed, Addy thought. It increased her interest in Agatha rather than the opposite.

"Let me introduce you to the other members of the spiritualist society," he said.

The slew of introductions went by in a blur; Addy couldn't imagine how to possibly keep track of everyone. But, unlike the dowager, everyone seemed pleased to meet both her and William. She smiled, tried to appear confident, hoping to convince them that she, too, was interesting and worthy of being known, not just a shadow to a celebrated husband. She had never felt such insecurity before, and she didn't like it.

Like the introductions, the minutes blurred by, and soon a butler ushered them into the dining room, its centerpiece a long table crammed with chairs to accommodate the forty or so guests. William sat at the place of honor at the countess's right, and Addy sat beside him. Next to her was a waifish middle-aged woman whose name Addy had already forgotten. But she seemed friendly, so Addy dared to ask her to repeat it.

"Yes, dear," the woman replied. There was a distinct lilt to her accent that Addy couldn't pinpoint. "I'm sure it's hard to keep track of everyone when you meet them all at once. I'm Mrs. O'Toole. My husband," she said, gesturing to the man next to her, who raised his knife at Addy in greeting. "We're set to be part of Thursday's séance, I believe. Do you assist your husband?"

"Yes. Well, I will now. In New York, he and Mrs. Alexi worked closely together. But, of course, I was always in attendance."

"Oh, I'm sure. Must be old hat to you now."

"It never gets old," Addy said, leaning to the side more than was necessary to let a bowl of soup be placed before her. "Plus, William's talents always seem to be growing."

"Wonderful. We're looking forward to it, aren't we?" She turned to her husband, but he was engaged in conversation with his other neighbor, only the back of his gray head visible. "Well, we are," Mrs. O'Toole chuckled. "How are you enjoying London so far?"

"It's remarkable. Though I still have much more to see."

"You'll have plenty of time, I'm sure. Now that we have Mr. Fairley here, we don't plan on letting him go anytime soon."

"I hope not." Addy smiled, scraping the bottom of her bowl with her spoon. "Are you from London, Mrs. O'Toole?"

"No, dear, I'm from Dublin." That explained the difference in her accent. Addy should have recognized it, with so many Irish in New York. Mrs. O'Toole continued, "Perhaps you'll see it while you're in this part of the world?"

"I would love to travel, but we're not sure if we'll have time."

Mrs. O'Toole smiled, and Addy relaxed. This was no different than charming any other dinner party back home. She was more than up to the task.

Conversation continued pleasantly enough throughout the meal, though William monopolized the countess, whom he had won over. As dessert was served, Mr. Pierce clinked his glass with a knife and stood. "A toast," he declared, "to Mr. Fairley, for crossing to the other side of the ocean to help us connect with the other side."

Addy smothered a smile, wondering how long he had worked at that line. He gestured to William, who stood, champagne flute in hand.

"I want to thank you all for your generosity, and particularly the dowager countess for her hospitality. I hope to help you all connect to the spirit world and show you manifestations the likes of which you have never seen."

The room rang with applause, and Addy felt herself equally swept along by his charismatic promises, the worries about finding her place in all this lost.

Chapter 11

Addy awoke late the next morning. Sunlight mixed with the noises of the street streaming through the window. She yawned and stretched, her mind still caught up in the hours of dancing after dinner the night before. She pulled the covers tight around herself, admiring the way the gold color of the sheets reflected the sunbeams.

William crossed the room to her, dressed in a silk robe. "I thought you might sleep all day." He smiled and kissed her as he sat on the edge of the bed. "But I couldn't bring myself to wake you."

She turned onto her side, traced her fingers along the pale skin on the back of his hand. "I don't remember the last time I was out that late. My feet ache." She paused. "They all seem to love you, though."

"Are you surprised?" he teased.

She shook her head and yawned again.

"Now, stop that," he said. "Get up and get ready. We have to prepare for tonight."

That jarred her into action. She jumped out of bed, enlivened by the prospect of her first event as his assistant and finally gaining access to the secrets of his trade.

Once she was dressed, Addy nibbled a piece of toast while she watched William lift the lid of the trunk he had denied her access to on their first day in London. But before he opened it all the way, he paused and looked meaningfully at her over his shoulder. "Now, you know that anything I tell you here can't be shared with anyone else."

"Don't be so dramatic, William. Who would I tell? Besides, what secrets can there be that anyone else could use who doesn't have your talent?"

Something flickered across his face as he turned from her, but he said nothing.

Addy leaned over to look into his face directly. "Must we really be so serious?"

"This is serious, Addy," he said, shoving the trunk lid the rest of the way up. "My reputation in London will impact my prospects everywhere else of significance."

"I know, but have a little faith. Of course you'll do well." She got up and rubbed the divot between his shoulder blades.

He shrugged her off. "That's very nice, but I need you to focus. Put away the toast, please. I don't want crumbs on my things."

Frowning, Addy jammed the remainder of the slice into her mouth and crossed her arms. "All right," she said, once she had swallowed.

"Good." He rolled up his shirtsleeves. "We'll have a big group tonight, and they'll want to see a lot of manifestations. We have to make a good impression. Not even a good impression—an *astounding* impression." He moved a pile of lace onto the bed, revealing the photographic plates Addy had glimpsed before.

She could barely discern the outline of figures on the plates. She frowned. "Who are those photographs of?"

"Let's worry about those when I do the spirit photography session next week."

Addy shrugged, by now used to his evasiveness.

Next out of the trunk came a loop of string, then the bag of powder she had spotted before. He turned to her, leaning one hand on the lip of the trunk. "Mr. Pierce is supposed to give us fifteen minutes before the guests arrive to see the room. Before we go in, they'll search me but not you. You need to hide the string and powder somewhere it won't be visible." Seeing Addy's confounded look, he added, "Under your clothes."

She took an inadvertent step back as if feeling a physical push from the force of his words. "Whatever for?"

William sighed. "People here don't want what Mrs. Alexi does, sitting quietly in her room and talking to spirits. We need to *show* them the spirit world exists. And if that doesn't make sense to you, then just do as I say."

Struggling to process what he was trying to tell her, she re-trod familiar ground. "So I hide the string and the powder."

"Yes. Here." He handed her the string. "I'll show you how to tie it." They crossed to the small dining table beneath the window. He knelt, and she followed. "Tie it once here." He indicated a spoke on the underside of the table. "And here." He traced a line from there to the base of the chair leg. "Then from here, you'll connect the line to three objects behind me."

"What kind of objects?"

"Something small—a vase, a candlestick, a piece of fruit. The kinds of objects that normally fall over at these things." He gazed at Addy steadily, and the power of his look cracked something in her understanding. The first shattering of belief.

She gulped. "What does the powder do?" she asked, not knowing what else to say, her voice quiet inside the sudden intensity of the moment.

William stood, but Addy stayed kneeling and rocked back on her heels so she was looking up at him. "It's phosphorescent powder," he said. "We'll put a small packet of it up my sleeve while we're preparing."

"Phosphorescent? So the spirit lights . . ."

"Yes," he said curtly. "Now, get up. Who knows how filthy that carpet is. Mr. Pierce and his ilk didn't exactly put us up at the Ritz." Addy complied without a word as her husband continued his instructions. "I'll want you to sit on my right hand tonight. This is the most leeway we'll have for any setup, probably. They'll do more tests later. For now, they want to believe." Again, the searching, testing gaze. "You do understand how important this is, don't you?"

"Yes, William," she said, leaning her fingertips against the tabletop for support.

"If you notice my hand or my foot move, for God's sake, don't say anything. They were in place the whole time."

"Yes, William," she repeated, picking at a crack running along the edge of the table. She suddenly didn't want to be his assistant quite so much.

The necessary items went under Addy's bodice that evening in strategic places she could reach later. As she walked into the countess's house, where they had been so elegantly received the night before, she felt like a guilty thing, a rat crawling beneath the floorboards. But she held her head high again and pushed on because she told herself even the deceit was for the greater good of the movement. Like William had said, these people wanted to believe. William just needed to give them a little push.

In the parlor William and Addy went through a round of greetings with the guests, many of the same faces as the prior evening. The countess sat detached from the proceedings in the same chair, with Lady Agatha parked beside her, still looking unimpressed. Addy made a beeline for the two women, determined to engage them this time.

She curtsied in front of them. "Ladies, thank you for having us in your home again." The seated women simply nodded. The packet of powder rubbed against Addy's rib cage. "Have you both attended séances before?"

"My mother has," Lady Agatha replied.

"I don't know why you put up such a fuss, dear," the countess said to her daughter. Addy couldn't imagine Agatha putting up much of a fuss about anything, but she made no comment. "It's all good fun to fill an evening," the countess finished.

Addy smiled. "I hope you'll find it's much more than that. I think Mr. Fairley will surprise you."

"I'm very much looking forward to it," the countess said, and Addy could tell she was dismissed again, though perhaps she had impressed a bit more successfully this time. She curtsied again and walked away.

"There you are," William said when she reappeared at his side. "I think we're ready to set up, aren't we?" The question was directed at the ever-watchful Mr. Pierce.

"Yes," Mr. Pierce said, "but you know I've got to look you over for form's sake, my boy."

William smiled indulgently, slipped off his coat, and spread his arms. Mr. Pierce riffled through the coat pockets and then patted William down. "May I see your reticule as well?" Mr. Pierce asked Addy. She handed it over, feeling invaded as he pulled out her few possessions one by one, then put them back inside. He gave it back to her and returned the coat to William. "All clear, it looks like," he declared for the benefit of those watching. "Let me show you the room." He waved William and Addy forward, and they followed close behind.

Mr. Pierce opened a dark-paneled door into an even darker room. "Candles will be the first order of business." He produced a pack of matches and began making his way around the room, lighting the wicks.

"Not too many on the table," William instructed, taking in the room with a glance. He led Addy behind a hand-painted Chinese screen in the corner. He had to loosen her laces slightly to reach the items stowed between her corset and underclothes, then quickly laced her back up.

When they emerged, Addy glanced nervously at Mr. Pierce, sure they had been caught. But their guide only said with a wink, "No reason to worry, Mrs. Fairley. I'm only here to supervise." Then he returned to lighting candles along the mantelpiece.

William nodded quickly in understanding, and Addy commenced tying the string as he had instructed her earlier. Her mind whirled as she came to the sinking realization that both these men were in on the joke, and no one had clued her in until now. Was anyone truly a believer? Worse yet, was there really anything in which to believe?

The thought slammed through Addy's consciousness, ricocheting through her fingers, causing her to spill part of the contents of the packet she had been opening. Particles clung to her fingertips and the front of her dress.

William was instantly at her side. "Addy," he groaned, but saw there was nothing to be done. "Here, put it in my gloves like we discussed, and you'll just have to act surprised when it starts glowing on you later, too. But be more careful next time."

Addy nodded furiously, trying to shake off the tears collecting in the corners of her eyes as she poured pits of powder into the fingers of his gloves.

"Almost time," Mr. Pierce warned from behind them.

Addy finished her task, and William slipped his coat and gloves back on. He stood behind the chair he had claimed as his. "Bring them in," he said.

He was ready to begin.

The group settled around the table and sang a hymn, just like the many other sessions Addy had attended. But this one felt profoundly different. She held herself straight, as if the solidness in her spine could translate to her resolve to make it through the evening. The group joined hands, and the powder she knew was on William's hand burned into her conscience. But she made no mention of it, only sat grim-faced in the dark as those around her received their messages, which she hoped were still legitimate amid the spectacle. The guests seemed satisfied with them, at least. She stayed silent later as she felt William's foot slip from his shoe to work the string and as a few droplets of water sent bright sparks flying into the air; she *ooh*ed and *aah*ed with the rest of them as the phosphorescence also highlighted her dress and hands. She had, she knew, become part of the farce.

Back at the hotel that night, the dark secrets of the séance room still hung over Addy and William, with Addy struggling to speak beneath their weight. Finally, William spoke as he packed away his tools. "You did a good job tonight. Thank you."

The praise Addy had wanted to hear for so long fell flat against her ears. She said nothing and continued brushing her hair, enjoying feeling its cool reality slide between her fingers.

William sighed. "Is there something you want to say to me, or are you going to pout all night?"

She set down the brush with a slight click against the glass top of the dressing table. "I don't know what to say, William. It's too big."

"What does that mean, 'it's too big'?"

It was Addy's turn to sigh. "Let's just go to bed. We can talk about it in the morning." She slid into bed, her back turned coldly toward his side. She heard him pause, considering; then he turned out the light, grabbed his coat, and went back out into the night.

Chapter 12

Addy woke in the morning with William tucked into bed beside her. She hadn't heard him come in, which was probably for the best. Any further conversation she would have initiated last night would have resulted in another argument. Now, with a new day starting, William's betrayal didn't feel quite so enormous.

She watched William's dark curls flopped across the pillow, the gentle rise and fall of his chest. By the morning light, she felt sorry for him. He had gotten caught up in something that surely could be fixed, or explained away, at least.

She got up, dressed, and stepped purposefully out, without a stir from William. The bakery down the street from the hotel would have the perfect peace offering to bring back for breakfast. The day was chilled but sunny, promising that spring had not completely forgotten them. She purchased a box of pastries—too many because she couldn't decide—and walked slowly back, the whole way trying to establish the right words to say.

When she returned, William was still sleeping, so she sat in front of the window with a novel and picked at her croissant. Watching people pass by, she was suddenly struck with the urge to *get out*—to see the rest of this new country, travel like she had planned to. But she knew they were stuck here for now, though only committed for two weeks. After that they could travel, her and William, and things would be better away from the pressures of the constant work and its required subterfuge. Yes, that was something she could look forward to.

Finally, William stirred. He rolled onto his back and looked across the room at her, holding a hand in front of his eyes to block the sun streaming through the lacy curtains.

"What time did you get back?" she asked.

He grunted and stretched. "You're talking to me now?"

She raised the paperboard box. "I went to the bakery for breakfast." The words were skittish and unsure, like feral cats skirting food left out for them.

"That's nice." He rubbed his face. "Anything else on the docket for today?"

Addy shrugged. "You're the man with the schedule."

"Nothing until tonight."

A knock sounded at the door. Addy answered it, accepted the letter from the bellhop, and closed the door. She walked over to the bed and offered it to William. "It's for you."

He perused it quickly. "Last night must have gone well enough. A journalist is requesting an interview and a chance to attend a séance. I'm sure we can fit him in somewhere." He sounded pleased with himself.

"That's nice" was all Addy could muster. It seemed their time to talk and come to terms would be brushed away by everything else that had to be done. "Do you want a roll or a Danish?"

"I think I could eat both," he said, leaping out of bed, suddenly energized by his increased prospects. Addy laid the two pastries out for him, and they sat across from each other in divided silence as he ate.

William and Addy met the journalist, Nigel Reynolds, for dinner a few days later, right before the séance he was to observe. Mr. Reynolds was a man of the old school—rotund, formal, with full graying whiskers. He immediately began reminiscing about his days covering the exploits of Mr. Home and of the Fox sisters during their time in England. With such fond memories, Addy hoped he would sympathize with their cause and not be too analytical of their methods. She was part of this charade now, and she would hate for their shame to be revealed in the press. She and William had not broached the topic again, but it spread inside her, seething, like a cancer.

Once he reached the end of his reminiscences, Mr. Reynolds launched into his interview questions, scribbling notes between bites of beef. William discussed his background and beliefs, his time with Mrs. Alexi. The lost daughter was not mentioned. Mr. Reynolds nodded throughout but made few comments.

Once he was satisfied with William's interview, Mr. Reynolds turned to Addy. "And you, Mrs. Fairley? You are a believer, I assume?"

"Oh, yes, of course," she said mildly, sticking a fork tine into the remains of her meat. "I met Mr. Fairley through Mrs. Alexi."

"And you were moved by his talents once you saw them?"

"Yes, I was very impressed."

"Now that you have seen him work so many times, are you still impressed?"

Addy gulped, feeling William's eyes on her. He must know she would support him. Now was not the time to jeopardize the cause over a lover's tiff. She plunged forward. "Very much so. Each séance is different—plus, the new spirit photography, which he is doing more of now . . . He has many talents." She smiled, as much to convince herself as her interrogator.

"Nicely said. And how do you find our English ladies?"

Addy sighed. Clearly the questions of substance were over. "Everyone has been very kind. And they're all very fashionable."

This pleased Mr. Reynolds, and he noted it down with a flourish.

Mr. Reynolds accompanied them from the restaurant to the séance. After William's big debut led by the countess, he was now appearing at other members' homes. With less at stake, Mr. Pierce had declined to accompany them to every event. Addy appreciated emerging out from under the shadow of their chaperone, but it also made her a bit uneasy, as if they might be thrown to the wolves.

When they arrived at the residence for the séance, Mr. Reynolds hung close by William and Addy, even following them when they entered the séance room to set up. Without Mr. Pierce, there was no one to object and maintain their cover. William shot Addy a significant look, followed by a barely perceptible shake of his head. She was surprised by how easily she already understood him. They couldn't force Mr. Reynolds to leave the room and risk the negative publicity. Addy remained silent. To appear busy, she arranged candles and moved chairs while William supervised. But with Mr. Reynolds's eyes on them, none of their tricks would be in play tonight.

William called the other guests in. Addy moved to take her spot at William's right, but Mr. Reynolds stayed her with a touch of his hand.

"Please, allow me to sit by our host as the guest of honor this evening."

She smiled and inclined her head. Since she had no tricks to manage, it wouldn't matter if she didn't sit next to her husband. By now everyone else was seated, and she was left with a spot three seats over from William. She couldn't help a grimace as she sat. This event would disappoint. She could only hope Mr. Reynolds didn't need the artifice to be convinced of the spirits.

The hymn, the trance. When William's eyes snapped open, he focused immediately on Mr. Reynolds.

"Father," he said, in a voice that sounded remarkably young and lost. "I never thought I would see you again while you were still in the physical world."

Mr. Reynolds fixed his gaze on William. His lower lip trembled for an instant before he straightened and returned to his purpose. "Tell me your name."

"Richard."

"Remind me how you died."

"You know I was ill for such a long time."

Mr. Reynolds blinked once, hard. "I miss you, my boy."

"I am with you always."

"It's not the same, though."

"It's not as different as you think."

William closed his eyes, and Addy could almost feel the spirit leave his body as he jerked against the back of his chair. Then he looked around the table. "Let's listen to the spirits," he said in his own voice. "To know that there really is not so much separation between this world and the next as we think." He paused. "Thank you."

The session ended. The guests rose and began to exit the room, whispering among themselves.

William stopped Mr. Reynolds and guided him away by the elbow. Addy kept tabs on the conversation from the corner of her eye as she said her goodbyes to the evening's other guests.

"I feel like your son has more he would like to say to you," William told him, "in a more private setting. Not all spirits like the big show. Mrs. Alexi trained me in her art of spirit letter writing using an object as a conduit. Perhaps you have something I could use to reach him again, like a pocket watch?"

Mr. Reynolds's eyes widened, but after an instant, he fumbled in his vest. He pulled out a pocket watch and handed it to William. "I would have given this to my son had he lived. It was my father's."

William clasped the gold watch tenderly between his palms. "Perfect. I'll send you the message as soon as I receive it."

"Perhaps I'll see you on Saturday, for the photography sessions?"

"Of course. Please come, and I'll give it to you there." He clapped Mr. Reynolds on the shoulder, and the older man bowed his head and took his leave.

William stood beside her, and she gave him a quick squeeze, her earlier anger disappearing under a wave of relief. William may employ tricks for show, but messages like the one he just delivered were meaningful to their recipients, and that was what mattered.

Two days later Addy met a small group of women from the spiritualist organization for afternoon tea at an elegant hotel. The group included Mrs. O'Toole, whom Addy had sat next to at the countess's dinner party. Addy relished the promise of female company, though she felt slightly guilty at her eagerness to escape William for an afternoon. She reassured herself she had nothing to feel bad about because the event supported his career.

The other women were seated around a lace-covered table when Addy arrived, and she felt like an honored guest when they rose to greet her. She unwrapped herself from her winter clothes and handed them to the host before settling into her seat. "Thank you so much for the invitation," she said.

"Don't mention it," Mrs. O'Toole said. "You and Mr. Fairley are both our guests, and I know it must be difficult to come to a new country and not know anyone besides your husband. I did that myself many years ago, when we came over from Dublin."

"I wouldn't complain too much. He's charming. And handsome," a young carrot-haired woman, Miss Lincoln, broke in. "Quite a catch," she added with a wink.

Addy laughed. "That's what everyone says about him. Yes, I'm very lucky."

"I saw the article Mr. Reynolds published about you two yesterday," the widow, Mrs. Bland, still blonde and lovely at fiftyish, said. "He seemed very impressed. Though I'm afraid other members of the press might not be so kind."

"We'll just have to convince them, won't we?"

"Hear, hear," Mrs. O'Toole said, with a small raise of her teacup.

"So, you met him as a client?" Miss Lincoln asked Addy.

"Who? Mr. Reynolds?"

"No, Mr. Fairley."

"I was a client of Mrs. Alexi's first, but yes."

"Does he ever give you random messages throughout the day?"

Addy's thoughts jarred against one another as she considered this. Though she had questioned him about receiving messages while they were at Westminster Abbey, she had never before noticed it as an omission that no messages came through outside the séances.

"No, actually," she began slowly, then continued more convincingly, "He must be able to stave it off until the séances."

"I think it's the ritual of the séances that brings the spirits out to communicate, isn't it?" Mrs. O'Toole asked gently.

"Yes, of course you're right." Addy nodded. "He has explained that to me before."

Miss Lincoln shook her head slowly. "I suppose us mere mortals without such a gift will never fully understand the nature of these things."

They all laughed.

"Tell me how you each came to spiritualism," Addy said, hoping to move the conversation along. She only half listened to their answers. Inside, she fumed over what she did or did not know about the ways of her ostensibly gifted husband. Her faith sat inside her like a block of marble, each question a nick of the artist's chisel. Only she wasn't sure she wanted to see what shape would be revealed once the work was done.

Addy returned to her own hotel, rubbed raw by her doubts over William and irritated that even without being there, he had still kept Addy from enjoying her time with the women as much as she had hoped. She tried to push those feelings away, but as soon as she entered the hotel room, she could tell that William was in his own irritable mood. Their negative emotions crashed into each other as she shut the door.

"Whatever's the matter?" she asked as she unpinned her hat.

William, sitting at the table, ran his hands through his hair. "That blasted Mr. Pierce won't give me an advance on our expense account."

"Why on earth do we need an advance? We—"

"Don't even pretend that you know our financial situation."

Addy clamped her mouth shut. True, he had kept her away from the money since they married, so she didn't know the current situation, but surely it couldn't be as bad as all that? All that money from her parents' deaths . . . ? "What do you need it for now, anyway?" she dared ask. "Aren't they covering the hotel costs?"

William sighed dramatically. "I have to give Mr. Reynolds his pocket watch back tomorrow."

"And . . . ?"

A beat of hesitation, then: "It's at the pawnbroker."

Addy just gaped. "What—"

"Don't start." He crossed to the window, looking at the view as if he could escape his problems in the streets outside.

Gears clicked in Addy's mind, their teeth fitting snuggly together. "Is that what happened to Tiffany's necklace? When she couldn't get it back right away?"

He spun around, glared at her, and stormed out of the room, his answer to everything, it seemed. Addy, unsteady, held her hand to her heart.

William returned late, after Addy had already settled in bed, reading by the light of the gas lamp.

"I got it back," her husband said, tossing the watch on the table.

"How?"

He sighed. "Let's agree that you stop asking so many questions."

Addy pressed her lips into a firm line, but nodded and returned to her book. She probably didn't want to know the answers to the questions she had, anyway.

The next morning William and Addy got ready in silence. After breakfast they headed to the photography studio Mr. Pierce had rented for their use. William placed the photographic plates from the trunk in a hatbox and rode with his arm draped protectively over it in the carriage. Addy watched the cold, dreary day pass by through the window, willing herself not to ask anything more about those plates.

A small crowd gathered out front, waiting for William to arrive, to make sure they got their turn to be photographed today. William waved to them like a visiting prince as Mr. Pierce ushered them inside. Addy ducked in behind the men, not wanting to be seen or acknowledged until she knew what she was participating in.

Once in the upstairs studio, William set the hatbox by the camera. A stack of fresh photography plates wrapped in brown paper had been provided. He carefully unwrapped them and rewrapped the paper around the ones he had brought, then placed the now-unwrapped new ones in the darkroom and shut the door. He scurried around, setting up the photo area to provide the best background. He moved a brown leather armchair, a chipped end table, and a tall potted plant, leaving a long velvet sofa discarded off to one side. Addy settled on the sofa, content to stay out of the way until her role as hostess began.

Eventually, William gave the order to let in the crowd, and Addy steeled herself to complete her social duties. She greeted everyone, took their names down in order of arrival in a small notebook William had given her, and instructed the overflow to wait in the stairwell until called. Addy smiled and charmed those waiting in the studio, and, in spite of her disenchantment with William, she couldn't help enjoying the attention and the small amount of fame afforded to her as the wife of the great Mr. Fairley.

One elderly woman clasped Addy's hand and held it to her chest. "Dear, I am so glad you two have come. I've been so looking forward to having a photo taken with my husband, Philip."

"Thank you so much. When did you lose him?"

"Two years ago next month."

"I'm so sorry. But I'm glad Mr. Fairley can help you in some small way."

As the old woman shuffled away, Addy hesitated; then, for a reason she couldn't quite articulate, she opened the notebook and scribbled next to the woman's name *Philip—elderly*.

Between sittings, Addy went over to William, who eyed her suspiciously. "What is it?"

"I took some notes that might help. Look." She opened the pages and showed him other notations she had made: *Son—Thomas—8, Mother—died aged 40*.

William peered over her shoulder, intrigued, absorbing what she showed him. "Addy," he said finally, after kissing her cheek, "you're a natural and you don't even know it." He took the notebook from her greedily and riffled through its pages. "Keep it up." He handed it back to her and gave her a gentle push back toward the paying guests.

A few minutes later a commotion started in the stairway. Addy went over and saw Mr. Reynolds pushing his way through the crowd. Most let him pass, a few sent him silent glares, but two men on the landing berated him for cutting in line. Once Mr. Reynolds reached the top, Addy leaned over and grabbed his arm.

"I'm sorry for the confusion, everyone, but Mr. Reynolds is a special guest today, so I appreciate you letting him through."

The two men grumbled but accepted it.

Addy ushered Mr. Reynolds over to an empty chair. "Mr. Fairley will be with you just as soon as he can."

A few guests later, Mr. Reynolds took his seat. William bent over him momentarily, and when he moved, Addy saw the pocket watch proudly hanging from Mr. Reynolds's lapel and a letter in his hand. William had pulled it off after all. And whatever he had done to impress their most important guest had surely been worth it.

By dinnertime both William and Addy were exhausted, and William closed the studio for the day, promising the half dozen or so remaining patrons that they would be guaranteed the first spots the next time he held a photography session. Their names went into Addy's notebook.

The door closed behind those last people, leaving Addy, William, and Mr. Pierce in a bubble of their own creation. Mr. Pierce clinked the money box, which he had been in charge of. "Quite a taking," he announced. "I think the cuts for the society and for you, Mr. Fairley, will be very good."

"Excellent," William replied, distracted by carrying the exposed photographic plates into the darkroom.

"I'm famished," Addy said, dropping into the armchair that had been used for the pictures.

"So am I," Mr. Pierce said.

"You two go. I need to start developing these since we only have the studio through tonight."

"I'll help. Mr. Pierce, do you think we could get something brought in?"

"I know a place that will wrap something up for us. I'll go for it. I need some fresh air."

After he left, William stopped moving the plates. "Good thinking today. We'll have to prep better next time so I can select the best plate for each person based on your notes."

Addy rubbed her forehead. She didn't want to get dragged further in, yet she couldn't see a way out. And she didn't want to see William fail or be ridiculed. "Yes, that was the idea." It was as much agreement as she could muster.

He stood looking at her for a moment, then turned back to the darkroom. Before he entered, he said lightly, "Let me know when Mr. Pierce returns with the food."

Shut out from the darkroom, as from so much else, Addy tidied the studio while she waited for Mr. Pierce. She settled into the armchair once she was done. A cat of guilty pride slunk into her lap as she thought back on her husband's praise of her duplicity. But in the end, she thought, the pride in what they were accomplishing outweighed the guilt.

Addy left the studio after they had eaten, but William stayed until nearly midnight to develop the photographs and cart them home with Mr. Pierce's help. Addy slept better than she had in days, her dreams full of mysterious faces she didn't recognize but gave names to—Walter the lost husband, Thomas the lost son. Her own lost ones did not appear. Her dreams jumbled when William finally came in, rearranging themselves like a rotated kaleidoscope, but she did not wake.

Over breakfast, William was brusque and businesslike, but for once he engaged her like an equal. "We must come up with a system for next time," he said as he picked croissant crumbs off his lower lip. "Something discreet that people won't notice. I think we could stack the plates by category—men, women, children, and so on—and just remember which is which. You have a good memory, don't you, dear?"

"I think so. I'll hand you the right plate before the person sits for the photo."

William snapped his fingers. "Perfect! The less written down or said out loud, the better. You'll just look like my assistant that way. But we'll have to change the order of the stacks each time so people don't notice what we're doing."

Addy swallowed the last of her tea and considered her next chess move. "William, if I'm going to help you with this, I think I deserve to be in your confidence. I have to know what's really going on."

He stiffened. "What do you mean?"

"The money, everything. What you do when you go out late at night."

"Surely a husband deserves to have some secrets from his wife."

Addy sidestepped that battle. "Let's start small, then. Tell me about the finances. How bad is it?"

William leaned back, hooked one arm over the back of his chair, struggling with his decision. Finally, he heaved a sigh and gave in. "When we got married, I had to use your inheritance money to pay off some old debts. And then our style of living didn't change as it should have."

"If you had told me, it could have. Although, really, it's not like we were living extravagantly, staying with Mrs. Alexi."

He rubbed his hands over his face and said, from between his fingers, "I know. But . . . it's complicated. And I have to keep up a certain standard of living for my clients."

"Not everything is about your clients."

His face reappeared from behind his hands like a child playing peekaboo. "Isn't it?"

Addy frowned. "What can I do?"

William shrugged. "Just help me. And do as I ask, please."

Addy nodded, but felt her stomach contract uneasily.

That afternoon the Fairleys hauled the developed plates to the countess's home, where the previous day's clients would collect their photographs. Addy had spent the morning wrapping each in paper with the person's name written across the front. Her fingertips ached with papercuts.

A line snaked along the sidewalk when Addy and William arrived, just as there had been the day before at the photography studio. As they passed through the crowd on their way to the door, a few people reached out and touched William, as if he had a healing power that might rub off on them.

One gentleman stepped forward. "Do you need help carrying all these in?" he asked, motioning to the remaining stacks of plates in the carriage.

"Yes, thank you," William said.

The first man, then two others, scooped up armfuls of plates and followed the Fairleys inside. Having apparently decided that they would now be the first to be served, the three men waited in front of the sofa as Addy tried to arrange the plates back into some semblance of the order they had been in when they left the hotel. But as the rest of the line began filing into the countess's parlor, crowd control became the more pressing point.

"Please form one line here," she said, herding everyone into a long tail heading out the parlor door. "When you get to the front, tell me your name and I'll give you your photograph. Then you can take"—she glanced around someone's head at the trays of scones and cakes that had been provided on a table and saw that there might not be enough for everyone—"one scone or cake that the Countess Greeley has so kindly provided for us. Then we ask that you please move back outside so others can come in."

Hoping that her message would be passed down the line, she rejoined William at the front of the queue. She took the first man's name, checked it off in her notebook from yesterday, then shuffled through the plates to find the right one. William stood beside her, engaging his public, which meant he offered no help. She shook her head. It was going to be a long afternoon.

Most people came and went as Addy had asked, accepting their photograph, absconding with a scone or two, and then leaving. But a few hung around, diving in when William had a free moment, always with that familiar touch of the arm before they talked. Some thanked him, some expressed hope that they would get to attend another session with him, some asked after his future plans. No one talked to Addy.

But an elderly woman stayed until the end, when the trays of sweets were only crumbs and the last few unclaimed photographs waited sadly on the floor. Like all the other clients, Addy vaguely recognized her from the day before but didn't remember much else about her. Addy thought maybe the woman had expected her husband to appear in the photograph. Eventually, the woman fixed her gaze on William until he went over to her.

"Is anything the matter?" he asked.

The woman stabbed a finger at the faint image of a man standing behind her in the photograph. "Who is this man? I've never seen a man who looks like this in my life."

William placed a hand on her shoulder. "I'm sorry you didn't see who you wished to, but we can't control the spirits."

"Then what good is this?"

William leaned in closer. "I tell you what: come early to my next photo session, and I'll focus on you specially, to make sure he comes through. How does that sound?"

The old woman frowned but nodded.

William patted her shoulder and walked over to Addy.

Mr. Pierce walked in from the street, nearly colliding into the old woman in the process.

"So sorry!" he shouted after her. He grinned as he walked over to William. "I talked to some people as they were coming out. I suppose I have to book another session at the studio after this success."

"Well, that woman clearly didn't think it was much of a success," Addy cut in, then started to suck on a freshly reopened papercut to keep more words from sliding out of her mouth.

"One unhappy customer is not the end of the world," William said.

Mr. Pierce looked between the couple. "Be that as it may, one unhappy customer could spoil things for us. Even if the rest seem happy enough this first time, to really impress them, we need to find a way to show someone that fits the basic description of who they want to see. They seem eager enough to interpret what they have now, but if we can wow them next time, we might just catapult you to fame, Mr. Fairley."

William smiled slyly. "As it happens, we have a new system. Mrs. Fairley came up with it, actually."

"Really? To be honest, Mrs. Fairley, I was never sure if you were in on this or not."

"Of course I am," she said confidently, not admitting how recent her illumination had been.

"Just give us another opportunity and there will be no questions this time," William said.

Mr. Pierce spread his hands. "I trust you completely."

Chapter 13

The next day a letter arrived from Arthur, breaking through Addy's London life like a hand moving through a cloud of mist. Her old life in Washington already seemed like somebody else's story. His letter was perfunctory, feeling out how their correspondence should continue. He did not mention his past proposal, but neither did he mention William by name. Based on what he said, life back home was much the same. She was surprised to feel a twinge of nostalgia at the thought of past mundanities.

William was out visiting clients with Mr. Pierce—low-key work that did not specifically require her presence—so she had opted to stay at the hotel, claiming a headache. She spent the time alone composing a reply to Arthur, making sure to sound pleasant and positive, describing the sights in London and the success of William's work. After signing it and sealing it up for the mail, she leaned back in her chair and tapped her pen against the desktop. She felt more burdened after writing the letter because she had had to hold back the truth.

She pulled out another sheet of paper and began composing a letter to Tiffany. Addy missed her friend, although Addy had not written nearly as much as she should have. She started this letter with the same pleasantries and descriptions she had shared with Arthur, but then drifted into touchier territory that she was not afraid to brooch with her old companion.

I fear that William's work is not as miraculous as I thought. As I have been initiated as his assistant, I have done some things that, while not lies, have certainly not been the truth. I also learned the truth about that necklace you had difficulty getting back from Mrs. Alexi. You were right to be suspicious. But he is still a good man, and we are doing good work here, making people realize that the spirit world exists. I hope you know, of course, that you cannot speak of this with <u>anyone</u>.

She folded the letter and took both missives downstairs to the front desk before she had a chance to change her mind.

When William returned and asked her how her day went, she left out any mention of the letters, hoping he wouldn't notice the guilt lurking in her expression. She needn't have worried, because for him, such a question was perfunctory. In the next instant he was off on his own topic, barely casting a glance in her direction as he described the many visits he had made that day. When he finished, he sat and faced her. "Mrs. O'Toole is quite taken with you. You impressed the ladies at lunch the other day."

In spite of herself, Addy blushed at the praise. She appreciated feeling that she was part of the spiritualist cause.

"Ah!" William said, reaching into his pocket. "I have something for you." He handed a small, folded slip of paper to her.

Addy opened it. She stared at the words for a long moment, trying to absorb them.

"You asked me about receiving messages outside of séances. I know it's because you want to hear more from your parents, and they haven't come through in a while. It's true I have to prioritize the clients' loved ones during séances. But I've been listening closely lately, trying to hear them as I go about my day. This nugget came through early this morning."

Stay the course, Mädchen, the note said. *Remember that we must always be moving forward.*

She traced the curlicue on the *d* with a finger. It matched exactly her father's handwriting. That would be easy enough to copy, she knew, but she was fairly certain she had never told William that her father had called her *Mädchen* when she was little, a relic of her father's German grandparents. Had she been too quick to assume that the subterfuge meant the rest of it wasn't real?

William reached gently for her arm and pulled her into his lap. She leaned against him. "Thank you."

He kissed her cheek. "We've got the photography studio booked for another day next week."

"I can't wait," Addy replied, folding the note and setting it gingerly on the table to tuck into her trunk later. Despite the reservations she had just given voice to on paper, she looked forward to the next session, when they would implement the system she'd devised. Did it matter if they used a few tricks to give people what they wanted so that they believed? It would be better if she stayed close to William and his work so she could make sure they kept that goal in mind. The aim was not personal fame or fortune, though she admitted that excited her. If she and William worked together, they could build a new movement, a new wave of belief, like the one that had swept the nation forty years before. Real success lingered just beyond their grasp. And with the two of them united, she knew they could reach it.

A week later the line of people wanting William to photograph them snaked around the block once again. As requested, the old woman who had complained about her portrait last time, Mrs. David, headed the line as their first patron that morning. Addy ushered her inside, leaving the other guests waiting on the stairs. She wanted William's full attention focused on converting Mrs. David this morning.

After Mrs. David sat, William held her hand and said a quiet prayer with her. Then Addy handed him the correct photographic plate, and he moved behind the camera.

They were off.

The day was even busier than the first session. Some familiar faces appeared, but there were many more curious new ones. Addy courted them all, talking to them innocuously as they came in and taking notes about their responses. She kept the stacks of plates in order, allowing no one to touch them but herself.

That is, until one gentleman threw a kink into the proceedings.

He came up behind Addy as she was talking to a guest. "I'm next, right?" he asked.

Addy swung around to see him, her pen still poised over her notebook.

"Name?"

"Alex Winters."

He was young and blond and handsome, with a confident air. She nodded to confirm he was next but stopped short of speaking when she saw what he held in his hand.

He held up the plate. "They're working you too hard, love. I grabbed my own plate to make things a bit easier."

Addy's thoughts ran quickly. She glanced at William, but his back was to her. Better to have one photograph potentially not meet the patron's explanation than to make a fuss about the plate and risk exposing the larger system, she decided.

"I appreciate that, but we ask patrons to stay back here, away from the photography area."

Mr. Winters grinned. "I'm not in trouble, am I?"

Addy tried one of William's charming tricks and gave him a little wink. "Not today, sir."

Satisfied, he took a step toward the back of the room. Fortunately, William was ready for him at that moment. Addy touched Mr. Winters's arm and pointed him in the right direction. *Thank God he won't be mingling with the crowd and making them all decide they want to pick their own plate,* Addy thought.

The rest of the day went smoothly. They closed up shop after 8:00 p.m. Addy and Mr. Pierce stayed with William until midnight, wrapping and labeling the photographs as he finished developing them. At that point, with Addy practically falling asleep on her feet, they dragged William out of the darkroom to discuss the situation.

"I'm going to be here all night," William said, tugging at his rolled-up shirtsleeves. "I'll send the plates on to the countess's as soon as I'm done."

"If that's the case, I don't think you'll be fit to meet everyone first thing in the morning," Addy said.

"I'll be fine."

"We don't want you to be *fine*," Addy said. "We always need you at your best when you're interacting with clients."

Mr. Pierce let out a guffaw.

Addy frowned at him.

"I meant no offense. I was just surprised to hear you be so practical about this. You're quite the professional assistant now."

"I've learned, I suppose."

Mr. Pierce held up one finger. "We'll push the meeting back from the morning to the afternoon." Hearing no objection, he continued, "I'll get messages together to send out to the paper and the people who came today for whom we have addresses. I'll let the countess know first thing in the morning."

In a sugary-sweet voice, Addy said, "You're always so useful, Mr. Pierce."

He bowed to her with a flourish and left to arrange the messages. Addy followed soon after to go to the hotel to sleep, leaving her notebook behind so the men could label the rest of the photographs on their own when Mr. Pierce returned.

Even with the delay announced to as many people as possible, when William and Addy arrived at Countess Greeley's the next afternoon, the parlor and entryway overflowed with guests. As the Fairleys squeezed inside, a few people started clapping—whether genuinely or sarcastically, Addy couldn't tell at first. But others quickly joined in, and soon the parlor resounded with genuine applause. William bowed and waved for them to stop, but Addy knew he relished the praise. She didn't hate it, either. Perhaps they should arrive late more often.

Finally, the applause ended, and the Fairleys milled about with the guests. Mr. Pierce leaned in the doorway to the back parlor. Addy saw that to appease the waiting crowd, he had gone ahead and handed out the photographs, so there was no real work for her to do. She watched as people pointed out aspects of their photograph to others or clutched the package under their arm. The brown wrapping paper littered the floor. She pursed her lips. Cleaning up the mess would probably fall to her later.

She gazed around the room. The countess and Lady Agatha hid upstairs during the chaos of these events. Considering the countess was the Fairleys' main patron, they saw very little of her. It was just as well, Addy mused. She didn't feel the need to be dismissed by the two women again.

Drawing her mind back to more immediate matters, Addy spotted Mrs. David and crossed the room to her to make sure she was satisfied this time.

"Did your husband appear?" Addy asked, nodding at the photograph.

Mrs. David clutched the photo to her chest. "He did. I cried when I saw it, honestly."

Addy hugged her. "I am so glad."

Mrs. David held on to Addy's arm as she pulled away. "You are both doing such wonderful work."

"Thank you," Addy replied, her heart thrilled to be included in the praise. Perhaps her work was integral to the movement after all. And maybe she could delegate the cleanup of the wrapping paper to the countess's servants. She had more important things to do.

Shortly after, Mr. Pierce sidled up to her. He held out the notebook she had left behind the night before.

"This ended up wrapped with someone's photo. Fortunately, I caught it before they opened it."

She slid the notebook under her arm. "How did it end up there? I left it with you and William to use, not give away." She meant it lightheartedly, but she could tell by the look on Mr. Pierce's face that the words carried more weight than intended.

The noise that came out of his mouth was almost a snarl. "Just take better care of your things. And maybe don't worry so much about your beauty sleep. Imagine what would have happened if someone read that."

Before she could retort, he walked away. She looked for William, who sent her a quizzical look. She frowned and turned her gaze back to Mr. Pierce. Just when her work was gaining traction, she got blamed for the misdeeds of men. Typical.

The next morning, Mr. Pierce arrived early at the Fairleys' hotel room. He brandished a newspaper as if he would attack them with it.

"Have you seen this?" he asked, pacing instead of sitting down.

William snatched the paper from Mr. Pierce's hand. Once he found the correct page, he sat down and read it, completely absorbed in the words. He finished and started back at the top, his finger seeking out favorite phrases. "Listen to this," he said. "'Mr. Fairley shows a skill that has not been seen in London in some time.'" He dragged his finger down the page. "'Respectable figures of our city have attended his events and leave singing his praises. We hear that his spirit photography is particularly remarkable.'" William looked up, his face aglow.

"You've done it," Addy said in awe, all her gripes from the previous days forgotten.

"*We've* done it," he said.

Addy beamed at the praise but then noticed his gaze was directed at Mr. Pierce, and her smile collapsed.

"Your support is, of course, integral, Mrs. Fairley," Mr. Pierce said, noticing her look.

Addy didn't change her expression; she wouldn't let Mr. Pierce appease her the way he did the crowds.

But William at least picked up the hint. He reached across the table and grasped Addy's hand.

"Absolutely. It was your system for the spirit photography that tipped us over the edge." He tapped the paper again and grew reabsorbed in it. Addy latched on to the brief recognition as he pulled his fingertips away. It was probably all he would give her.

The next morning two more papers had picked up the story, and the following day, three. Soon the Fairley name was on every tongue in London. New invitations came every day.

Then, at the end of the week, came one that Addy had never dreamed they would receive: the Society for Psychical Research wanted to test her husband to see if his talents were real.

The Society for Psychical Research had only officially existed for ten years but was already well known. Its investigators aimed to bring science to the séance—to determine what in these purported miracles was fact and what was fiction. To draw their attention meant that William's skill had piqued their interest. It would take much more than a few strings and some preexposed photographic plates to fool them. But she knew that William would have a plan to ensure the investigation's success and that her participation would somehow be required.

She had read the note while William was out, too excited by the return address to wait to open it. She twirled the folded paper between her fingers as she waited for her husband's return. Her thoughts slurred heavily, dragging her first to one decision, then to another: whether her aid would make her merely helpful or culpable. Whether culpability would be worth it in the wider context of the movement. When the hotel-room door finally creaked open, she was still muddled, unsure.

"It's happened," she said as he set a parcel on the table. "The Society for Psychical Research wants to test you."

"I knew it would come soon!" He grabbed the letter out of her hand and read over it eagerly. His eyes were still on the paper as he said, "And don't say 'test.' That makes it sound so ominous. They will be there simply to observe."

"But it won't be so easy to fool them. They will check everything, and they'll know all the tricks."

"You're right. We'll need a plan—and an accomplice besides you that they won't expect."

"Good. Because I'm not sure I want to take part."

"Addy—"

"It's not right, William."

"We've come so far. We're almost at the end of our funded time in London. Let's just make this one last thing a success; then we can go to Paris and start over there."

"*Now* you're promising me Paris?"

"It makes sense now. Don't give up on me after all we've come through."

Addy squeezed his proffered hand but stayed silent, whirling in the sludge of her thoughts like a toy caught circling an emptying drain. She had upended her entire life for

love of him. Did giving up on the charade mean giving up on him? She wasn't sure, but she knew once she found the answer, it would determine her ultimate decision.

Two days before the investigation, Addy received a reply letter from Tiffany while William was out yet again. The words inked onto the pages were cudgels, hammering Addy's sensibilities and pride.

Addy,

I hope we have been through enough together that I can address you as a friend rather than as an employer.

I was sorely disappointed to receive your last letter. I always had my suspicions of Mr. Fairley, and it pains me to know that you have gotten caught up in his deception. For that is what it is, no matter what he would have you call it. He is deceiving people for money.

Addy particularly felt this blow, as she knew the deception had not even arrived at its stated goal: there was no money. She gritted her teeth and forced herself to continue reading, feeling like a penitent flagging herself with a whip in punishment for some mysterious sin.

I understand your devotion to him, and I hope he has earned it. You probably feel like not participating in his work would be a betrayal. But I encourage you to follow your own conscience. I know you're strong, and he should respect that in you. Please know I am always here for you. And, of course, my lips are sealed. But I think Arthur would be more understanding than you think, if you were to share some of these things with him.

Reaching the end of the page, Addy could take no more and gave up on finishing the letter. She threw herself face down onto the bed and wept, feeling more conflicted and desperate than at any time since her parents' deaths. She was trapped in a room of her own making, and she wasn't sure she had the courage to do what was necessary to escape. She didn't see how she could avoid participating in her husband's career, when it was what had brought her to London in the first place. And there were the shreds of truth that she desperately believed underlay everything he did. She couldn't abandon the faith that had been her salve during the last horrendous year.

After crying herself to exhaustion, Addy washed her face and went out. She turned her footsteps toward one of the city's many museums that she had planned to visit when this trip was just a dream they were building in their New York apartment. In reality, sightseeing had fallen by the wayside of William's work. Now she needed to escape into the streets again, away from the endless litany of things she was supposed to do and be.

Once at the museum, she wandered the exhibits, though when she was done, if someone had asked her, she couldn't explain anything she had seen. Her subconscious mind had been working too hard and had overridden retention of anything she had consciously thought. Even so, she was no closer to an answer.

She emerged from the building into a bright but chilly afternoon. She purchased a paper cone of fish and chips and sat on a bench at the end of a small park, picking at the fried batter and watching a boy and his father play with a kite. She had never had a strong desire to be a mother, but in that moment she felt how much simpler it would be if she and William were just spouses and parents, unconcerned with fame and a need to deal in bigger ideas like life after death. It would be easy to teach a boy to fly a kite. To teach him to speak with spirits was so much more difficult. She wasn't sure if she was up to the task.

Addy sighed and bit into a french fry, enjoying the way the first crisp bite gave way to an oily savoriness. Once her meal was finished, she rose and tramped back to the hotel, leaving the boy and his kite behind.

William was there when she returned. He jumped up as soon as she entered, eager to share his news. "Where have you been? I met with Mr. Pierce and—"

"William," she said, with the same weariness she felt in her legs, "can we have one conversation that's not about your work?"

He looked taken aback but acquiesced and waved her to the table. "Of course. I didn't mean that I didn't care about your day."

"It's not even that," she said as she sat across from him. "I just need to not think about all this for a little while." As she spoke, her eye caught the crumpled pages of Tiffany's letter resting on the end of the table. She had stupidly left them out, and she hoped to God William hadn't read them. She casually reached for the letter and tucked the pages into her reticule for safekeeping. William didn't bat an eye. To redirect the conversation, she said, "I went to a history museum today and ate fish and chips."

"How very British of you." He grabbed her hand and kissed it, rubbed her thumb between two fingers. "I'm sorry we haven't had much time to be tourists lately. But you know I appreciate everything you do for me."

"I know," she said, though she wasn't sure she wanted to be appreciated if it caught her up in all this. "Things will be better in Paris, won't they?"

"Yes, soon we'll be in Paris and all will be well." He reached across the table and kissed her, then settled back into his chair. "But we do have an amazing opportunity."

"Which is what?" Addy asked dryly.

"A chance to join someone else's séance for once." He grinned. "To reinvigorate our purpose."

Addy couldn't keep the corners of her mouth from perking up. "Anyone in particular?"

"A Mr. Kraft. He was a student of the famed Mr. Home."

"Really? When?"

"Tomorrow night. I may or may not be able to go, depending on how much I still need to prepare for the society's investigation. But I'm sure you'll enjoy yourself either way."

"I absolutely will."

This was her chance. To connect with her own loved ones again. To be a spectator instead of a conspirator. To appreciate the miracles of spiritualism again.

Addy wasn't surprised the next afternoon when William told her he couldn't go to the séance with her. In fact, she felt a bit relieved, happy to have this experience to herself.

She left early and sat on a bench in a nearby square. She pulled Tiffany's letter out of her reticule. Finally, she was prepared to read the rest. She told herself that whatever Tiffany could say would not be strong enough to make Addy waver in her faith, though a voice of doubt crept in underneath her thoughts.

I also want to finally share something with you. You asked me what my spirit letter from Mrs. Alexi contained when I first received it. At the time, I was conflicted about it, and didn't feel ready to share it with anyone. But now, after talking with Arthur, I think it is best I share some of it with you.

Addy grimaced. Why was Tiffany mentioning Arthur so much? And why were they still discussing Addy like they had some control over her when she was thousands of miles away?

The letter mentioned the necklace, of course, and how they had given it to me. But with the necklace in Mrs. Alexi's possession, she obviously knew of its existence, and to guess that it was given by a lost loved one is no leap at all.

She wrote about messages from "my parents" as if they were one unit—while the truth is that my father had so much more to apologize for than my mother. I know it's said that spirits can learn lessons on the other side, but I find it odd that if my father had learned something, he wouldn't mention that when he contacted me. The letter did mention my brother, which shook me at the time but could be a lucky guess.

What I'm saying is that I don't want to put all of your faith into these messages and the people who give them. Maybe there is something there, but there are a lot of cranks, too. Besides, you didn't listen to your first message from your parents. "Do not marry," I think it was?

I hope this will not ruin our friendship. I really do want to support you, and of course you can believe what you want. But I do not want you to blindly follow someone who does not deserve it.

I love you.

Tiffany

How dare she? Addy thought, but the anger quickly dissipated. She could admit that Tiffany's doubts mirrored Addy's own on occasion. But while doubts were allowable, a loss of faith was not. She would take Tiffany's advice into account, but for now Addy had her appointment with Mr. Kraft, a true spiritualist who would remind Addy of the reason why she supported the faith—she was sure of it.

As she made this resolution, another page she hadn't seen slipped from behind the others. It was written in Arthur's hand.

Dear Addy,

I asked Tiffany to include this information in her letter, but she said she didn't want to get involved.

Addy scoffed. Tiffany had involved herself in every other way. Why stop now?

I've made some inquiries about William's past life through a connection in Boston and was able to get in touch with the sister, Jane. She confirmed she is the caretaker of his daughter, whom she has refused to let him see for several years. She was insistent that she did not want him in Harriet's life because of his connection to Mrs. Alexi. She wouldn't say more than that. I urge you to consider what must underlie such a monumental decision as keeping a child from her father and what that means for you. If you ever need a sanctuary, we are here.

Best,

Arthur

Addy crumpled the page in her fist. Part of her was relieved to have the story William had told her independently verified, but mostly she fumed at Arthur for continuing to interfere and to try to control her. Addy knew exactly what had caused Jane's decision: society's common prejudice against spiritualism. And Addy certainly wouldn't hold that against William.

She stood and marched on to Mr. Kraft.

When she arrived at Mr. Kraft's residence, she tried her best to blend in, making small talk with the other guests only when they directly engaged her in conversation. She felt small after reading Tiffany's letter and preferred to hide in the crowd for now. Fortunately, no one seemed interested in the wife of the famed Mr. Fairley when they had Mr. Kraft to focus on.

The party was large—a dozen guests—and they gathered around a dining table that could have fit several more. Addy's mind hadn't stored anyone's names during the brief snatches of conversation, so she invented her own labels for them for reference: Blue Cravat Man, Painfully Thin Woman, Walrus Mustachio. Blue Cravat heard from a lost parent; Walrus connected with a dead daughter. Throughout, objects flew around the room, a candlestick nearly whacking Addy in the head at one point.

It was thrilling.

"It's us, Adalinda," Mr. Kraft finally intoned. "Your parents."

Addy scooted forward to the edge of her seat, pulling her neighbors' hands closer to the center of the table in her eagerness.

"Don't worry what the letter said."

Addy sucked in a breath. They must be referring to the letter Tiffany had just sent her.

"Don't worry," Mr. Kraft repeated. "You have to follow your true purpose."

There was a long pause, during which a bell tinkled continuously in some unseen nook.

Mr. Kraft's voice rose to a higher pitch, like he was channeling a woman's voice. Addy's mother.

"I want you to still have faith in God."

Addy thought back to the last morning her and her parents were together. They fought about spiritualism's worth alongside Christianity. Mr. Kraft's statement, with its insistence on faith, validated that her mother was present. But her mother's close-minded faith bothered Addy no more now than it had when her mother was alive. Addy had faith in God. And now she had no doubts that God could facilitate more miracles between this world and the next than Addy's mother wanted to believe.

The medium's voice dropped again. "We love you."

Mr. Kraft's shoulders sank, indicating her parents' spirits were gone. But they had validated their presence, and her path, which was all she needed.

The spirits were still real.

If only William's machinations were, too.

The next morning, when Addy woke up, William was already pacing across the room, clutching a sheet of notes for the investigation that night.

"Have you slept at all?" she asked.

"Of course," he said, but finished another circuit of the room before he paused to look at her. "Did the séance last night help you come to your senses?"

She sat up in bed and took a few seconds to craft an appropriate response to what seemed an odd question.

When she didn't answer fast enough, William slapped his pen and paper down on the table, interrupting Addy's thoughts.

"Addy, I know you've been conflicted about all this, but you have to be there tonight. How would it look if my wife weren't there to support me at the biggest event of my career?"

She recalled her parents' message from the previous night. Tiffany's words flashed through Addy's thoughts, but, as her parents had advised, she ignored them as best she could. She had come too far to not support William now, and they were working toward a higher purpose, after all.

"Fine," she said. "I'll go. But that's it."

"That's all I ask." He reached one hand out to her imploringly.

She got out of bed and let him envelop her in his embrace. For the first time in a long while, she felt safe and understood.

The séance with the Society for Psychical Research took place at the countess's house that night. The gathering was small and intimate: just the investigator, the Fairleys, Mr.

Pierce, the countess, and three other guests, including the O'Tooles. The investigator was a smooth, plump man with shaven cheeks and thinning hair that he didn't seem quite able to control; locks of it stuck out at odd angles even though they looked like they had been oiled down carefully before he left the house.

He introduced himself as Mr. Quail with a strong, pumping handshake for each of them.

William threw Mr. Quail his most charming smile, but the investigator didn't give it more than a passing glance.

"Shall we get down to business?" he asked.

Mr. Pierce appeared at this cue and began ushering everyone into the séance room, but Mr. Quail stopped him with an upheld finger.

"Now, you know we must do the searches before anyone enters the room."

Mr. Pierce bowed. "Of course, Mr. Quail. As you request."

"Why don't you and Mr. Fairley join me in the dining room?"

The three men shut themselves into the room across the hall from the parlor, where everyone else waited. Mr. O'Toole came up to Addy and put a hand gently on her arm. "Don't worry, Mrs. Fairley, this is all pretty standard stuff."

She forced a smile. "Of course."

"We all know Mr. Fairley wouldn't be caught in any shenanigans."

"He appreciates your support, I'm sure." She couldn't think of anything else to say to continue the conversation. Her limbs were heavy, like a dream where you can't move or breathe. Mr. O'Toole drifted away, leaving Addy standing off to one side with her arms crossed.

After a quarter of an hour, Mr. Quail's balding head emerged. "Mrs. Fairley, could you join us—and perhaps bring another lady in with you?"

"Me?" she asked, and reached a hand out, searching for a friend. She hadn't expected to be dragged into this. William's only request had been that she attend.

Mrs. O'Toole grabbed Addy's hand and took charge. "Yes, dear," she replied, comforting Addy. Then, to Mr. Quail, she said, "We'll go in."

Once they were in the room, Mr. Quail explained his request. "I've already searched your husband and Mr. Pierce and looked over the séance room and found nothing too mischievous." Addy glanced to her left and saw William replacing a cuff link and then buttoning up his vest. "I'm afraid I'll also need to do a search of your person, though

Mrs.—O'Toole, is it?—can do it for propriety's sake. Since you might be assisting your husband, you see."

"Me?" Addy repeated, then caught control of herself again. "I hardly think that's proper."

"It's not unusual," Mr. Pierce said. Addy glared at him. "I'll step outside, of course." He hurried out into the hall.

Ignoring her protests, Mr. Quail said calmly to Mrs. O'Toole, "Just down to her petticoat, please."

Addy wasn't ready to give in. "What if I refuse?"

William stepped closer. "Mr. Quail, what if my wife just didn't attend the séance?"

Mr. Quail paused. "Yes, I suppose that would be fine."

William turned to his wife. "Addy, why don't you wait outside—or even go back to the hotel, if you want?"

Mollified but still agitated, she shuffled her feet and considered. After all this fuss, to not even be there . . . "All right. I'll wait for you back at the hotel."

Mrs. O'Toole squeezed Addy's hand as she turned to leave. *Sorry,* she mouthed, and Addy nodded in response. At least she wouldn't have to participate in whatever William had planned. But she still felt guilty leaving him at such a critical moment. However, when she turned around at the door, she saw him busily getting everyone into their seats and doling out a little quip for each of them. It didn't seem like he would miss her at all.

A few hours later, Addy was reading a paragraph in her novel for the third time, trying to force her distracted mind to catch at the words' meaning, when William returned from the séance. She closed the book and sat up straight as he walked in, her heart quickening for news.

William sighed, tossed his keys onto the table, and peeled off his coat.

"How did it go?"

"You saw how he searched us. There was no way to set up."

"Nothing came through?"

"I managed to get some messages out, but nothing spectacular to impress him."

"Aren't the messages the most important thing?" she asked, scrambling to find a truth she could accept. "Maybe people should stop expecting the rest?"

"You know that's not how the world works."

She folded her hands in her lap. "Thank you for not making me go through that humiliating search."

"You wanted to leave anyway, didn't you?"

She avoided the question. Her feelings were more complicated than that. "Will he let you see the report before it's published?"

"Yes, it should be ready in a few days."

William sank into a chair and gripped the arms tightly as if needing to steady himself. "In the meantime, let's plan for Christmas in Paris. Won't that be nice?"

With all that had been happening, the impending holidays hadn't even crossed Addy's mind. "We'll be leaving that soon?"

"Our contract here will be up; we may as well move on."

"Do we have the money?"

"Let me worry about that."

"With respect, I'm not sure that strategy has worked well for us so far."

A storm surged across his face, forcing his brows to knit together in rage. "Don't question me so much!" He slammed his hand down onto the end table between him and Addy, and leaned over her. The threat reverberated through the room, but he did not follow through.

Addy stood and walked calmly to the window, crossing her arms so he wouldn't see her trembling.

"I'm sorry," he mumbled from the table.

Addy kept her silence.

When they woke the next morning, frost lined the window, matching the iciness between William and Addy. They existed in silence until William left to meet with Mr. Pierce. Addy was glad he did not ask her to come; she couldn't put on a pleasant face now. She spent the day reading and napping, writing letters and tearing them up because they said too much.

When William came home, he dropped an envelope on the table. Addy looked at it but didn't want to give him the satisfaction of asking what it was. Besides, she wasn't supposed to question him anymore, she thought dryly.

He waved a finger at it when she didn't acknowledge him. "Our tickets," he said.

She remained mute.

"To go to Paris."

She couldn't suppress a smile. She hadn't let herself believe it would really happen. "When are we going?" She touched the edge of the envelope gingerly but left it lying on the table.

"The day after tomorrow."

"So soon?"

"The report will be out then, and our time here will be over."

"Is it really so bad as that?"

"Mr. Pierce paid me what he owes me."

That was it, then. William cared about the money, and now that it was dealt with, he was ready to move on. Addy looked forward to the fresh start. She took in the unorganized mess around the room, wishing she had Tiffany to help her pack. But it would give her something to do. A way to keep her mind from questioning even more things about her life. She picked up the first item of clothing and began.

The next morning, Mr. Pierce arrived, bearing a copy of Mr. Quail's report. His normally eager and commanding manner was subdued. He waited in the doorway until William, dark circles hanging under his eyes from lack of sleep, went over to him, like a puppy greeting his master.

Mr. Pierce handed him the few typewritten sheets of paper.

"Nothing bad, but not much good, either, I'm afraid. Inconclusive." Mr. Pierce surveyed the room, noticed the half-packed trunks. "Leaving already?"

"Yes," William said, rolling up the papers in slightly shaky hands. "Now that we're done here, we're moving on to Paris. My wife has always wanted to travel."

"An excellent idea."

"We are forever grateful for your hospitality."

"We thank you for sharing your talents with us for a time. When do you depart?"

"Tomorrow, early."

"You'll break a few hearts, but I'll tell any remaining clients they can always catch you abroad. Mrs. Fairley, it's been a pleasure." He kissed her hand.

Addy hesitated, then said, "Thank you for all your support of my husband." She had a sinking feeling that they wouldn't have made it half so far without him.

"Of course. Best of luck in the next stage of your journey." Mr. Pierce leaned back on one heel but didn't turn to look at William as he talked, as if he couldn't stand to face him. "There were a few clients that asked me about some personal items you had taken from them to conduct the spirit writing."

"All of that has been taken care of."

"Good, good." He hesitated again, then turned and left.

"He certainly didn't seem sad to see us go," Addy said, once they were alone again.

"It's time for us to go. We know that, and he knows that. There's nothing worse than a guest that stays too long. Now, help me finish packing."

Chapter 14

In the morning William and Addy woke with the first stirrings of the city. The bellhop took their trunks down to transfer them to the train. Addy dressed slowly, for once relishing the chill seeping into her skin through the cracks around the window since it was among the last sensations she would have in London. William, too, moved slowly, but hardly seemed serene. He had the energy of a racehorse eager to start yet held back by the bit.

Then they were ready to add their movement to the anonymous bustle of London's streets. When they left the hotel, a faint night still reigned. Light peeked from below the horizon to cancel out some of the low-slung stars but not enough to light their way. Then, all too soon, they were chugging out of the city that Addy felt she had barely gotten to know at all.

They rushed through Dover to catch the boat to Calais, the Dover streets quieter than London's but still a blur to the travelers. William and Addy stepped onto the boat wrapped in their individual thoughts. Addy knew she should be ecstatic to finally be on her way to Paris, that city of dreams, but instead, a faint dread approached her like the dawn that crept up on them. William let her be, though he, too, probably had his own clouds to contend with.

The day turned out clear, and a vibrant morning broke as they crossed the Channel, revealing the low cliffs of France as they neared the coast. Addy and William stood at the railing despite a cold wind to watch this new continent come into view.

Eventually, William said, "A place to start over." His grip on Addy's forearm mirrored his firm tone.

"I hope so" was all Addy could summon in reply.

A few hours later their final train pulled into Paris, and they soon walked foreign streets. It was briefly overwhelming, being surrounded by half-understood chatter, but Addy's brain adjusted as they rounded the third corner, trying to find a carriage, and she was able to pick out words and conjugations that had been drilled into her as a student but that she had never heard in the real world.

An English-speaking porter corralled them, eager to receive a tip for providing directions to their hotel. Out of his element for once, William shoved a slip of paper with the hotel's address at the man, who quickly guided them to a carriage and conferred with the driver. William handed the porter a coin before stepping into the cab, and the man hurried off to find his next customer.

Once they were shut into the cab, Addy noticed how oddly full William's purse looked after what he had revealed about their financial problems. Perhaps Mr. Pierce had owed him that much, she reasoned, though her stomach did a little flip-flop nonetheless.

The trip through the city was loud and jostling, with dust floating in through the open carriage windows. Outside, women bustled past holding the hems of their dresses off the ground, men carted heavy items across the road, and ragged children scurried by in search of handouts. It could be life in any other city. But as the carriage turned and crested a hill, Addy saw the skyline for the first time. Ancient buildings lifted their dignified heads above the streets, while in the background gleamed the new marvel, the Eiffel Tower, taller than Addy imagined a structure could be. She gaped in childlike awe, the coins clinking in William's purse momentarily forgotten.

"What do you think?" he asked, watching her crane her neck to keep the marvels in view.

"It's incredible," she breathed. She grabbed his hand. "You were right. This is just what we need."

"I knew it was what you wanted."

She hadn't had time to form a reply to this noncommittal response when the carriage ground to a halt and the driver yelled something incomprehensible.

The couple exchanged glances.

William shrugged. "This must be it." They clambered out to find the driver already pulling down their trunks. Coins once again exchanged hands, and then they were left on their own on the sidewalk. Addy turned toward the hotel. A young man hurried out to help with the luggage.

While he carried in the trunks, Addy took in the squat building. It stood wider than its neighbors and only three stories high. It exuded an air of languishing aristocracy. It had seen better days, but lovely cornices and carvings adorned its eaves, announcing that it had originally been built by and for people of means. The lobby they stepped into was the same—gorgeously appointed but dated, the air slightly musty and stale.

The man at the small front desk to their right was young and short, with close-cropped, curly dark hair. He checked them in with absolutely charming English he had clearly learned from a book.

"I demonstrate you the room," he declared, leading them up the stairs. One flight up, he turned off the landing and unlocked the first room on the hall. Another moldering burst of air was unleashed as the door swung open, but it quickly dissipated.

The room was small, with a table and chairs in front of the fireplace, a desk, a bed, and a wardrobe cramped into the space. Addy had to turn sideways several times to make it to the window to avoid knocking into anything.

William nodded his acceptance, and the clerk handed over the key. The Frenchman bowed. "Good morning," he said as he departed.

"Leave it open," Addy instructed as William moved to close the door. "We need to air this place out." She pushed up the window. "Look," she called back to her husband. "How quaint."

William crossed the room, banging his leg into a corner of the desk along the way. He placed a hand on Addy's back and peered over her shoulder at the view. The room looked out on a small courtyard with just the right amount of barely tamed greenery threatening to hide the paving stones from view.

A scuffle behind them announced the arrival of their trunks. They thanked the bellhop, and he, too, bowed, closing the door behind him. Addy sighed. "Leave it, I guess. Maybe the open window will help."

"I think it's just old-building smell."

"Well, old-building smell stinks."

William went and perched on the edge of the bed. "So, Paris is not all you thought it would be?" he teased.

Addy straddled him and kissed his forehead. "No. Only in Paris would the smell somehow be charming."

"There is no place I would rather be than in Paris with you."

Addy beamed. Determined to start over, she pressed against him as he began to searchingly run his hands over her. Her mouth found his, liberating a need for him she hadn't realized had been building up with her over the last tension-filled weeks. He lifted her hips to settle her on him, and soon their bodies were moving together until release stilled them.

As the afternoon light faded to sepia, Addy and William emerged from the hotel for their first foray into the Parisian streets. They bought treats from a baker eager to sell his end-of-the-day remnants and chewed the pastries as they sauntered through the neighborhood. The sugar melted on Addy's tongue like the ambience of the city sinking into her skin. Just as she popped the last sweet bite into her mouth, they passed a dressmaker's shop. Addy stopped to admire its wares through the window.

"Go on in and look," William said from beside her.

She did, fingering the laces and trying on a hat while William hung by the door. The shopkeeper directed her to a dress he insisted she must have—deep-green silk that perfectly complemented her complexion. "It's lovely," she said, but tried to make it discreetly past him to the exit since she knew they couldn't afford it.

"No, no," the dressmaker said, sensing her intent. "I will tailor it just for you. Perfect!"

To Addy's surprise, William chimed in from behind her, "Get it."

"We can't afford it . . ."

"Things aren't as bad as all that. You deserve it."

Addy was skeptical, but she couldn't refuse a French dress. She let herself be swept up in the moment. She was quickly measured and instructed to come back in three days.

As they left, Addy started to speak, but William cut her off.

"Let me worry about it. I have leads for clients here. It will be fine."

"Where did you get that money?" she asked after a moment's mental struggle.

"I'm handling it!" he said, grabbing her arm a touch harder than was strictly necessary to hold her in place.

Addy bit her lip and chastised herself for imperiling their fresh start. She let it drop.

When he saw that she was not going to argue further, he released his grip. "Now, you go back to the hotel. I have to meet a contact. And, Addy," he said as she started to walk back the way they had come, "if anyone comes by our hotel room while I'm out, don't answer the door."

She halted. "Why?"

"Safety, of course," he said with a lilt of a laugh. But Addy sensed a falseness underlying his good mood, and she was uneasy when she made it back to the hotel room and shut the door behind her.

When Addy awoke in the morning, William lay in bed next to her. He was staring up at the ceiling, his head on his hands. Addy reached out touched his shoulder. He startled, his hands flailing out from behind his head.

Addy laughed.

"Sorry," he said, covering his heart. "I didn't realize you were awake." He grabbed one of her wrists and kissed it.

"Lots on your mind?"

He grunted as a reply.

She climbed out of the old high bed. By the bathroom door, she stepped on a loose floorboard, which emitted a surprisingly loud creak. Out of the corner of her eye, she saw William's gaze dart toward the noise.

When she emerged from the bathroom, he was up and getting dressed, so she followed suit. As she started to construct her hair for the coming day, her hand slipped and knocked her box of hairpins to the floor.

William jumped again this time.

"Jesus!" he yelled.

Addy frowned at him, pausing in her quest to pick up the pins. "What's the matter with you this morning?"

Again, he gave the same grunt in response.

She rubbed the light bruise encircling her arm as she watched William finish preening himself in front of the mirror, remembering his rough handling of her the day before. Not wanting things to devolve into another argument, she decided to keep the subject neutral. "What's on the docket for today?" she asked.

William drummed the fingers of one hand on the table and rubbed his forehead with the other. "I'm meeting a group of expat English tonight. Mr. Pierce made the introduction." He glanced at Addy. "You should come, of course."

"Of course," she replied, smoothing her dress across her lap. "Until then, we can go sightsee?"

"You go. I have a headache, and I have to prepare."

"How am I supposed to go out by myself all day?"

"Addy, you of all people should know that this is no longer the age of chaperones. Take a carriage or an omnibus into the city center. It will be fine."

"All right," she said, standing and readying her reticule. She pulled out a small travel brochure someone had given her before they left London. "I have this to guide me, and my French is good enough."

"See? Just watch out for pickpockets." William wrapped an arm around her shoulder. Not expecting the gesture, she didn't look up as he leaned in, and he ended up placing a kiss on her ear.

She flushed with sudden awkwardness as they disentangled themselves.

"Well," she said as she placed her hand on the doorknob. "Have a good day."

The Paris Addy stepped into had readied itself for Christmas. A special magic hung in the cold air. The street vendors sold their wares as gifts for others rather than oneself. Garlands and wreaths decorated the old buildings. A crisp hint of snow scented the breeze, anticipating a change in the weather along with the arrival of the holiday season.

It was beautiful. But Addy couldn't enjoy it because her mind kept dragging her back to what might be happening in her hotel room. William was keeping some secret from her, she was sure, but she feared asking him to reveal it. She knew the secret might finally force her to choose between her love for William and spiritualism and her abhorrence of his methods. If such a decision came, the choice she made would determine the course of her life.

An omnibus pulled up to the curb, rattling Addy out of her thoughts. In slow, careful French, she asked the destination. Fortunately, the driver was patient with her. Satisfied the conveyance would take her in the right direction, she paid her fare and sat next to a working-class girl in a plain dress. Addy smiled at her, but the young woman returned only a scowl. Addy fixed her gaze in her lap for the rest of the ride.

When Addy arrived back at the hotel room in late afternoon, she headed straight to the fireplace to warm herself. She had walked back instead of taking the omnibus to better enjoy the scenery, and as soon she entered the hotel, she had realized she was chilled to the bone.

William sat at the small table, a few of his tools of the trade scattered around him. He was scribbling furiously and didn't stop when she walked in. After a few minutes he set down his pen and looked up.

"How was it?"

"Lovely" was all she said.

Distracted, he did not press her further. "We have to leave by six."

"All right."

She left the fireplace but didn't take off her gloves or coat. She settled in the chair across from William.

She gestured at the mess on the table. "Is everything ready?"

He frowned and rubbed his hands together but nodded. "This is just an initial social meeting. I won't be doing a séance."

She almost asked him why he had his equipment out, then, but knew he probably would interpret that as prying. Instead, she circled back to the mundane. "Did you eat while I was gone?"

"I had them send something up from the restaurant across the street."

"That's nice."

William's eyes brightened, and he suddenly seemed to really see her. "I'm sorry I wasn't able to go with you today. Tomorrow, perhaps."

"Yes, maybe tomorrow." She stood. "I'm going to wash up and change."

William nodded weakly, already back in his own mysterious thoughts.

That night they put on smiling faces as accessories to their best clothes and headed to the rendezvous with the British Parisians.

Five couples greeted them. A middle-aged diplomat and his much younger wife, the Boxers, hosted the evening at their apartment and introduced themselves to the Fairleys first. *Obviously a second marriage, at least for him,* Addy thought as they shook hands.

Next was a young banker, Mr. Nimitz, with his French bride, then three elderly couples whose names Addy knew she wouldn't be able to keep straight. All three elderly men were of the same height, with a swish of hair attempting to cover bald spots, though one's nose was his defining feature while another was his almost total lack of a chin. But their wives caught Addy's attention. She could tell by their long, slim necks and barely rouged faces that they had all been beauties in another age. Now they wore diamonds around their high-necked dresses with an ease that showed they were used to being pampered. Addy felt her lack of elegance terribly and wished the dress she had splurged on the day before had been ready sooner.

Mr. Nimitz seemed to be the leader, and he naturally took on the role of Mr. Pierce, leading the conversation and handing out champagne as they stood around the elegant parlor. "We're glad you could join us," he began. "France doesn't have as many home-grown spiritualists as England or the States. We have to make do with those who deign to visit us." He smiled at his own weak joke.

"We're very glad to be here," William said modestly, "and to have such an eager welcoming committee."

Mr. Nimitz inclined his head in acknowledgment of the compliment. "Mr. Pierce recommended you. I know him from my London days."

The diplomat, Mr. Boxer, broke in. "Though I must say, we were just delivered the article about the investigation the Society for Psychical Research did with you. A bit disappointing, wasn't it?"

Mrs. Boxer swiped at his arm, hissing at him to be polite.

William stretched his mouth into a tight semblance of a smile. "Of course it was. But you must understand, the spirits do not like to be questioned. They are much more likely to appear to those who believe."

"Yes, that must be it," Mr. Boxer said with a wry lift of his eyebrows.

Mrs. Nimitz stepped forward to save the day, moving between the men to rest her hand on Addy's forearm.

"How do you like Paris so far, Mrs. Fairley?"

Relieved, Addy replied, "It's beautiful. The fashion and the food and the architecture are all amazing. But there is still a lot to see."

William jumped in. "Mrs. Fairley has been out more than I have so far. Unfortunately, I've been stuck inside, working. But even the neighborhood around our hotel is charming. As are the ladies here."

He lifted his champagne glass to Mrs. Nimitz and Mrs. Boxer in turn and then made a small sweeping gesture to indicate the three elderly women observing with their husbands from just outside their little circle. The one in a white dress blushed under William's handsome smile, caught herself in the act, and cast a quick glance up at her husband to make sure he hadn't seen. Addy suppressed a smile.

Not accepting the turn the conversation had taken, Mr. Boxer dragged it back toward his preferred topic. "Shall we get a séance from you tonight, Mr. Fairley?"

"I'm sorry, Mr. Boxer, I'm not quite ready. I was under the impression this was more of a social call."

"Quite right," Mr. Nimitz said. "For God's sake, Richard, he's not on trial here. We're not the SPS."

Mr. Boxer shrugged and gave it up, but still looked unconvinced.

Silence reigned for a few awkward moments until Mrs. Boxer, as if hoping to make up for her husband's behavior, said, "Tell us about America."

This, William and Addy could do easily, and the conversation continued smoothly for the rest of the evening, though William and Mr. Boxer threw glances at each other across the room that said a challenge was afoot.

Mr. Boxer's insistent doubt threatened their prospects in the new city, and William fumed over it on the ride home. His gaze never wavered from a spot he had fixed on out the window. Addy said nothing for fear of stoking the fire, but also sensed the silence building his emotions to a boiling point.

It was in this mood that he stepped into the hotel. As they headed for the stairs, the clerk at the front desk waved them down.

"Mr. Fairley!" The clerk came out from behind the desk to speak with them without shouting.

William spun on his heel but did not respond.

"Mr. Fairley, you've had some friends come by looking for you."

William took one step forward so he towered over the diminutive Frenchman. "Friends!" William bellowed. "Who?"

Surprised, the clerk took a few seconds to catch his words. "They didn't say. They just wanted to know if you were staying here."

William's cheeks reddened. "What did you tell them?"

"I—I told them yes, of course."

"Idiot! Were they French or English?"

"English, sir." The worker must have encountered this sort of irrationality in his guests before, because after his initial surprise, he did not look scared.

William swore and bounded up the stairs.

Addy hung back and apologized to the clerk, then raced upstairs after her husband.

When she reached the door, William was inside, throwing clothing into their trunks.

"William! What on earth is going on?"

"We have to go."

"What? Why? Who were those men?"

"We have to go."

"No," she said, though the word faltered in her mouth.

He gave his head a shake as if tossing her off his shoulders. "Stay if you want, but *I* am leaving." He slammed one of the trunks closed and dragged it into the hallway. Then he turned back to the room. "Here," he said, and tossed her a gold coin from his purse—then two, three, four. With a yank at the trunk, he was gone.

Addy stared at the empty hallway in disbelief as the coins clinked to the floor.

Part III

Chapter 15

Addy sat on the edge of the bed, rolling the coins over in her hands, finding comfort in their hard solidity against her fingertips. If she let go of them, she felt she might disappear in a puff out of this life, back to that fateful afternoon when she ran down the street toward the fire—the day everything changed.

Here she was at another moment of change. William was gone. She knew this time he was not coming back. Their clothes lay strewn across the floor, still intertwined, but otherwise she and her husband were now separate. The reverberations of his trunk scraping down the hall still echoed in her ears. She didn't know what she ought to do.

In this state of hazy indecision, she crawled under the bedcovers, still dressed, and descended into a haunted sleep.

She awoke with a start to the sound of men's voices. Sunlight illuminated the chaotic scene. Three French police officers and two men in tweed suits stood muttering in the center of the room. Addy realized that in her disbelief the night before, she had forgotten to close the door. She was grateful she hadn't bothered to change into her night things but still amazed that they would dare come into the room while a lady was sleeping.

One suited man, short and balding, noticed her. "Mrs. Fairley, I presume?" he asked in an English accent.

He held up a hand as Addy scrambled out of bed. "Don't worry. We're not here to hurt you. We're looking for your husband. Do you know where he might be?"

Addy opened and closed her mouth a few times before any sound came out. "He left last night."

The other gentleman in a suit stepped forward. "Forgive my colleague, Mrs. Fairley. My name is Inspector White; this is Inspector Carter."

Addy shook both their hands.

Inspector White continued, "We're detectives from Scotland Yard. Obviously, our other colleagues are French police."

White gestured toward the other three men, who paused their search long enough to nod toward Addy.

"Please, sit down." Inspector White led Addy to a chair. "Perhaps we can call down for some tea," he said to no one in particular. But soon a steaming cup appeared before her, delivered by unnoticed hands.

White pulled up the other chair and sat next to her while Carter hovered in the background. With a nod from White, the police officers ambled into the corridor to wait. Addy smelled smoke as they lit cigarettes.

Addy took a tentative sip of the tea, disconcerted by Inspector White's solicitousness. She eyed him cautiously and kept her words to herself.

Not letting her reticence dissuade him, White plunged ahead. "Do you know perhaps where your husband has gone?"

"No."

"Will he be back?" Inspector Carter asked.

Addy shook her head and set down the teacup and saucer. "I don't think so." Her head suddenly ached fiercely.

White's hand moved over Addy's. Surprisingly, his gentle touch was comforting rather than intrusive. "Why did he leave?"

Regaining some semblance of herself from the strength of the tea, Addy asked, "Why are you here?"

Her two interrogators exchanged meaningful glances. "I told you," White said gently. "We're looking for your husband."

"But why? What has he done?"

White leaned back in his chair to reconsider his approach. He pulled a cigarette out of his pocket. "Mind if I smoke?"

"Yes," Addy replied harshly, already sick of whatever game he was trying to get her to join him in.

He slowly put the cigarette away. "All right, then. I understand your concerns. Why don't you come with us back to the station."

Addy physically recoiled. "What? No. I—"

He patted her arm. "Don't worry. It's just that I can't discuss confidential matters here, you see," he said with a wave around the room, as if demonstrating his statement was obvious. "We'll get you a nice breakfast. It will be fine, I promise. All routine."

Before she could protest again, he stood. "We'll give you a few minutes to dress."

The two men walked into the hall and shut the door, leaving her alone.

Still dazed by last night and this morning's events, she pawed through the mess of her dresses on the floor and selected one. As she changed, she looked around the room for what she suddenly feared might be the last time. She picked up her reticule and carefully placed the coins William had left her in the bottom of it.

Then she walked into the hall to meet her fate.

The two detectives rode with her to the police station, chatting about innocuous topics the whole way—the weather, the Paris scenery, a mangy dog galloping down the sidewalk alongside their carriage part of the way. Addy squeezed her palms together in her lap in an attempt to hold her nervousness there rather than express it on her face.

Eventually, the carriage rattled to a stop. Addy glanced behind her as she entered the building, casting a final gaze on life outside in case she was not released. In the same instant, she chastised herself for that thought, but with the muddle of events swirling around her, she couldn't fully rein her emotions in.

She was directed to one of the policeman's offices, and the two detectives left her alone while they procured breakfast. The room was cluttered but homey. Cigarette smoke wafted around the mahogany desk piled with papers. It seemed everyone smoked in Paris. Addy hated the smell, and held her handkerchief to her nose to block it out. It did no good.

She occupied herself by continuing her examination of the room. A half-consumed cup of tea balanced on one pile of papers next to a crumb-covered plate. A small window sat in the back wall, its only view that of the building next door.

Feet scuffled behind her. Inspector White appeared and cleared a space on the desk for Inspector Carter to set down a cup of coffee and a croissant.

Addy took a buttery bite of croissant and a burning sip of coffee.

Inspector Carter sat beside her while Inspector White swung into the chair behind the desk.

"Better, Mrs. Fairley?" White asked after she had had a chance to eat.

"Quite, thank you."

Inspector White nodded at his partner, who stood to close the door.

"Now, Mrs. Fairley, I have to ask you some more questions. I can't just tell you what your husband is accused of because I have to determine what you know. Do you understand?"

"Yes." She turned her body square to Inspector White, intuiting that Inspector Carter was peripheral to the proceedings.

"Good." He picked up a pen and rapped it against the desk several times. Then he abruptly set it down, folded his hands, and looked her in the eyes, ready to begin.

"What do you know of your husband's work?"

"He's a medium," she said carefully.

"Now, you have to do a little better than that," he said, but with a friendly twinkle in his eye.

"What is it you actually want to know, Inspector White?"

He changed tactics. "How are your husband's finances?"

"Poor."

"Really? He hasn't come into any money recently?"

Addy paused. "Yes. He came into some money before we left for Paris."

"Do you know how he came by this money?"

"I assumed Mr. Pierce—our benefactor in London—made a final payment to him before we left."

"But you don't know."

"No. Like many wives, I am left in the dark about these things." For once, she was glad of it.

Inspector Carter leaned an elbow on the desk beside her, physically inserting himself into the conversation. "Would you say your husband is an honest man, Mrs. Fairley?"

"You want to know if he uses any tricks in his séances."

Carter inclined his head but didn't answer.

"Of course he does. But that doesn't mean everything he does is false."

Inspector White resumed the questioning. "Did you ever help him with these 'tricks,' as you call them?"

Addy squirmed. "Yes . . . but that's not a crime, is it?"

White looked thoughtful, his forehead crinkling. "It's certainly questionable, morally, but no, it's not a crime. And that's not why we're interested in your husband. Has he ever taken property from his clients?"

"They sometimes give him objects to borrow so he can channel their loved ones." A burst of sweat collected in Addy's armpits.

"And these borrowed objects always made it back promptly to their owners?"

Addy chewed her lip.

"Let me reassure you that we are not interested in arresting you," White continued. "We simply want to find Mr. Fairley. So, please, answer the question." His voice was firmer now, laced with a hint of a threat.

"They were always returned, but I believe, on occasion, they were pawned for ready funds in between."

"Ah!" The detectives shared another glance. "As far as you know, this modus operandi hasn't changed."

"No."

Inspector White shifted in his seat. "I think you're being straight with us, Mrs. Fairley. So, I can tell you that we followed your husband here from London because he stole a number of very valuable objects that the owners thought would be returned before he so conveniently fled to Paris."

Addy's right hand fluttered to her throat, and she collapsed in a faint.

Chapter 16

For the second time in her life, Addy awoke from her faint in a strange place with strange men looking on and life-altering news echoing in her ears. For a moment she thought she was back in Washington, the day after her parents' deaths, everything in between nothing more than a feverish dream. But as her head cleared, she saw the surroundings and the circumstances were quite different, and quite real.

She pushed herself up onto her elbows. She was stretched out on a wooden bench with Inspectors White and Carter conversing in whispers nearby. When they noticed she was awake, they rushed to her side.

"Mrs. Fairley," Inspector White said, "I certainly did not mean to upset you to this degree."

Addy shook her head and sat up the rest of the way. "I'm fine. It was just a shock, is all."

"Perhaps you would like a cup of tea."

"No, thank you." The English seemed to think everything could be cured with a cup of tea. She rubbed the sore back of her neck, which must have hit the chair as she fainted.

"We could go back into the office," White said, "if you feel all right to walk."

She nodded and stood, pointedly not accepting his arm. She walked proudly back into the room on her own and sat in the same chair. The two men also settled into place, recreating the earlier tableau.

Addy was embarrassed at the weakness of her initial reaction. She must be stronger from now on. "So," she began, "you accuse my husband of this, but how do you know he did it?"

She knew immediately she had erred by Inspector White's pitying look.

"Mrs. Fairley, based on what you said about your husband's past behavior, I don't think you're particularly surprised by these allegations. And in this situation, there is really only one person that could be the culprit. But you're correct that he has a right to a trial to prove his innocence—or his guilt. But we need to find him before that can happen."

"You see our conundrum," Inspector Carter said, turning toward her. "Perhaps you'll help us."

Carter's eyes were surprisingly green, like two halves of a lime, Addy noticed as she gazed into them, contemplating the strange request he had just made. The moment had finally come when she had to make a final decision about the man she loved and had once admired so deeply. The admiration shattered like a china vase. Her love was still one intact piece amid the shards, no longer part of anything larger but a reminder of the beauty that had existed before everything crashed to the floor.

She turned her gaze to White instead. His eyes were brown, flecked with gold, calm yet expectant. She sighed. She would try one last battle tactic before her strength and will were exhausted. "Why should I help you?" she asked, cool and aloof.

"Because if you help us," White replied, "I think you'll find that we'll be able to prove that you knew nothing of your husband's treachery."

She sighed again. Here it was, then. Time to trade her life for William's. It pained her to do it, but she knew that given such a choice, William would not hesitate. She knew he would, however, always have a backup plan, and agreeing to the detectives' terms would buy her time to craft one for herself.

"All right," she said. "What do I do?"

The detectives explained that they had the means for tracking William; it was once they found him that they would need Addy's help. Unless, of course, he contacted her first, but Addy found that possibility increasingly remote as the hours ticked by without a word from him. Once the detectives got a lead on William, Addy would need to keep him there until an arrest could be made. Perhaps, the detectives hoped, they could catch him in the act of some grander criminal scheme. To do so, Addy would have to win back his trust, lull him into a sense of safety, and report back to the detectives about William's activities and plans.

She agreed to this surreal scheme because she had no better option. She only hoped she could pull it off.

White and Carter wanted her to remain in the hotel in case William returned or sent a message. Assuming she was destitute, they also offered to pay her expenses while she was unofficially in their employ. She kept the weight of the coins in her purse a secret, a holdout account should she ever need to access it.

When Addy finally left the police station, darkness was descending over Paris like a protective cloak. She was alone in a foreign city. More alone than she had ever been, in fact. But, still, standing in the bright evening air of a city preparing for one of the loveliest holidays of the year, she felt both terrified and invigorated. The only person she had to rely on now was herself. It was, really, what she had always said she wanted.

She stood on the first corner past the police station, passive as the rest of the city moved around her. She considered what she should do next. Remembering the dress she had ordered and paid for so blissfully a few days ago, she turned her feet in the direction of the dressmaker's shop. As soon as the package was in her hands, she marched to the nearest pawn shop and sold it outright. She had no need for silks such as that now. As soon as the Nimitzes and the Boxers heard of William's flight and the accusations surrounding him, Addy's ostracization from Parisian spiritualist society would be complete.

She felt more confident as she stepped outside with the bills and coins folded in her bag, an addition to her hidden account. With it, she was once again independent and could strike out on her own, if necessary. Not that the funds would last for that long. She would need to find some alternate means of income at some point. But for now, she was as set as she could be. She returned to the hotel, tidied up, and waited.

The next day Addy inventoried her remaining belongings to find anything worth selling. Some of her things had been mixed up with William's in the trunk he had dragged after him, but she was left with most of her dresses and underthings. She had never been one for adornment, so she had no real jewelry to speak of. Suddenly, she felt shortsighted for not having invested in something physical before handing her entire inheritance over to William. At least then she would have had something to claim as her own. Though, who knows—those items could have ended up at the pawnbroker's, too.

She pulled each dress out of the trunk and folded it neatly onto a pile beside her. When she lifted out a last, gray garment, it revealed a writing box at the bottom of the trunk. Her heart quickened. It must be William's. She had never seen it, which meant it either contained nothing important or a secret.

She lifted the box, weighing it carefully in her hands. In the few instants it took to set the box in her lap and open the lid, her mind raced through possibilities of what it would contain—money, proof of William's guilt, evidence of his life before Mrs. Alexi.

Stashed inside was a jumble of papers. She shuffled through the stacks, and her chest deflated. She dug through them once more to be sure.

There was nothing else.

She shut the lid. It seemed a gross violation to read what he had hidden. But...

She opened it again. He owed her something at this point, even if it was just his secrets. She pulled out the first page and scanned its contents.

Everything in the box was about Mrs. Alexi. Letters from her, ledgers of accounts, statements of debts, bank receipts from funds William had wired to her.

Addy sat with the papers spread around her, trying to make sense of her first cursory glance through them. Her mind still swirled, unable to grasp the storyline, see who was the villain and who the hero.

She pawed to the bottom of the stack. There was nothing left to do but start from the beginning and work her way forward. She found the earliest date and began a careful read.

Hours later her back ached from sitting rigid and tense for so long, and she still hadn't read through everything. Her stomach growled. She stood up stiffly from the chair and walked down to the lobby to ask the concierge to have some food brought up to her. She hated parting with the few extra coins charged for not going to get the food herself, but she didn't want to leave the room unattended while the papers were everywhere. She didn't trust the detectives not to search through her things at every opportunity. Not that what she had learned so far would help their case—if anything, it shifted the blame from William to Mrs. Alexi. But she didn't want them in her and William's affairs any more than they had to be. At least not until she understood the whole picture and could decide what to do with it.

She returned to the room and dived back in. When the food arrived, she moved to the little table while barely averting her eyes from the page. She read through the rest of the papers, managing to drip sauce on just one of them.

When she finished, the sun had set long ago. She leaned back and released a long breath she hadn't realized she had been holding in.

She was angry at both William and Mrs. Alexi. For getting themselves into what was clearly a codependent mess and dragging Addy into it now, too.

The story, as best she could ascertain, went like this: From the beginning of their work together, William had supported Mrs. Alexi. He had first given the money from the sale of his bookstore in Boston to pay off some of her debts. That had not been enough, and soon he was scrambling to find new clients, new sources of income, new ways to flip money quickly. Mrs. Alexi had a long history, it seemed, of spending above her means, of maintaining a certain lifestyle no matter her actual funds so she could acquire ever more wealthy clients. She had also paid off some unhappy clients to keep their silence so her reputation wouldn't be damaged.

Mrs. Alexi's letters to William wavered between motherly love and demands that he fix the mess she had gotten herself into. The letters that had arrived since Addy and William had been abroad leaned more and more on the side of demands.

Because William owed Mrs. Alexi his life, he had acquiesced. The wrong decision, perhaps, but made with the best of intentions.

In New York, he had resorted to pawning clients' keepsakes for quick cash. Now, with Addy's inheritance spent and no options left, he had devolved to theft.

Addy thought back to that last accusatory letter she'd received from Arthur. His meddling had helped after all as she now fitted more pieces to what William's sister had told Arthur. Jane must have seen William giving all his money to Mrs. Alexi when the money should have supported Harriet. Even though William had signed Harriet over to Jane to live as Jane's own child, surely she would have expected some level of financial support for the favor. In that context, Addy couldn't blame Jane for cutting off communication between William and Harriet. But, having broken ties with her brother, Jane couldn't have known about his questionable activities since.

The tension in Addy's shoulders fell away like a shed snakeskin. Arthur's suspicions had been wrong. The falling-out between William and his sister was because of that most common and banal of reasons—money.

Money was at the root of all this. Money and forced guilt. William's perceived selfishness had not really been selfishness at all. He had thieved out of a sense of loyalty and dedication to the spiritualist movement. None of this had been about Addy; she was simply a pawn in the game of chess between William and Mrs. Alexi. Addy saw that William deserved her sympathy, if not her complete forgiveness.

But the question of what Addy should do about her current situation still lingered. She yearned to run to William and tell her what she had learned, what she now understood. But he was God knows where, and she had no method for reaching him.

The detectives were the more pressing matter. They would expect her cooperation as she had promised, but Addy needed to have her own plan. For now, she would keep these papers safe and tucked away from prying eyes. They were her insurance policy to deploy at the right moment if needed. They contained enough damning evidence to convict both William and Mrs. Alexi.

For Addy, Mrs. Alexi was now a means to an end. She had built William's career but destroyed him as a person in the process. Addy would be smarter. Mrs. Alexi drove William by a sense of what she felt he owed her. Addy would now drive Mrs. Alexi by what she owed Addy—her entire inheritance, for one; her and William's good names, for the other. And she had the perfect collateral with which to do it. Like Mrs. Alexi, Addy would have no qualms about calling in favors from those in her debt.

Addy had always yearned for her independence. She had lost it for now, but she saw a way that she could regain it and keep the upper hand. She would save herself and William. When—not if—she succeeded, life would be normal again.

No, not *again*. For the first time, maybe.

Addy went to bed with the dawn and only awoke when a knock sounded at the door. Fortunately, it was the concierge instead of the detectives. He handed her a folded sheet of paper, then left with soundless steps down the corridor.

Reality crashed in. The note was from the Boxers, inquiring about scheduling the first séance with William. The lie for Addy's reply, pulled from threads of the truth, came surprisingly quickly.

I am sorry to tell you that William had to return to America suddenly because he received notice his sister is very ill. Having just arrived in Paris, I decided to stay on. My sincerest apologies for the disappointment.

She sent the note along without a second thought. Soon enough, word of the charges against William would cross the Channel into France. In the meantime Addy would keep up the facade. She had been doing it for months, anyway, and she was starting to think that she might be very good at it. Which, given her current circumstances, boded well for her future.

Addy was reading in an armchair that afternoon, enjoying the peace and quiet, when the porter knocked and presented her with Mrs. Boxer's card.

Addy didn't hesitate. "Ask her to wait five minutes; then let her up."

Addy scrambled to make herself presentable before her guest entered. She had just finished pinning up her hair when she heard footsteps and rushed to the door. "Mrs. Boxer! How kind of you to come!" she said as the door swung open.

"Forgive me for not letting you know I was coming, but after I got your note last night, I just had to come see you." She sat in the chair across from Addy, her posture perfectly straight. "Did he really leave you all alone in a strange country?"

Addy broke into a soft smile. If her guest only knew. "It was my choice, I assure you. I couldn't stomach the thought of going back to America so soon."

"But is it really proper for you to be staying in a hotel on your own? You must come stay with us."

"No, no, I'm fine, really."

"I insist. It's the least we can do. Besides, a little female companionship never hurt anyone. All my husband thinks about is French politics and what they mean for England. Quite dull."

A knock sounded at the door.

Addy rose to answer it. "Excuse me."

Inspector White stood in the hall. Addy gave a minuscule shake of her head and angled her body so he could see her guest. However, she didn't move fast enough to keep Mrs. Boxer from glimpsing him.

"Who's this?" Mrs. Boxer called from across the room.

White removed his hat and ever so subtly pushed his way inside. "Inspector White, ma'am. Police force. We were told that Mrs. Fairley here was staying on her own, so I'm just checking on her. Like to keep an eye on the English speakers around here."

Addy moved carefully away from the door back toward the other two, but remained outside of the conversation.

"How decent of you," Mrs. Boxer said. "I was just telling Mrs. Fairley she must come stay with me. I'm sure you'll agree that it's not right for her to stay here alone."

"That's up to Mrs. Fairley, but it's kind of you to offer." He looked from one woman to the other. "How did you make her acquaintance?" he asked Mrs. Boxer.

"We had her and her husband to dinner the other night. I was hoping to see Mr. Fairley in action."

"Ah. Well, we can keep an eye on her for you and save you the trouble."

"Please do consider it, dear," Mrs. Boxer said to Addy as she stood to leave.

"I certainly will. Thank you for coming."

Once the door closed behind Mrs. Boxer, Inspector White sat. "What have you told her?"

"He had to rush home to see his sick sister."

"Very good."

"Sooner or later they'll see it in the papers."

He steepled his fingers thoughtfully. "I don't think so. We've worked to suppress the story so we don't tip him off any more than we already have."

"What should I tell her about coming to stay?"

"If he comes looking for you, it will be here. You see my predicament."

"I'll make some excuse."

"Good. But be friendly with her, by all means."

"Yes."

"He hasn't contacted you, has he?"

"No," Addy said.

But she felt the scratch of a scrap of paper stuffed in her bodice as she shifted her feet.

The same boy who had delivered the note to her that morning stood on the corner down the block from the hotel. Addy had waited a sufficient length of time after Inspector White left before slipping out, and she was glad to see the messenger still there. She offered the boy a small slice of baguette, the bit of paper burrowed within. With the newspapers called off the story, William might breathe a little easier, and the two of them might have more time to plan their next move.

Addy had received William's note that morning as she walked to get breakfast. Seeing the familiar handwriting, she had cried in front of the little boy. William had not abandoned her.

She had rushed up to the room and unfolded the note. It wasn't long, but William gave her an apology and a declaration of love. She now knew where he was headed, and she was part of his plan once again. With her inheritance squandered, there was no reason for him to contact her unless he truly wanted her as his partner. He had remained loyal to her, and she would do the same to him. The detectives wanted to destroy everything she and William had built. She had invested too much time and energy into their creation to let that happen.

However, William did not explain himself in the letter. On that point, she saw she had the upper hand. Her heart yearned for him, but she must protect herself and her future. She reined in her enthusiasm. She mustn't let him off too easily.

In her response, she struck a deal. She would help him out of love, she said, but she required a promise securing her future from Mrs. Alexi so she would be taken care of no matter what happened. If William did end up in jail, Addy would need somewhere to go. She mentioned the papers she had found in his abandoned trunk and assumed no more needed to be said. He would understand the power the proof held over both him and his mentor. She told him of Carter and White and the deal she had struck with them so he would see the value of the inside knowledge she could offer. She had hesitated to send it, wanting to make sure she had thought through everything rightly, but after the appearances of Mrs. Boxer and Inspector White that afternoon, she knew she had to act. Hence the return visit to the messenger boy. She had set events in motion and, like a row of dominoes, had to wait to see where things would fall.

As she went about her errands over the next two days, she kept an eye out for the boy, but having done his duty, he did not reappear. It made sense that it would take longer to receive a response, as William moved farther from Paris and the message had to be relayed in a more complicated manner. But the illogical part of her brain worried over the delay like an oyster worrying over the irritating bit of dust in its shell. And she couldn't imagine what pearl would come of this.

She made her excuse to Mrs. Boxer and stayed on at the hotel. As much as Addy would have liked the companionship, it was the best way forward that she could see. Better to be on her own for now and keep her secrets to herself. But Mrs. Boxer wouldn't completely release Addy from under her wing, so Addy found herself at a subdued lunch at the Boxers' with the Nimitzes as the only other guests. As they munched on sandwiches, the conversation couldn't escape the situation with William.

"Have you heard from him?" Mr. Nimitz asked.

"Yes. His sister is not doing well, I'm afraid."

"And how much longer do you plan on staying in Paris without him?"

"No specific plan for now. I'm enjoying it so much."

Mr. Nimitz frowned, but his wife jumped in before he could respond.

"Mrs. Fairley, I have a proposal for you."

Addy raised an eyebrow.

"Surely you've learned a lot about spirit communication from your time assisting your husband. Is there really nothing you can do for us? I was so disappointed we didn't get to have a session with him."

"You mean, lead a session on my own? I've never tried. And my husband is the one with the natural gift—"

"Yes, but women often get stuck in their husbands' shadows"—she tossed a cheeky smile at her husband—"so how do you know if you don't try?"

Addy's heart picked up the pace, but she kept herself from getting too excited. She didn't even know if she wanted to do what William did—especially considering how he did it. But to build her own career promoting the cause she most loved would assure her an independent future. She took a deep breath. "I appreciate your confidence in me, of course. But it isn't quite so easy . . . If we do try it, it would have to be with a small group, maybe just us. I don't want to make any promises to anyone about how it will go." She paused. "And with that being the case, the session would be complimentary, of course. In exchange for all your hospitality."

Mrs. Nimitz reached across the table to clasp Addy's hand. "Of course. Thank you." She beamed at the others, but their frowns showed they didn't share her level of enthusiasm.

"Give me a few days to prepare, please."

Mrs. Nimitz nodded in agreement, undeterred by the others' doubts.

Addy swallowed. She had to get another message to William right away.

The most obvious problem was that William had taken the supplies with him, Addy mused when she got home, though most of the items could be replaced easily enough. She needed to start off small in her first session anyway.

She made a list, feeling purposeful for the first time in weeks. As she finished, she glanced at the clock and noticed that she was about to miss the possible afternoon messenger rendezvous. She hastily scribbled a note and headed outside, as she did every day, just in case there was news.

Today there was. The boy stood aimlessly on the corner, trying to appear as if he were waiting for no one at all. She watched his light-brown hair emerge from between two men crossing the street until he was in front of her. She took the note he offered and quickly stuffed it in her reticule. She handed him her own scrap of paper, then went home to read William's letter. She could tell it was longer than the others had been, and she couldn't wait to hear William's voice, even on the flatness of paper.

When she unfolded the page, another slip of paper fell out. It was a brief telegram from Mrs. Alexi, agreeing to Addy's terms. Addy had won, then. She would never again be circumvented by these two. She would lead the drive to make them all respectable, successful purveyors of the spirit realm.

She smoothed the telegram out on the table, pleased with herself, before moving on to William's letter. He said he was impressed by her resolve and her approach.

I knew I married you for a reason, he wrote.

Addy had a reason for her marriage now, too. Once she sorted out this situation—granted, it was rather a large situation to sort—William would be her stepping stone to the life she had always envisioned. In the future, she would make sure theirs would be a partnership, built of love and belief.

William dedicated most of his letter to detailing his plans for evading Scotland Yard. He inquired less about how Addy was coping on her own, but to be fair, she had already shown herself more than capable. She sucked in her resentment and focused on the matter at hand—how to reunite with William and keep him safe. In this situation, he was most important, she reasoned, though a small voice reminded her that he had brought this on himself.

After reading the letter twice, she burned it in the fireplace. William's plans would be easy enough to remember, and she didn't want any evidence of their communication. If Inspector White wasn't already having Addy watched, he would soon.

Addy calculated the response times between messages and realized with a sinking heart that there was no chance of a response before she would have to perform the séance she'd promised the Boxers. She really was on her own. But she was up to the challenge, and she would make devoted spiritualists out of them all. Just because William had ruined his chance to convert these Parisians did not mean she would ruin hers.

Chapter 17

A few days later Addy noticed him—a tall, nondescript man in a dark suit who appeared everywhere she did. Sent by Inspectors Carter and White, to be sure. She ignored him and went about her preparations for the séance. There was nothing wrong with her taking over the legitimate side of her husband's business. She wouldn't be deterred.

She gathered copies of spiritualist publications she had acquired and borrowed a few more from her new friends in Paris. Reading through them reminded Addy of what was possible and made her ambitions grow. She would start simple but precise with this first séance so there was no room for error. But plans already swirled for how she could build ever more remarkable sessions. This was her one chance at a career, and she would make it worth it.

Having made this decision, she shopped for supplies. She was carrying a basket of materials back home through an afternoon that threatened rain when she met Inspector White in the street in front of the hotel.

He bowed. "Mrs. Fairley."

"Inspector White." She pushed past him to continue inside.

He followed her amiably, hands shoved into his pockets, his pace slow.

Once in the hotel room, she set down her things. "I'm surprised you feel the need to visit. Your henchman could tell you everything I'm doing without you ever setting foot on this street."

"You wouldn't expect anything less of me, would you? You've been awfully silent during our partnership, and I have to make sure our interests are still aligned."

"Why wouldn't they be?"

He riffled through the contents of the basket. "What are these for?"

"I'm holding a séance tomorrow night. For a few close friends."

"Really? You told me you weren't terribly involved in your husband's business. That he had all the talent."

"This will be my first attempt. I need to support myself somehow."

"Our arrangement isn't to your satisfaction?"

She put her hands on her hips. "Why did you come?"

He gestured to a chair. "May I?"

"Of course."

Addy stayed standing.

"I think it's time we devised a plan," he said, unbothered by having to look up at her. "There's no getting away from it now, Mrs. Fairley."

"I thought the plan was to wait until he contacted me."

"Hasn't he? Or do you send secret intercontinental messages to all your friends?"

Addy straightened. "How long have you been watching me?"

"From the beginning, of course. I gave you a chance to tell me and you didn't. So now you will do what I say."

He held up a hand to halt her protests.

"You may hold your séance. But in two days' time we'll all be on our way to Rome. That is where he's headed, isn't it? No answer? Well, you'll just have to tell him you couldn't wait to see him any longer."

With that, he stood and swept out of the room.

Addy's hands shook as she closed the door behind him.

How had she been so naive? She should have guessed White would use her as a pawn in his game, just as William had tried to do. Well, she was sick of it. She would outsmart all these men and become the one dictating the moves.

In the lonely quiet, her resolve wavered only a little.

***

Addy spent the afternoon preparing for the séance and writing a final letter to William that took many drafts. Her and William's plan would require a few tweaks but was still workable, assuming the letter could reach William before the detectives did. She finally sealed the letter and addressed it using the first note from him, which she kept hidden in her dress. This note, too, she burned. She wouldn't need it again.

The evening mail brought a letter that, as soon as she read it, Addy realized she had been half expecting all along.

Tiffany and Arthur were engaged.

She was happy for them, of course—they were both people she loved, though love could be complicated. But the letter still felt like proof that Tiffany and Arthur had been working against her ever since she had left for New York.

They advised Addy to return home and live with them. While they didn't say it outright, Addy guessed Tiffany had betrayed her promise and told Arthur of Addy's qualms about William's methods. Addy was grateful she hadn't told Tiffany about William leaving her. If she had, Tiffany and her betrothed might sail across the sea and drag Addy back home with them no matter what.

Addy considered her options. If she had chafed at Arthur's oversight before her marriage, to return to it defeated and proven wrong would be unbearable. Perhaps it was stubbornness on her part, but she had to make her own way.

If Addy had any doubts left about her path, they dissipated like a spirit vaporizing after a manifestation. There was no going home, no going back. Her own independent future lay with William and the spirits. She just had to figure out how to fix everything.

At 5:00 p.m. the next day, she gathered everything up and headed for the Boxers'. Inspector's White's lookout was nowhere to be seen but probably lurked somewhere. She was sure he had only let himself be seen the day before to frighten her. But now she wasn't worried by what he might relay to White. She had her own plans that were already in motion.

This time, the Nimitzes hosted the event. Both the Boxers and Nimitzes greeted Addy warmly when she arrived, fussing over her and making sure she was well. After reassuring them she was fine and that she was in touch with William, she said, "I'll need one of you to be my assistant. Who shall it be?"

Mrs. Nimitz stepped forward. No one moved to protest.

Perfect.

"What shall I do?" Mrs. Nimitz asked, sounding like an eager child being initiated into a new game.

"Come with me into whatever room we'll be using, and I'll show you."

Mr. Boxer showed them into a back parlor. "Don't pull any tricks, Mrs. Fairley," he said with the same wry smile he had used when challenging William the first time they had met.

"Have a little faith, Mr. Boxer," Addy said as she entered the room with Mrs. Nimitz. Once they were inside, Addy set down her basket and closed the door behind them.

She hadn't prepared any obvious tricks with string, like William had. Her focus had instead been on researching her guests to give them what they would say was irrefutable proof. Her tricks would be small, simple highlights.

Addy channeled William's confidence and delivered directions to Mrs. Nimitz. "We'll sit around the table. I want you to sit next to me so you can tell everyone my hands and feet are in place." Then Addy turned to the real reason she had asked Mrs. Nimitz to join her in the room. "I have an unrelated request to make of you." Addy pulled the letter out of the bottom of the basket. "I need you to mail this for me. It's for a friend, but I can't be seen sending it, you understand?"

"Yes, but why?"

Addy shook her head, indicating that she couldn't, or wouldn't, answer.

"All right, then." Mrs. Nimitz accepted the letter and slipped it into her pocket. "I'll send it in the morning."

"Thank you." She clasped her friend's hands. "Now, I think we're ready. Let's call the others in, shall we?"

Addy slid into her seat. She deftly grabbed a handful of powder from her basket and kept it in her fist as she pulled on the gloves she had purchased just for this occasion. Mrs. Nimitz sat and placed a hand over Addy's.

Their small party did not completely fill the circular table. Across from Addy, an empty seat watched her. She imagined William sitting there, judging everything she was about to do but urging her on as well.

She started to take her neighbors' hands, but Mr. Boxer suddenly stood. "Who has checked around here to know there won't be some sort of trick?"

His wife shushed him, but Addy amiably stood and stepped aside. Surprised by her easy acquiescence, the bravado left him. He moved Addy's chair and quickly glanced under the table, but there was nothing to see. The others watched him uncomfortably. Unsure what to do next, he opened a cabinet shoved against a nearby wall. Then, declaring himself satisfied, he returned meekly to his seat.

Addy's hands sweated in her thick gloves just as she had hoped they would. She began the séance and led the hymn in a wavering voice. Once that was done, she closed her eyes and blocked out everyone besides the spirits. She could feel their energies around her, waiting to come through. A peaceful power flowed through her.

She brought to mind all the notes she had taken over the last few days. She had done her research. She would not be caught making incorrect assumptions about which departed loved ones the guests wanted to hear from, like William had been with the two young ladies on their voyage to England.

"Albert," Addy whispered as the group's voices trailed out the last notes of the hymn. Addy softened the *r* in the name as she said it in a passable attempt at an English accent.

"Ruth?" Mr. Boxer asked.

Addy smiled to herself in the dark. The most skeptical member of the party, and she had hooked him right away.

"Albert, I miss you. But I see you are happy."

"Yes, my dear. I hope you aren't upset I married again."

"Of course not. She is beautiful, and so young."

"She is. But I still love you, too."

"And I, you. Tell the children I love them."

"I will." His voice faltered with emotion.

Addy let the silence continue for a long moment, keeping them wondering who would appear next. But she, of course, knew.

Next appeared Mrs. Boxer's mother, then Mr. Nimitz's brother. She kept their messages plain, generic enough not to arouse suspicion. No one would remember those messages afterward, if her final display went as planned.

"I feel a strong spirit who wants to speak next," she said, her voice low and evocative. "No matter what happens, you must keep the circle unbroken." She brought together Mr. and Mrs. Nimitz's hands, who were sitting to her right and left, respectively. In the next instant she jerked her head back and darted her hands out of her too-large gloves, a move she had practiced obsessively over the last few days. Now, with the phosphorescent powder exposed to the heavy sweat of her hands, her palms and fingertips glowed in the open air.

The others gasped in delight. A slight twittering followed.

When Addy was ready, she shouted, "Stop!" Then, through the ensuing silence, she called in a high voice, "Annette."

Mrs. Annette Nimitz gasped and covered her gaping mouth with her hands, all thoughts of an unbroken circle forgotten. "Adele!"

"What do you want to ask me?" Addy replied.

"You are at peace?"

"Yes, the spirit world is always at peace." Addy lowered her hands in front of the candleflame in the center of the table, releasing another puff of powder as she did so, to remarkable effect. She could feel everyone holding their breath as they took in the spectacle.

Addy turned back to Mrs. Nimitz and let forth the sentence she had practiced so carefully in French: *"I am with you always. Continue your work with the spirits."*

Another little gasp escaped Mrs. Nimitz's mouth. Her husband rubbed her back comfortingly but looked bewildered himself. Satisfied with the performance, Addy relaxed her body and closed her eyes, folding her hands in her lap. A moment later she opened her eyes, her triumph complete. She quickly returned her hands to her gloves as everyone stood and regathered themselves.

Addy accepted everyone's praise with what she hoped was a dignified and humble air. Even Mr. Boxer shook her hand and for once had nothing to say.

Before leaving, she again took Mrs. Nimitz aside.

"I must ask you another favor," Addy said.

"Anything!"

"I need a little money—a loan. Just until William can wire me some more from America. He's so preoccupied with his sister, you know."

"Don't say another word. Wait here." Mrs. Nimitz dashed upstairs and returned quickly with a stack of bills. "It's the least we can do for you," she said as she handed them over.

Addy squeezed her patron's hand. "Thank you."

The two women rejoined the rest of the group.

"When shall we see you again?" Mr. Nimitz asked.

"I hope to go back to America soon, but I will come by before then."

He shook her hand firmly with both of his. "Excellent."

"It's remarkable," Mr. Boxer said from the fringes of the group, apparently having collected himself sufficiently to play his usual role. "How unsure you were of your abilities and how well they came through." The tautness of his stance showed he didn't mean it as a compliment.

Addy beamed and ignored the undertone of his statement. "I'm so relieved you think so. I suppose I learned more from Mr. Fairley than I realized. And the spirits smiled on us today." She put on her hat. "I must go," she said, waving as she stepped into the Nimitzes' waiting carriage, which they had placed at her disposal.

With Mrs. Nimitz's ready cash and the encircling snare of Inspector White, when Addy got home, she knew she couldn't wait any longer. She had to kick over the first domino in their plan and hope William would be there at the end to catch the last one.

In the morning she packed her trunks and gave her notice at the hotel. Then she marched to the police station. When Inspectors White and Carter greeted her, she said simply, "I know where to find William. We must leave tonight."

Chapter 18

The detectives showed their surprise at Addy's sudden pronouncement, but they didn't press her about the circumstances of her revelation until the trio was comfortably seated on the last evening train heading south from Paris. Then the two men stared at her, sussing her out. She picked at a loose string on her left glove to avoid their gazes. She had rehearsed her part many times in her head, and it wouldn't do to have nervousness set her off on the wrong foot.

Once she had gathered herself, she looked up with a beaming smile. "I've never been to Rome, you know."

Inspector White's returning smile was placating. "Yes, my dear, but I hardly think there will be time for sightseeing, given the circumstances."

She looked nonchalantly out the window. "Perhaps I'll stay on after you all have taken care of your business."

She saw the men exchange glances out of the corner of her eye.

Inspector Carter cleared his throat. "I must admit, I'm surprised to see you so calm about your husband's pending arrest."

She shrugged. "He abandoned me."

"Indeed he did. Tell me, how exactly did you come to find out your husband's location?"

"He sent me a note through the messenger boy, like you saw. He asked me to come to him."

"Just the one note?"

"No, I had to reassure him first that I was on his side. Isn't that what you wanted me to do?"

White took over again. "Yes, you did well in that case. Has he acquired any clients in Rome, do you know? Anyone else he may be targeting?"

"There's a big séance there in four days' time. That's why we had to leave tonight. That's when he'll take valuables from his supporters."

"Excellent work. I'm impressed."

"Thank you." She looked at the men coyly. "I don't suppose you employ any female detectives?"

White chuckled. "No, but we'll keep you in mind if we ever do." He clapped his hands. "How about we find the dining car?"

They all agreed and walked one after the other down the unsteady aisle.

They spent the night in Nice and caught the first train to Rome in the morning. Addy's thoughts were already in Italy with William. For now, her loose ends were tied up. She sent Mrs. Nimitz a letter from Nice stating she had to catch the next ship to America for her sister-in-law's funeral and needed the money Mrs. Nimitz had loaned her for the journey. Addy promised she would pay it back. And she would, sometime. When, exactly, depended on how the next few days transpired. On whether William could pull off the escape he and Addy had orchestrated.

Either way, Addy would be fine. She was prepared to strike out on her own. But still, she hoped that William awaited her as anxiously as she did him. Without his devotion, all this would be for naught.

As the trio trundled through the Mediterranean countryside, green hills clothed in a damp wintry mist, Addy was almost able to forget the impending confrontation. Her chaperones occupied themselves with their newspapers, and Addy kept her head in a book—one of her Marie Corelli novels that she had loved so much and that had started her on this spiritualist journey. It was a familiar comfort. She thought back to the days of reading in the living room while her mother sewed. It seemed like another lifetime now, subsumed by her life with William. But she didn't regret the shift for a minute; that previous, stifled life had been no life at all. The last few weeks, she felt almost like one of the heroines from the books. Now, no matter what happened, she would know she had been alive.

Addy looked up from the page and noticed Inspector Carter watching her, but he quickly returned his eyes to his paper. Addy shrugged it off; in a few days she would be done with both of these men for good.

When they arrived in Rome late that night, rain lashed down and the wait for a carriage was long. In one far-off corner of the skyline, an orange light burned above the buildings, hinting at flames. Addy huddled in the station away from the weather while the men waited in line. She felt this was an ominous welcome to the city.

She awoke in the morning, tired and aching from the jostling of the long train journey. She breakfasted in her room, and afterward Inspector White came in with the morning's paper. He tossed it down in front of her.

"I see you were telling the truth about this event. It's in all the papers. He's rented out a theater."

Addy looked at the page, recognizing William's name in the half-page ad amid the unfamiliar Italian words. She tapped the page with a finger. "Why would I lie?"

"I'm sure you could have many reasons. But we'll be there to catch him in the act." He adjusted his stance. "I'll have to keep a close eye on you the next two days, just in case."

Addy smiled. "I would expect nothing less of you, Inspector White. But surely while you're keeping an eye on me, we can do a bit of sightseeing?"

He chuckled. "Of course." He bowed and exited, leaving the paper on the table. Addy contemplated it for a long time, willing the foreign words to give her some idea of what fate it may lead William to. But when her eyes finally left the page, she was none the wiser.

That afternoon, Inspector Carter collected her for lunch. As they left the hotel, Inspector White came in from the street.

"What's the news?" Carter asked.

"He's certainly not laying low. There's a rotating door of people coming to see him."

"You've been watching him already?" Addy asked.

"It's hardly a secret where he's staying."

"You know he asked me to come here. He'll be expecting to see me."

"We'll get to that," White said, "don't you worry. Now, where were you two off to?"

"Lunch and an afternoon tour of the city," Addy said. "Join us?" she asked, as if any of them had any choice in the matter.

White inclined his head politely as he turned to go back outside with them. As if none of this was a charade and they truly were three friends vacationing together.

The afternoon was pleasant, a stunning contrast to the day before, bursting with the most sun and warmth Addy had seen in months. Carter came into his own on the tour, expounding on the history of the ancient buildings they passed, pointing them out with the tip of the cane he carried but never seemed to need. Addy murmured her appreciation, content to take in the sights and play along that they were all just friends out for a pleasant tour. By the time the light began to fade, catching shadows in the crooks of buildings and narrow alleys, Addy's feet ached and she was already sick of Italy. It kept her from returning home with her husband and escaping these dull middle-aged Englishmen. Her European tour was over before it had even really begun, but she saw now other things could be more important than the plans she had made for herself in her previous existence. Her life could be bigger and more meaningful than she had ever dared dream. If all these men would only get out of her way.

They dined at a restaurant on the edge of a bustling square. The atmosphere was lively, and through it Addy could feel the pulse of William's energy, crossing the city to get to her. She yearned to slip away and get even a few moments with him, but she knew she couldn't risk it. In two more days, it would be over and they could be together again. She consoled herself with this.

The next day, she toured the city again with Inspector Carter and his gargantuan knowledge of its past. Inspector White presumably still stalked their prey while Carter kept an eye on her. When Addy and Carter returned to the hotel in the evening, she penned letters to Arthur and Tiffany, congratulating them on their impending nuptials and informing them that she wouldn't be returning Stateside anytime soon. She kept the tone mundane and left out any further details. She guessed the detectives would read her outgoing mail, and she didn't want to give them any clues about her plans for the future. Eventually, word of William's escapades would reach the American papers, and when that happened Arthur and Tiffany would expect Addy to cut ties with William and all the spiritualists. But Addy knew what choice she would make. She couldn't go backward. The door to her old life had slammed behind her. She would rely on her own wits and Mrs. Alexi's promises going forward.

Afterward, all that was left was to sleep and wait for morning and the final day.

Addy awoke to foreign sounds slipping through the windows and a weak sun brightening her bedspread. She could tell that a cold front had passed through overnight, and she stayed wrapped in the covers despite her eagerness for the day to begin. A bird lilted outside, a comforting noise in the midst of the screeching and slamming of the city. She closed her eyes and focused on the birdsong, pinning her hopes on its uplifting notes.

Eventually, she got up and dressed. Inspector White knocked close enough to the instant she fastened the last button that she wondered if he were watching her somehow, even here in her hotel room.

"I have three tickets for tonight's performance," he said as he entered her room. "Sold out, you know."

Addy's heart bloomed with pride in spite of impending events. William really had made a name for himself.

"We leave at six."

White turned to leave but paused with his hand on the doorknob. "I've spoken to the venue. They know we will be there and that he shouldn't be allowed to leave. All to be handled discreetly, of course. We do still want to catch him in the act of a crime. That will be foolproof evidence for the jury." He peered at Addy over his shoulder, and she held his gaze.

"See you at six," she said.

He would not rattle her, she determined as he left.

But as the door closed behind him, a nausea rose in her stomach that sent her back to bed for much of the morning. She cradled one hand around her stomach, knowing what the sickness meant. What transpired tonight would affect not only her but her child's future.

The carriage departed at six o'clock that evening carrying Addy, the two detectives, and an Italian policeman who could make the arrest. The latter—young and handsome, with a drooping mustache—sat silently with a pleasant smile on his face. His entire English acquisition seemed to consist of "yes," "please," and "hello," all of which he had employed profusely when meeting his three companions. Addy liked him and wished he didn't have to be caught up in this.

Addy also caught Inspector White smiling across from her.

"Inspector White, if I didn't know better, I'd say you were enjoying all this," she chided him.

He smiled even bigger. "It's a lovely Italian evening, and we're going to the theater. By all accounts, your husband is very talented. I like a good show as much as anybody." Seeing Addy's grimace, he said, "I'm sorry if you don't want to see him again, but just think, before the night is through, he'll be taken care of and you can go back to your old life."

For a detective supposedly possessed of the powers of deduction, White proved terrible at reading his subjects. Addy smiled flatly in response and decided to join the Italian in studied silence. She was glad to be an enigma to these men. It boded well for her future in the spiritualist arts.

The lobby of the theater was hectic, a bustle of people bumping into each other, waving across the crowd to separated companions, clutching tickets between gloved fingers. Addy enjoyed the forced anonymity. For an instant she pictured herself running through the crowd, holding up her pink skirts, running to find William backstage, escaping. But in the next moment Carter's hand was on her arm, directing her to their seats.

Once seated, she gazed around the packed space and felt a twinge of pride at what William had accomplished. This should be his triumph, she thought bitterly, converting all these people to believers, and the police were going to make sure it was his downfall. She knew she couldn't let that happen. For the sake of her growing family's future.

The lights dimmed, the curtain rose. Applause as a man appeared and spewed off a monologue in Italian. Then he turned to the side of the stage and clapped as William entered, waving.

Addy caught her breath, struck by the sight of him again like a kick to the back of her chair. He looked even more handsome, well to do, and confident than she remembered. His exile hadn't troubled him much, by the look of it. A pair of young women in front of her tittered over William's good looks. Addy swallowed the jealousy down. In this moment, he was supposed to be nothing to her, she reminded herself. She must keep up the ruse.

William crossed the stage, passing in front of a large, round table set precisely in the center. Addy knew Rome's elite had paid dearly to be one of the chosen few to participate in the séance onstage. William reached the edge of the stage and began his introductory speech, his voice booming and solid as an old-growth oak. The Italian drifted off to one side to serve as translator.

"Ladies and gentlemen, thank you for coming. I am honored to share the spirits with you. As we conduct the séance, I ask you to be quiet and respectful. Our wonderful volunteers are actually trying to connect with their loved ones. Enjoy. And believe."

Addy joined the rest of the audience in thunderous applause. While it continued, the Italian host patted William down, making a show of proving nothing was hidden within his clothes. Then the lights dimmed further, the low gas lamps giving the room an eerie effect. Addy glanced at her chaperones, one on either side; they both fixed rapt attention on the stage, but whether their interest was in William's crimes or gifts, she couldn't say.

Next, they brought out the "volunteers." As each one was announced, they received almost as much applause as William had. Addy focused her attention on an older gentleman in coat and tails, an American businessman visiting Italy, or so his introduction claimed. But Addy recognized Mr. Belk, and his presence meant their plan was progressing well so far. He looked confident and calm as he bowed to the audience and then took his seat.

Perfect, Addy thought. So far, everything was proceeding as planned.

The hymn to start the session, sung by the whole audience, enchanted Addy. She felt herself swept away, just as she had in her first séance. A respite before the storm to come.

The revelations to the volunteers built slowly—a few select words to one of the participants from a channeled family member, a candle levitating off the table. Then a pair of stagehands rolled out a large cabinet. The manifestation would be the pièce de résistance. Addy's heart thrilled in anticipation.

The Italian assistant tied William's hands with a flourish, then locked him in the cabinet. The singing began again, reverberating off the walls of the theater. The Italian raised his arms to encourage the crowd to sing louder, and they responded. Then he opened the cabinet. William was gone.

Had the moment of his escape arrived already?

A fresh gasp from the crowd told her it hadn't. Three hundred necks craned to the back of the theater, where a ghostly figure in an old-fashioned wig now stood.

Inspector Carter leaned over to Inspector White. "Trapdoors," he said.

The young women in front of them shushed him.

"I'll tell the staff to go watch the trapdoors," White said, and stood.

Addy clutched the armrest to stop herself from grabbing his arm and detaining him.

He can't go back there yet, she thought wildly. But there was nothing she could do. A trip to the bathroom now would be too conspicuous. All she could do was watch White shuffle down the row, banging into people's knees.

Addy stared at the ghost, willing William to cut things short and escape now. But she knew he would never leave his moment of triumph unfinished. His spectral form called to the American in tails on the stage in a voice much reedier than usual.

"Do you believe?" he asked the man.

"Yes!" Mr. Belk said. In the next instant, he levitated just as the candle had earlier, rising above the table until he floated on his back above it. The crowd gasped and cheered. Addy alone glanced to the rear of the theater. The bewigged ghost had vanished.

The lights cut off suddenly, signaling the end of the performance.

The applause dragged on for several minutes. Eventually, the host stepped out in a spotlight, waving the crowd to silence so he could give the closing speech.

But Addy didn't get to listen.

Inspector Carter yanked her up by her elbow. "Let's go," he hissed in her ear. "He must be pulling some trick."

Addy smiled in the half-light and followed.

When they arrived backstage, it was in chaos. The show's workers bustled around, trying to do their jobs beneath the outsize bellows of Inspector White directing the search for William.

"What's happened?" Carter asked as he and Addy jogged up.

"He escaped us, but he can't have got far yet. You"—he pointed at the Italian policeman—"call more officers. Now!"

The Italian looked unsure for a heartbeat, then, deciding he understood the tone of the command well enough, ran off to make the call.

"We've got people watching his hotel, so we'll know if he goes there," White said. He turned to Addy, his gaze fierce. "Tell me you didn't tip him off."

"How could I? You've been with me the entire time."

"Where would he go?"

"I don't know."

Carter stepped between them. "We need to get eyes on the port, train stations—anywhere he might go to try to leave the country." He grabbed Addy's shoulders and bent to look into her eyes. "Think! Is there anywhere he might go? Anyone he knows here?"

Mr. Belk interrupted, loudly playing his part. "What's all this racket?" he bellowed. "Where's Mr. Fairley?"

"I'm sorry, sir," White said. "We're looking for him."

"Has something happened? He was supposed to meet us to give us back the objects we lent him this morning."

White's attention was suddenly directed entirely on the stranger. "I'm sorry, sir, but you've probably been the victim of theft."

"This morning?" Carter broke in. "I thought he was meeting with you all after the show?"

"He changed it at the last minute. What's this about *theft*?"

"Damn!" White swore. He jerked forward, then back, seeming unsure in which direction to send his pent-up energy. "Mrs. Fairley, you have to stay here. This could get messy."

Carter turned as if to say something to the gentleman but rushed off with White instead.

"Wait!" Addy called after them. "You can't leave me here!"

The two men hurried off without a glance back. Addy watched until they disappeared. Then she turned to face the remaining man.

"So, Mr. Belk, are we all set?"

"Yes, come with me."

Chapter 19

Addy hurried down the hall after Mr. Belk until they reached the rear exit. She glanced behind her as he pushed open the door. It looked like, in the chaos of events, nobody would notice her missing right away. The pair emerged outside into a thick winter fog. Mr. Belk stood close to her in the heavy air so they could see each other clearly as he filled her in.

"Mrs. Fairley—"

"Please, call me Addy, after all the help you've given us." She set a hand on his arm. "And I'm sorry I was never very friendly to you in New York. I was so wrong about you. William needs his loyal followers now more than ever."

He reddened slightly. "Well, thank you, Addy." He cleared his throat. "William has transferred everything to me. The last items from this morning are in my hotel room."

Addy knew Mr. Belk's hotel was on the other side of the city from William's, so it wouldn't be watched or suspected.

William had somehow convinced Mr. Belk to absorb the money William had accumulated and, in exchange for a small cut, to use those funds to serve as their benefactor so the stolen money and items wouldn't be traceable. While Addy hated the duplicity, she admired the loyalty William inspired in his followers. And William had promised her it would be one final act, the last crime that would set them up in their new lives. She had grudgingly accepted it as necessary, but would use her knowledge of it to ensure the like never happened again. The threat would linger that Inspectors White and Carter could always be tipped off again later, after William's escape.

Mr. Belk continued, "I've got a man waiting for William at the rendezvous point who will disguise him and get him back to America. Once you are allowed to go back home, I'll contact you so you know where to find him."

Addy nodded, overwhelmed, even though she had planned for everything so carefully. "But they're chasing him now," she managed to get out.

Her and William's savior set a reassuring hand on her shoulder. "Don't worry. William is sharp. For now, you stay here and play along. I'll be with you the whole time. And Mrs. Alexi will be waiting for you both on the other side of this. She has pledged her support, you know."

"She better have," Addy murmured under her breath.

Mr. Belk looked at Addy quizzically but didn't ask her to repeat herself. On this night, he must know that she couldn't be held accountable for what she said. Instead, he reached for the theater door and held it open for her.

They slipped back inside and went to the dressing room to wait.

The hours dragged by, and the backstage area emptied, leaving Mr. Belk and Addy stuck alone in a frozen moment, waiting for news.

Eventually, it reached midnight. Mr. Belk broke through the ice.

"This is ridiculous. Surely they can't expect you to wait here all night. I'll see you home. I need to get back to see if my man sent the signal it's over."

"But won't the detectives expect me to still be here when they get back?" After being on edge for so long, her resolve was cracking, fear setting in, making her reticent to move.

"They can't fault you for going home and going to sleep. Just don't leave the hotel room, so you'll be there when they come looking for you."

Outside, the fog still hung heavy in the air. At the late hour, they had to wait awhile for a cab to appear. Eventually, one emerged from the mist and took them first to Addy's hotel. Mr. Belk walked her into the lobby, then continued on his way to his own hotel.

Once in her room, Addy undressed shakily, brushing her hair over and over in a daze. For half the brushstrokes, she was sure the delay was a good sign, meaning they hadn't found him, while for the other half, she was certain something terrible had happened.

She forced herself to get in bed and eventually fell into a fitful sleep. Not long after, a knock resounded through the room. She leaped out of bed, wrapped a robe protectively around herself, and opened the door a crack.

"William!" she gasped.

He stood in the hallway, a slash of blood above his right eyebrow. *I'm sorry,* he mouthed to her.

Before she could respond, the door was pushed roughly open by some unseen force, revealing Inspector White gripping William's elbow. Behind them stood Inspector Carter and the Italian policeman, his cheery smile long gone. All were dirty and bruised. Looking down, she saw handcuffs around William's wrists.

"Mrs. Fairley, thank God you're here," White said as he pushed the group farther into the room, forcing Addy back so she nearly tripped over a chair. "I would hate to think you had any part in your husband's escape."

"What's happened?"

White tossed William toward a chair like a rag doll. William sat without resistance, resting his head in his bound hands. He wouldn't look at Addy.

White stood tall and proud. "We caught him at the edge of the city. Waiting to meet someone at the crossroads, it looked like. We missed catching him in the act, but we're searching his hotel and the theater now. Either way, he'll be going with us on the next train back to England for trial."

Addy held a shaking hand to the neckline of her robe. She couldn't handle William sitting there, so dejected and subjugated. A thought crept in about herself—if she would be charged, too—but she shoved it away, feeling guilty for worrying about herself now. Besides, they wouldn't find anything in their search, thanks to Mr. Belk. When she spoke, she tried to sound unconcerned with her estranged husband's fate.

"And what shall I do?"

Carter took over, giving a little bow. "We can escort you back to England, too, of course. While you can't testify against your husband, your presence on the prosecution side of the courtroom would be very meaningful for the public."

Seeing Addy's strained expression, White added quickly, "That can all be decided later. For now, allow us to see you safely back so you have some time to think."

Addy nodded.

Another hand rapped at the door.

While Carter answered it, Addy stole a glance at William and finally succeeded in catching his eye. She had hoped to tell him their news when they were safely reunited, but she couldn't let him be dragged away without knowing. She cupped a hand around her belly. His eyes widened as the understanding sank in.

The moment shattered as Carter allowed in a group of Italian officers. He walked over to William, looking a tad too pleased for Addy's liking.

"Mr. Fairley, these men will take you to the station for a formal booking; then we'll collect you in the morning for the train."

William stood, holding Addy's gaze for a moment, his meaning inscrutable. She hoped he was pleased with the news, despite the circumstances. Then he walked out, and was lost to her.

"Now, Mrs. Fairley," White said, "I hope you'll understand we also need to search your room, just in case."

"Now?"

The men nodded, and Addy perched on the bed while they rummaged through her few belongings, moving furniture with loud squeals against the floorboards. She, too, rested her head in her hands. Any hope of sleep for the night had dissipated like the fog with the dawn.

Her mind cleared. She barely registered the men pawing through her belongings as she decided her own fate. She would accompany the detectives back to England to save her own money as long as she could. Then she would catch a steamer back to New York, where Mr. Belk and Mrs. Alexi would make sure she was provided for. There was no point in her staying in England. She chafed at Carter's suggestion that she join the prosecution's side against her husband in the courtroom. She would do no such thing. She would cite her pregnancy, the need to return home, to avoid the strain of a trial.

She shifted her position on the edge of the bed, bringing one leg up under her. The English jury would likely convict William of something, but no crime that would put him away for life.

The men began to leave, satisfied with their search. Addy barely acknowledged their goodbyes as she closed the door after them.

She turned and surveyed the room, her things haphazardly strewn everywhere. She sighed. Sleep eluded her, so she may as well clean up.

As she tidied, she contemplated her future. William would be released in a few years' time. Long enough to establish herself as the toast of New York spiritualist society, a martyr to the cause after the witch hunt against her husband. When William returned to her, they would be equal partners in the eyes of the world, but she would make the rules. True belief in the spirits, no theft, no unnecessary subterfuge. The way she'd always wanted it.

In an odd way, she had won.